THE UNGODLY HOUR

OTHER BOOKS BY LAURY A. EGAN

FICTION
Jenny Kidd
Fog and Other Stories
The Outcast Oracle
Fabulous! An Opera Buffa
A Bittersweet Tale

POETRY
Snow, Shadows, a Stranger
Beneath the Lion's Paw
The Sea & Beyond
Presence & Absence

THE UNGODLY HOUR

BY
LAURY A. EGAN

interlude press • new york

CONTENT WARNINGS

This book contains discussions of homophobia, violence, sexual violence, domestic abuse, child abuse and molestation, death of parents, as well as depictions of homophobic protests and homophobic bullying, sexual harassment, attempted sexual assault, sexual sadism, and violence.

interlude press • new york

PREFACE

Mykonos attracts those who appreciate exuberant music and nightlife, art galleries and shops, beaches, and excellent cuisine. Although my experiences there were extremely happy, since I'm a contrary writer, my imagination wandered from its sunny streets to its dark alleys, creating a story that balanced romance, tolerance, and joy with murder, bigotry, and fear. Despite my artistic liberties, I hope readers will fall in love with the island, travel there, and stay a week or longer. This book is dedicated to Mykonos and its residents.

My three visits provided much of the background for settings and locations. Some of my favorite bars and restaurants were included, though some night spots, local businesses, and several areas in and above the town were invented or substantially altered. The plot and all of the characters are entirely fictional.

CHAPTER ONE

The black-robed figure entered the viewfinder just as Dana Fox squeezed the shutter. He hadn't been there a second before. He wasn't there a second after. A Greek monk wearing a long black cassock and a stovepipe hat with a cloth draped from its top.

Dana had risen before sunrise to photograph the streets of Mykonos Town before they became clogged with tourists. At this hour, it wasn't common for locals to run errands because the stores weren't open, but she presumed the priest had been called to visit a dying parishioner or to deal with a sudden tragedy. Regardless of the reason for his presence, the man had marred her architectural composition. Dana lowered her head to look through the camera and took another shot, then waited until the sun inched higher, illuminating one of the buildings. After taking two more photographs, she hefted her camera and tripod, laying them against her shoulder as one would a wayward child, and grabbed the strap of her camera bag. Walking west, Dana documented several scenes all the while luxuriating in the precious moments of tranquility before the island came boisterously alive.

As the sun ascended in the clear sky, pouring its generous golden light through the funnel of narrow streets, more people stirred. Shop owners unbarred wooden shutters, drew up security gates, and picked up trash and broken glass. Men on rickety three-wheeled scooters brought in fresh bread, green bottles of wine, and vegetables grown in small gardens. Donkey carts laden with gallon tins of olive oil, bags of yellow lemons, and plastic jugs of drinking water made stops at restaurants. Soon, the tourists would begin to straggle lazily out of their hotels, though most would sleep late after dancing in conga lines at tavernas and clubs the night before. Mykonos had a loosening effect on even the most staid visitors—ouzo and bouzouki music transformed them into high-kicking, irrepressible Zorbas. As a seasonal renter, Dana had observed these hedonistic behaviors for the last three years, often falling sway to the lure of the midnight life, at straight bars and gay bars, depending on her mood.

After finishing the black-and-white roll, she rewound it, placed the canister in her khaki Dompke vest, inserted color film, and shot a series featuring a domed church, one of many brilliantly white structures clustered near the horseshoe-shaped harbor and up the hill past the three famous windmills. Then, feeling hungry, she headed for Kostas' Blue Dolphin Café. As usual, Kostas was surveying his small slice of white-washed walkway, hoping to inveigle some tourists into rotting their teeth on his expensive baklava.

"*Kalimera*, Miss Fox," he said. "*Ti kanete?*"

"*Kalimera. Ime kalá*," Dana replied that she was well. "You may call me Dana, if you like." She had suggested this informality before.

He dipped his shaggy gray head in a polite nod and gave her a cheerful smile. "It is a beautiful day, is it not?"

"A splendid day. And I would love some of your splendid coffee."

"But of course," Kostas replied, offering her a wobbly straight-back chair.

Dana studied its chipped white paint and uncertain thatched seat, figuring that it probably had been in this condition for decades and that she was not likely to be the straw that broke the proverbial "camel's back." It creaked unhappily as she sat down.

"And perhaps a croissant with lavender honey?" Kostas inquired, knowing her customary order.

"*Efharisto.*" While her Greek was serviceable in social situations, she needed to improve her fluency, even if most Mykonians answered her Greek with English.

He nodded, disappeared into the dark interior, and returned with a white mug, a bowl of sugar packets, and containers of cream.

Dana stirred some sugar into the coffee and sat back, enjoying the warming sea air. She was happy with her morning's work. As much as she loved to teach photography workshops, she loved being out with a camera more, having the feel of metal beneath her hands, seeing the world at whatever view the lens dictated—from the dizzying perspective of a super-wide angle or the voyeuristic perch of a long telephoto. It was a lonely occupation, much like any artistic pursuit, but it filled her with joy.

Her workshop met at nine. Six students—Americans, like herself. Today's assignment was Mykonos' most famous chapel, Our Lady Paraportiani, which lay west of the port. An amalgamation of five churches, its baroque geometry was a magnificent example of Cycladic architecture, though to Dana it resembled piled scoops of vanilla ice cream worthy of a giant's dessert, an undignified analogy she wouldn't mention to her students.

After finishing breakfast, Dana left payment hidden under the edge of her plate. She ran her hand through her short hair, knowing from past experience that the wind had blown the curls into twitchy yellow chaos since her morning shower, and applied pale pink lipstick. Standing, she bent a shoulder to the camera bag strap, grasped her tripod, and set off down several passageways to the office of *The Pelican*, a daily paper that squeezed local news between dozens of ads. The owner and editor-in-chief, Tassos, was an easygoing fellow who ran a photograph of hers if she captured a newsworthy image. On occasion, when he had space, Tassos printed one of her fine arts photographs and listed Dana's gallery—The

Meltémi. This arrangement was satisfactory all around because the gallery owners were pleased, and they in turn increased their advertising.

As she passed through the newspaper's open doors, Dana was greeted by the odor of cigarette smoke as well as by the receptionist. Anna wore a dour expression accentuated by thick black eyebrows that ran horizontally above large brown eyes. Although it had taken Dana time to befriend her, Anna was now a valued source of gossip and news.

Dana took her usual place on the corner of Anna's desk. "What's up?"

"Ah, Dana. You haven't heard?" Her voice became hushed.

"Heard what?"

"About the murder!"

Dana became instantly alert. "Oh, no! Who was killed?"

"A man named Malcolm Hall. A Brit. Staying here for two weeks at the Hotel Moros." She fluttered her wrist back and forth.

"Gay?"

She nodded. "Only twenty-four years old. Very sad."

"That's terrible! Does anyone know who did it?"

"No, but Yannis photographed the body for the police. He's in the darkroom printing. Perhaps we'll have more information soon—from him or from Tassos."

"Where and when did it happen?"

"Sometime between 4:30 and 6:30 a.m., according to the police. The body was found on Agion Saranta."

"Hmm. I was near there about then."

"Up so early?" She gave Dana a teasing look.

"Yes. Working," Dana countered her implication, smiling. "I wanted to take some shots with minimal lighting, when the town was quiet. I didn't see anyone. Oh, except for a monk who walked into one of my photographs." Dana thought about the black figure at the bottom of the lane, who had been visible for only a few seconds. Perhaps the unintended inclusion of the priest might produce a humanizing contrast to the street scene.

"Maybe I'll print the photo after class," she told Anna.

"If there is anything of interest—"

"I know. Bring it to Tassos." Dana smiled again and came to her feet. "I'll see you soon."

She grabbed her gear and left the office, musing on the death of Malcolm Hall. Despite its onslaught by eight-hundred thousand tourists each year, Mykonos was a peaceful island, and murder was extremely rare. Theft was the commonest crime, perpetrated primarily by Americans, urchins who drifted around the streets in dirty clothes looking for a free beer or a hit of marijuana. Dana assumed that the young man had been killed accidentally during a robbery.

As she neared the harbor, Dana was surprised to find the waterfront choked with people. Curious, Dana edged through the onlookers, some of whom were standing in the sun in front of two tavernas; others gathered in the shade of the restaurants' striped awnings. Because she was tall, she could see over the crowd. A small brigade of religious protesters were marching two abreast down the curving promenade. The men and women carried anti-gay signs and large wooden crosses and seemed to be chanting verses of scripture and homophobic slogans, though it was difficult to hear them over the jeers and chatter.

"What's going on?" she asked a woman who was standing beside her.

"A bunch of crazies shouting."

Dana moved forward for a better view. From their dress and speech, it appeared that the protesters were American, mostly middle-aged, their faces flushed with heat and religious fervor.

"Repent and be saved!" they cried. "Jesus loves you!"

These comments were met with derision by some of the gay men and women who had rushed to the scene. At this early hour, most of the gay population was still in bed. However, those who were out for a morning coffee or stroll were not amused by the incursion and greeted the bigoted words with increasingly virulent taunts.

"Go back to the Dark Ages!" one guy yelled.

"You don't belong here!" another shouted, which elicited applause and loud agreement.

Dana could tell the situation was coming to a head. The crowd, which had seemed amused at first, was now growing angry and beginning to press forward. The marchers kept repeating inflammatory phrases, ignoring the change in mood around them and the derogatory language being hurled in their direction. As the two groups became more agitated, the tourist police arrived from their building at the end of the harbor and swarmed around the religious protesters. Dana edged to the side of the promenade and noticed a man in his early fifties standing by a café table. He was wearing a crimson shirt, a white clerical collar, and a blue-and-white-striped seersucker suit. His American roots were obvious in his choice of patriotic colors; his Midwestern accent was clearly discernable when he raised a microphone to his lips and made an impassioned plea, beseeching all homosexuals to come forward so they could be saved by Jesus Christ. Bibles were on a table near his hand, ready for dispersal.

Dana shot his picture as well as several others of the protesters and the crowd. Then, realizing it was time for her class to meet, she hurried past the Town Hall and up Kastro Hill to Paraportiani.

—

THE MAN WATCHED the tall blond woman replace the lens cap on her camera and walk toward Kastro Hill. Although he had tried to turn his head away, he was sure she had taken his photograph once, possibly twice—and for the second time that day. Cursing his inattentiveness, cursing her, he began to leave the café intent on following her. As he did so, he was accosted by a restraining hand.

"You have not paid, sir," the taverna owner told him.

"How much?" He pulled his arm away. He hated to be touched.

"I must go inside to get your waiter."

The man gazed toward the azure-domed church at the edge of the port. He wiped the perspiration from his brow and sat down at the table, gritting his teeth in frustration. Nine endless minutes later, a folded rectangle of paper was slipped under his spoon. He counted out the requested number of drachmas, picked up his belongings, and vowed to find the photographer's film and destroy it—the photographer, too, as a precaution or, perhaps, for his pleasure.

CHAPTER TWO

As Dana approached the church, she admired its free-form curves painted in the dazzling whitewash used throughout the island. A composite of walls, staircases, and domes, the building peaked to a bell tower. The bell, however, was gone. What remained was an opening that seemed like a doorway to the bright, cloudless, blue heavens: a worthy subject for her students.

Most of her photographers were struggling up the hill, laden with bags and tripods, necks ringed with cameras on straps, and town maps hanging from back pockets of photo vests—it was impossible to do the job properly without a lot of equipment. Dana greeted Mike Garfield, who was sitting on a bench. He was fifty-two and had reaped the financial rewards of the burgeoning construction market in New Jersey. Photography was a new passion, and he was busy taking workshops to jumpstart his skill. Mike was a friendly soul with a frequent smile, squarely built, red-haired, freckled, and nursing a terrific sunburn.

Dana set her gray bag and tripod on the walkway and watched her other students—Julian Witten, Carolyn Hargreaves, David Ambrose, Teresa Corso, and Virgil Laine—arrive from the harbor and town, though Julian was stopping to snap photographs, clicking away as if the sun were in danger of being permanently extinguished. He was the jackrabbit of the group, always impatient, visually gobbling as many sights and scenes as he could. In his mid-thirties, fair of hair and complexion, Julian was lean—no doubt due to his constant agitation. When he stood before Dana, he was breathing heavily and annoyed about something, a state Dana had observed yesterday.

"*Kalimera*!" Dana said, once everyone was gathered together. "I hope all of you are up for today's assignment? Our Lady Paraportiani." She pointed at the church. "One of the fascinations of Greece is the amazingly intense light, the deep-valued sky. *Photography* is a word derived from the Greek, one that means 'writing with light.' And that's what the class is about. We're going to use Paraportiani like a studio model and observe the sun as it moves over it every hour or so, creating shadows and patterns, illuminating the curves."

"What else are we going to do?" Julian wanted to know, his eyes darting around the chapel, furiously composing mental pictures.

"You can shoot other areas, but the problem is how light and shadow change architectural forms. Today, we will patiently *make* our images, not quickly *take* them." Dana replied, staring meaningfully at Julian.

David Ambrose stood next to his wife, Hasina, who was listening but not enrolled in the class. Both were African-American, tall, and drop-dead handsome. He stepped forward. "Dana, should we shoot color or black-and-white?"

"I'd suggest some color slides for the critique, although you might get some striking monochromatic images also," Dana replied.

David nodded. He then kissed Hasina and wished her happy shopping. When she left, Dana returned her attention to the class.

"Now, as I said yesterday, because the sky here is such a bright color and a dark value, it can be a significant part of your composition. Look at the negative space—in this case, the sky—and try to maximize it. Pay attention to its shapes as much as you consider the positive shapes of the building."

"What about the shadows? Are they considered shapes?" Teresa asked. She was in her late thirties, slender, with black, shining hair. Like

David's wife, Hasina, Teresa drew lengthy looks from every male she passed, at least from those attracted to the female form.

"That's a great question, Teresa," Dana replied. "Yes, shadows are a significant aspect of the problem. Shadows can echo positive shapes or —not to get too esoteric—can become positive shapes themselves, depending on their dominance in your photograph."

Just then, Luca Alessi, Teresa's boyfriend, rushed up from the port. He placed a shopping bag on the ground and accosted Teresa, grasping her thin gold necklace and pulling her toward him.

"Don't!" Teresa whispered.

He smiled. "Oh, come on, babe."

She pried his fingers away. "I'm in class."

Luca dropped his arm over her shoulder. "Let's go swimming... or go back to the hotel and—"

Teresa disengaged. Luca stared at her, wearing a mock pout, as if she'd hurt his feelings. Then he laughed, turned toward Dana, and flashed a perfect white smile. "Sorry. I don't mean to disrupt anything."

Dana approached. The guy had sparkling brown eyes and an Italian complexion enhanced by sunbathing beside the hotel pool, where she'd noticed him yesterday. He had been wearing skintight black bathing trunks; his skin gleamed with suntan oil. Luca was a very good-looking guy who exuded sexiness.

"That's okay," she said, "but if you wouldn't mind... "

"No problem." He shrugged, kissed Teresa's cheek, and left, bag in hand.

Dana let a moment pass before speaking to the group. "Come and go as you wish, but when you return, shoot the area that has become interesting. It may not be the side facing the sun, so walk around the circumference. I'll meet you at the Olive Café at one," she said, pointing down the street. "It's a courtyard over. Any questions?"

"Where are you going to be?" Julian asked.

"Was there something you wanted to know?"

Frowning slightly, he shook his head.

As the others hefted their gear and climbed up to the church, Virgil Laine remained by her side. A blond-haired twenty-nine-year-old, Virgil loved to dance and party. His ebullient, slightly elfin grin belied a more serious side, an artistic nature that was quietly blooming. This morning, Virgil wore a striped T-shirt that appeared to have been painted on his biceps and pecs. In contrast, his shorts were nearly knee-length and hung loosely from his narrow hips. He was the only person Dana had known before the workshop because he lived with his wealthy, older lover, Émile de Szasi, who was a generous patron and friend of Dana's.

"That Luca is a real trip." Virgil pocketed his sunglasses in his tan vest.

She wasn't sure if Virgil was complimenting Luca or making a more negative observation, so she simply nodded.

He drew closer and, in a lower voice, said, "Dana, did you hear about last night?"

"About Malcolm Hall?"

"Yeah." Virgil's shoulders slumped. "Émile got a call this morning. We met Malcolm a few days ago. He was a nice guy. We're really upset."

"Do you know what happened?"

"No, not yet."

"Well, if you learn anything, let me know, okay?" Dana asked.

Virgil agreed to do so, then joined the other photographers.

Dana watched for a few minutes in case someone had a problem. She drew in a sharp breath when Carolyn's tripod and camera tipped over and was very relieved that Mike caught the combo before it hit the flag-stones. Carolyn was the oldest member of the class, a retired elementary school teacher, whom Dana had privately nicknamed "Miss Bumble." A large bandage on Carolyn's knee marked an encounter with the ground on the first day of class.

When everyone was settled, Dana headed toward her apartment, worrying about the murder and who might be responsible. Most likely the killer wasn't local, though this was a hunch based solely on the good feeling she had about the island's inhabitants, both those who were

Greek and those who were seasonal residents such as Émile. She thought about the hundreds of passengers disgorged from cruise ships —staying a few hours or a single night—and the tourists who arrived via plane or ferry and remained for several days or a week. Dana hoped that the murderer was one of these brief visitors and had already departed.

Her workshop ran for seven days, beginning on Wednesday, when all of her students except Virgil had flown to Mykonos from Athens. That afternoon, the participants had registered at the King Minos Inn and convened in the meeting room below the lobby, where she had given a lecture and slide show to present the themes of the class. Early yesterday, everyone had packed into a van and trundled about the countryside, visiting the two monasteries at Ano Merá as well as several beaches in order to do some seascapes. Each student had shot several rolls of Ektachrome film that had been developed by the photo shop in town and then received a critique last night after dinner before the group had ventured out to play in the discos. But between the session last night and the one this morning, Dana couldn't account for the whereabouts of any of her students or the two people traveling with them—Hasina and Luca. She prayed that the timing of their arrival with Malcolm Hall's death was merely a coincidence.

—

Dana's apartment was located in the Alefkandra section or Little Venice—so named because the doorsteps of the whitewashed houses huddled together along the narrow, curving stone promenade abutting the sea. Her building was distinguishable by its aqua door; like some of the neighboring houses, it had a second-level balcony jutting above the walkway. The ground floor was a windowless fortress of whitewashed concrete designed to withstand the incursion of the Aegean, though on rare occasions seawater leaked inside. The space contained her darkroom as well as a washer/dryer on a raised pedestal.

Dana entered, appreciating the room's coolness, left the tripod by the door, and slowly climbed the spiral staircase to the living room and galley-style kitchen. Here, Dana's photographs covered the walls, the frames fitting together like a puzzle, with scant inches of space between. On the west wall were two French glass doors leading to the balcony and two large windows, all providing breathtaking views of the sea. The open balcony, with its waist-high railing, was Dana's favorite spot in the house. It contained a small square dining table and three captain's chairs.

She lowered her camera bag onto the sofa and sighed. The seductively beautiful living room sometimes made her feel sad, reminding her of the solitariness of her life, of her many failed relationships. Years ago, she had given up attempts to date men, but her long-term relationships with women hadn't been extremely successful, either. Now, at age forty, Dana was beginning to doubt whether her future would include a partner. And, except for her grandfather, who spent part of the year in Europe, her parents and other close relatives were gone.

She thought back to the Saturday before her thirteenth birthday, a night indelibly imprinted in her mind. Her father, mother, maternal grandmother, and she had been invited to a lawn party at an estate above Nantucket harbor. The women wore pastel chiffon dresses; the men were handsome in white dinner jackets. Chinese lanterns swung on posts, and a Big Band orchestra played. Everything was perfect until the ride home on the Madaket Road, which curved in big arcs through the wetlands. Her father was at the wheel, her mother in the seat beside him; Dana and her grandmother were in the back. It was a black night growing blacker, as the lights of town were extinguished by intervening hills. At one point, her mother asked her father to slow down. With one hand on the wheel, he turned to her and laughed. A second later, the heavy Mercedes skipped off course and went sailing in the air, then crashed down, glass shattering, red blood everywhere, water seeping in, the air thick with the smell of black sea muck and gasoline.

Over the years, Dana had imagined what happened—that she had climbed through the open car window, dredged herself from the water, and crawled up the embankment to the road. The truth was that she couldn't remember anything except the flying car and the crash, a sequence that was frequently resurrected in nightmares.

Her father survived the accident; her grandmother didn't. Her mother lived in a coma for an agonizing month until she succumbed. Dana suffered a broken arm and glass wounds, one of which had etched a vertical scar below her right temple.

Dana poured water in a coffee mug and drank thirstily, all the while telling herself to forget the accident; to forget the years after her mother's death when her father began abusing alcohol, his brand of penance, yet she couldn't. For the thousandth time, Dana regretted her failure to rescue her father from self-destruction. They had always been close. Both athletic, they sailed, played tennis, and skied, but, despite their earlier bond, he had disappeared into a bottle and died from sclerosis during her last year at Bennington College. Numb from the pressure, sorrow, and remorse, Dana had shut down, beginning a dark period whose tentacles stretched to the present, to mornings like this. Although a therapist had helped after her father died, Dana had never been able to relinquish her wariness or eradicate her fear of falling into darkness and death, like on that Nantucket night.

She sighed again, tired of feeling so detached and alone, especially on an island where romance and revelry greeted her everywhere. She ascended a narrow staircase to her bedroom, which featured three windows facing the water. Dana loved smelling the sweet sea air and listening to the bray of ships' horns, the lap of the waves, and the cry of seabirds. Unfortunately, it was also necessary to contend with singing drunks and lovers' arguments since the promenade below served as a thoroughfare to a series of popular clubs and piano bars.

She went into the bathroom to splash cool water on her forehead and cheeks. Tired blue eyes stared back from the mirror; their usual dark color seemed faded, their brightness dulled by too many late nights, too little sleep, too busy being busy. Although she did her best to be cheerful and enthusiastic, especially with her students, she recognized that she was struggling. Annoyed with how she felt, Dana scrubbed her face dry with vigor and aggressively brushed her hair, which did little to tame its willful curliness.

Then, as she had so often during the last three days, Dana pictured the mysterious woman she had seen at Caprice the night before the workshop convened, when she had been mixing pleasure and business with Émile. They were finishing their second round of Metaxas and discussing his purchase of three more of Dana's photographs, when a woman walked by on her way from the ladies' room to the bar in the adjacent section. The first word that came to Dana's mind had been a simple and declarative "Wow!" Early thirties, a stunning figure with the narrow waist of a model and the flared shoulders of a swimmer, the woman moved with grace, making eye contact as she passed behind Émile. In the soft candlelight, the woman's ironical smile captivated Dana as did her full lips and dark brown eyes. The effect of the face was windswept, with angular cheekbones and a narrow chin, which was divided by a gentle cleft. Her straight black hair was brushed back from her forehead and gathered in a barrette. After pausing, the woman had continued into the next room.

Dana had wanted to rush after her, but Émile hadn't seen this beautiful vision and was making an offer for her work. As soon as she could politely do so, Dana explained what had just occurred. Always eager for a lark, Émile rose and accompanied her to the bar. The woman was gone.

Émile had beckoned the bartender, who said that the woman was new to the island. He didn't know much about her except that she was an Athenian and her name was Cybele.

Now, as Dana stood in front of her bathroom mirror, she noticed that her eyes—a moment ago lifeless—glistened. Although they hadn't met, Dana sensed this woman would become her lover, perhaps more. If she could find her again.

She applied makeup to cover the craggy scar that glowed white against her deep tan. People often asked why she didn't undergo plastic surgery, remarking that her face was otherwise so beautiful. When Dana heard someone express this sentiment, she knew they would never understand her. It was a kind of test—their reaction. Would Cybele perceive that the scar was a reminder of her losses, a fault line on a geologic map?

She returned to the kitchen, wishing that her path would cross Cybele's again, which was likely on this small, nine-mile island unless Cybele had only been a visitor.

"Quit daydreaming!" she told herself.

In the living room, Dana drank more water, rewound the color film from her camera, and placed the canister in an empty coffee can in the refrigerator to protect it from the heat. She withdrew the black-and-white roll from her vest and went downstairs to the darkroom. After sliding the black curtain across the exterior door, she turned off the lights and threaded the film on a reel before inserting it into a stainless-steel tank and securing the lid. With the lights on, she added developer, agitated the container, and emptied the tank before proceeding with the stop bath and fix stages to the final wash. Opening the lid, she removed the roll of negatives and clipped it to a clothesline, donned white gloves, and held the film up to the light. The Greek Orthodox priest was there on frame 21, very small. Printed, he would probably still be almost unrecognizable. Although it seemed pointless to make enlargements, she decided she would. Dana prepared the trays and chemistry and went upstairs to wait until the negatives dried.

—

CYBELE KARABÉLIAS was sitting at her desk at the police station typing notes from interviews with three protesters. The tourist police had responded initially, but the regular squad had taken over and incarcerated several picketers. It had been decided that a short jail stay might discourage their disruptive activities.

Although Cybele understood the importance of filing reports, she was restless to be outside. Junior police officers were often asked to do tedious paperwork for their superiors, but it seemed that she had been singled out because she was the only female recruit. The two new male officers were not at their desks, she noted.

She added the date, September 8, 2000, signed the last page, and leaned against her chair, allowing herself to slip into a fantasy about the blond woman from Caprice. The club catered to a mixed clientele, as did most places on the island, so her presence there didn't confirm her orientation. Yet Cybele had sensed her interest and felt a strong magnetism drawing her to the woman. Once again, she regretted making such a fast exit. It had been late—past midnight—but the hour had not been the primary reason for her retreat. She had panicked. And now all she could think about was how the woman had seemed so composed until they had exchanged glances. Then the woman's blue eyes had sparkled.

In Athens, because of her traditional family, Cybele had been forced to maintain a heterosexual life, but the deception had become intolerable. In August, she had accepted a job on the Mykonos police force, coming to the island to find out who she was and who she wanted, to confront her sexuality, yet Cybele had avoided the gay discos and the provocative glances of lesbians on the streets because she felt anxious and inexperienced. And now here she sat, pen in hand, while somewhere nearby walked a woman she desperately wanted to meet. Frustrated, she opened another file and counseled herself to be patient.

—

DANA PRINTED the negative on eight-by-ten-inch paper, first uncropped, then at two increasing enlargements to concentrate on the monk, whose bearded face was cast in shadow and was only a grainy semi-profile. His black cassock fell to his shoe tops, and the cloth attached to his hat hid his hair and the back of his head. A cross hung around his neck. Dana couldn't gauge his height and weight, though he seemed average in stature.

Disappointed by the minimal quality of the image, Dana placed the three prints in the diagonal drying rack, covered the trays of developer and fixer chemistry, and returned the negative to its paged sleeve. With ten minutes left before lunch at the Olive Café, she grabbed her straw hat from a peg by the door—today promised to be high on the UV hit parade—and began walking to the restaurant. For no reason that she could elucidate, she sensed a malevolent aura surrounding the man in the photograph.

CHAPTER THREE

DANA AND HER STUDENTS finished their meal, and the bill arrived. A slip of paper in longhand, it featured a cryptic series of prices toted up with no explanation as to the correlating food item. Mystifying for two people, it was a nightmare for seven. With the assistance of the waiter, the confusion was resolved, probably with the result that the taverna was overpaid. Dana shrugged. Sometimes things went the other way.

As she led her group back to Paraportiani, the sun was high in the south, beating down without any cloud diffusion. She was grateful for her hat, even though the chippy breeze was trying its best to snatch it. Walking around the side of the church with her students in tow, she pointed to the geometric shadows on the walls and ground.

"Pay attention to the shadows' shapes," she reminded them.

Everyone nodded and frowned, studying the situation. David and Mike asked a few technical questions, which Dana answered. Once she was satisfied that they were ready to begin, she said, "Drop your film at the photo shop for development before three and pick up your slides by six. Select about twelve images for the 6:30 critique at the King Minos Inn. Afterward, everyone is free for the evening."

Julian set up his tripod and began shooting while everyone else was still mulling over the problem. Dana caught David's eye and smiled, sharing amusement over Julian, then watched him skirt the far side of the church away from everyone. Patient as always, David would let the other photographers finish and would return when fewer bodies blocked the scene.

Carolyn had affixed her camera to the tripod and placed it, yet again, on uneven pavement. She was pushing strands of frizzy brown hair under her headband.

Dana hurried over to stabilize the tripod's legs on flatter ground. "Try here, Carolyn, and watch out for the wind. It can knock over your camera. Keep a hand on it."

A moment later, Virgil raised his index finger to catch her attention. He was standing farthest from the church.

"Now, Dana, I know I shouldn't pester you with questions, but I am absolutely lost here. I want so much to get this view-thing down." He took a step closer to Dana and whispered theatrically, "How clever of you to suggest Paraportiani as a subject. You know this is hallowed ground, where all the boys come in the wee hours."

Dana couldn't help laughing. "I had heard rumors."

Virgil covered a smile. "I mean, it is totally sacred! The boys are thick as fleas here after two in the morning. Not the only place—just about any spot will do—but this is a sure thing."

She was tempted to ask him if he was one of the patrons but decided she didn't want to know. Émile was probably aware that Virgil was catting around, but it felt disloyal to Émile to encourage Virgil to tell her details. Changing the subject, she asked, "How are you going to approach the church?"

"Oh, dear! Very carefully!" Virgil giggled, his eyes mischievous. "No, actually, I'm going to wait for everyone else to leave, and then I'm going to use that new lens Émile bought for me. By the way, I wanted to tell you how much I'm enjoying the class. I really want to do well. Although Émile thinks my work is fabulous, I see many areas where I need to improve. In fact, Dana, would you be willing to help me after the class ends? We'll pay you for your time."

"I'd be delighted, Virgil. We can talk more about it in a few days. Maybe you would like to learn to use the darkroom too?"

"Absolutely!" he exclaimed. "You know, I was thinking…well…" his voice become hushed, "…could I do some nudes? Like Robert Mapplethorpe does? You know, a hot Greek Adonis posing by the sea? For Émile?"

Dana chuckled. "I'm sure he'd be thrilled." She patted Virgil on the back. "I'm going to stop in at *The Pelican* in case they know more about the murder."

Virgil nodded and Dana began descending the hill. When she arrived at the newspaper, the staff was gathered, gesturing and talking over one another. Everyone had a cigarette in hand or one burning in an ashtray or both. In the thick of things was Yannis, their photographer, who stood up when he saw her.

"Dana—just the person we need," he said. "The police don't want us to run my pictures of Hall's body in the paper. They say it would give away too much information. But I say, 'so what?' I am a reporter and I did my job. I should be able to publish my own work, right, Dana?" His expression alternated between pride and indignation.

Before she could answer, Tassos cut in. "I'm sure you took some excellent shots, Yannis, but the police are threatening me. They say you were only allowed to take the photos because their photographer wasn't available."

"They never told me that!" Yannis protested. "We paid for the film, the development, the prints. The photographs are ours!"

Dana stepped between the owner and the photographer. "Yannis, I know it's unfair, but in America, the police could order you not to publish any photos if you were working for them."

There were a lot of muttered remarks about the fascism of the United States and comments about Greece being the first true democracy.

"Where are the prints you took?" Dana asked.

"The police have them," Anna replied. "And the negatives too. Before any of us saw the photographs—except for Yannis."

Yannis grinned, flashing a bright gold tooth. "Yes, but a few may have been mislaid." He shrugged innocently.

Dana shared a smile, one photographer to another, understanding his reluctance to give up his work. "Maybe you can compromise with the police. I don't know what they wanted to hide from the public—"

"I do," Yannis replied, with a dark look.

"Well, if you can't publish your images of the crime scene, perhaps you could use Malcolm Hall's passport photo instead." There was a buzz of agreement that this was a reasonable solution. "Maybe if you run the portrait, someone who saw him that night will contact the paper."

"Hall was very handsome. Blond hair, blue eyes," Yannis said.

"Then I bet a lot of men saw him," Anna replied in a knowing manner.

Tassos slumped into a nearby chair. "Dana, we have trouble with the police, yes, but also the Tourism Ministry. They don't like us to report anything that will scare the tourists."

"I can understand that," Dana replied. "However, the story will run in the *International Herald Tribune* and the Athens newspapers sooner or later, won't it?"

Tassos lifted his chin in agreement. "Yes, probably."

"This is stupid!" Devin Scott cut in. "They can't stop us from reporting the news." He was an American, sour-faced, with scraggly dark hair on his head and lining his upper lip and chin. The newspaper had recently hired him to sharpen their style and to improve their English usage and because he was an aggressive investigator. He seldom socialized with the staff, preferring to stay in his office, which was filled with the blue haze of cigarette smoke.

No one responded to Devin.

"What can you tell us, Tassos?" Dana asked.

"Very little except that the killer used a wire to choke Malcolm Hall, and Hall's clothes were missing."

"Anything else?"

"Not that I am allowed to say. Or write," muttered the owner, shaking his head. "Dana, did you print the photographs you took this morning near the murder scene?"

"How did you know about them?"

Anna put up her hand. "I told Tassos and some of the reporters after you left."

"Well, as a matter of fact I did. They're home. Nothing of much use, I'm afraid. I also took some of the protesters."

"Yannis already has photos of them and the minister," Tassos said, lighting another cigarette.

Dana coughed and explained she needed to check on her class.

—

When she returned to the church, only David was present. Even though she was boiling hot, David looked cool in a starched white shirt and seemed unaffected by the heat. His calm, unhurried approach to life was enviable, conducive to creating thoughtful compositions. David also worked hard and was eager to experiment, making him the perfect student.

After he asked several questions, Dana reminded him it was almost three, and he needed to drop off his film at the store.

David glanced at his watch. "Time flies when you're in the zone!" He grinned, gathered his gear, and hurried down the hill.

Dana chuckled, knowing exactly what he meant, having lost thousands of hours in creative absorption. She walked a few blocks to Makis' bar, selected a chair under a yellow umbrella, and ordered iced tea. While she waited for her drink, Dana's thoughts turned serious, to the killer who was wandering freely in town. Tomorrow's paper would reveal what had happened and would shock those visitors and residents who weren't aware of Malcolm Hall's death, though most locals would know by then. Dana stared at the people around her, searching for a suspicious face, someone who could strangle another human being, but all she saw were hot, sunburned tourists. She finished her drink and placed money on the table.

As Dana came around the corner to her building, she noticed her front door was partially open. She was positive it had been locked, but, on closer examination, wedge marks were visible on the wooden frame. Stepping cautiously over the threshold, she flipped on the light. Her darkroom was a riotous mess. The notebooks of negatives and prints lay open on the worktable. Strips of negatives curled like brown snakes on the floor. Listening for any sound upstairs, Dana held her breath. Because of the ancient construction, the slightest movement in the rooms above could be heard. All was quiet. Nevertheless, she climbed the staircase slowly, ready to run.

In the living room, her anger grew when she saw the contents of her camera bag sprawled on the couch and the backs of her two Nikons flipped open, gathering dust on the shutters. A blackware vase was in pieces on the floor, as if the thief had become frustrated. Dana took the stairs to her bedroom two at a time. Nothing there was disturbed.

What was the person looking for? It was obvious that burglary hadn't been the primary goal because a thief would have taken her expensive Nikon cameras and lenses. Even so, Dana was relieved she had been wearing most of her valuable jewelry—a gold cuff bracelet, her father's Hamilton watch, and three gold rings. She then thought about the darkroom and the cameras and deduced that exposed film, negatives, and prints were the target, most likely related to Malcolm Hall and the pictures she had taken earlier.

She flew downstairs. The prints were missing from the drying racks. The negative page was gone. "Damn!" she shouted.

After fuming and cursing, Dana called the police and Nikos, her landlord.

—

About fifteen minutes later, there was a firm knock on the door. From the balcony, Dana peered over the railing and saw a uniformed policeman, Myron Tsoublekas, who was talking to someone hidden by the overhanging balcony. As she descended the stairs, she considered his name, Myron, which meant "fragrant." Myron was anything but sweet-smelling: the overpowering combination of tobacco, garlic, and sweat usually made her retreat a step.

Dana opened the door and was stunned to see the woman from Caprice standing behind Myron. The woman was equally surprised to see her—a faint blush darkened her tanned face. Wearing the same uniform as Myron, she was crisp in a pale blue shirt framed at the shoulders with epaulette bars; her legs were clad in pressed navy trousers. She was even more beautiful than Dana remembered.

The policewoman introduced herself as Cybele Karabélias. Reaching into her breast pocket, she withdrew a white business card and gave it to Dana, who stared at it, noting the police station's address and phone number.

Looking up and meeting Cybele's direct gaze, Dana was momentarily struck speechless, dazzled by the woman who stood before her. "You spell your first name with a 'C'?"

The question seemed to amuse Cybele. With a trace of a smile, she replied, "In English, yes."

Dana nodded and invited them in. Myron entered first and Cybele followed, trailing the sensuous scent of sandalwood as she stepped into the darkroom. The two officers surveyed the damage and pulled out notebooks to record details.

"Do you know what's been stolen?" asked Cybele in a deep, musical voice. Her accent was British.

"I think the thief was looking for the photographs I took this morning. I was out with my camera before sunrise…very near where Malcolm Hall's body was found."

"So you have information about his death?" Myron asked.

"No, not really. Only a little…from the staff of *The Pelican*. Anyway, as I was taking a shot of the street, an Orthodox monk walked into the picture. I thought nothing of it at the time, but after I heard about the murder, I decided to develop the roll of black-and-white film and make a few eight-by-ten prints."

"Was he in a photo?" Cybele observed Dana with large brown eyes.

"In one frame. At the bottom of the street. His face was in profile and in shadow. His head was partly covered by a—I don't know what the cloth is called—"

"An epanokalimavkion. The hat is a kamilavkion," explained Myron, frowning. "That is strange because only a few holy men live on Mykonos. At the Monastery of Panagia Tourliani and the Monastery of Paleokastro, several kilometers outside of town. They could have business here, at a church or with a parishioner, or might be visiting from the mainland." He gave a little snort. "But I doubt a priest would break into your apartment."

Cybele smiled at Myron, who was a very devout man, and then turned to Dana. "How many prints did you make?"

"A full-frame shot and then I enlarged the figure twice, but the detail was poor."

"And all of the prints and negatives are gone, Miss Fox?" Myron inquired.

"Yes. Probably when the thief found the prints and the negatives, he knew that was all there was—if it was the person I photographed this morning. Both my cameras were opened and checked for film. Would you like to see?"

The two officers followed Dana upstairs and made more notes.

"A bit of temper," remarked Cybele, pointing to the broken vase.

"It would seem so," Dana agreed. "It was a museum replica. Not valuable."

While Cybele picked up the shards, Dana had a moment to study the policewoman. She was in her mid-thirties, a few inches shorter than Dana, graceful, and very, very attractive.

Cybele straightened and took in the room. "Is this your work, Miss Fox?"

Dana snapped out of her admiring reverie. "Yes."

The policewoman hid a small smile, as if she had caught Dana's examination, and then surveyed each wall. "The images are quite impressive. I understand from Officer Tsoublekas that you also teach photography?" This time the smile was unconcealed and warm.

Dana felt the heat of Cybele's interest. "I have a seven-day workshop in progress."

"I see. Did any of your students know about the photographs you took this morning? Or did you show the prints to anyone?"

"No. The only person who knew I had been in the area was Anna at the newspaper. She told some of the reporters and the owner—"

"And maybe someone else," finished Cybele.

Dana agreed. "I spoke with Anna early, before my nine o'clock class."

"We will report what happened and will interview the staff of the paper and make calls to the monasteries and churches," Myron said, closing his notebook. "I suggest you replace your lock. Perhaps you may also wish to add a bolt…for when you are home alone."

As Dana was explaining that her landlord was coming by to repair the door, Myron's police radio blared. He excused himself and walked onto the balcony.

"So, was it an accident that you came along with Myron?" Dana asked as soon as the policeman couldn't hear their conversation.

"The fates were kind," Cybele said with a hint of flirtation. "We were assigned to come."

"That night at Caprice…I was discussing the sale of some photographs. When I finished, I followed you into the bar, but you'd already left."

Cybele smiled. "It doesn't matter. Everything has worked out as it should, yes?"

She nodded. "Yes, it has. And, please, call me Dana." She was silent, feeling awkward. "Would it be possible to see you? For dinner tonight?"

Cybele laughed lightly. "Yes, it would be possible. I'm off work soon. If you like, I could bring a roast chicken and a salad?"

"That would be fine, but I'm happy to take you out."

"No, I would prefer a quiet evening." Her gaze lingered on Dana's face.

"A quiet evening it is. I have wine … I'll take care of the rest," Dana offered. "My workshop meets at the King Minos Inn at 6:30. Shall we say about 8:30?"

"Until later," Cybele replied, with a playful smile.

—

AFTER A RESTORATIVE SLEEP, the man was satisfied with his night and day, although his satisfaction was tempered with the knowledge he would soon feel urges, as the sky turned black and the stars pierced the heavens. Part of him wished that he could forget; part of him was eager to remember, to re-experience the thrill.

He planned to eat a late dinner. Then it would be time for hunting, for pleasure.

CHAPTER FOUR

AFTER MYRON and Cybele left, Nikos arrived to replace the lock. He was in a garrulous mood, greatly disturbed by the break-in and fretting over Dana's safety, yet soon he returned to his favorite subject: his many mercantile ventures on Mykonos and on the mainland. Dana listened to him with half an ear because he was always devising byzantine deals and loved nothing better than to explain their intricacies over cups of the oily black espresso he served in his shop. Finally, she steered Nikos toward the broken lock so she could leave for class at the King Minos Inn.

As Dana climbed the steep road that ran above the windmills, all she could think about was Cybele. Distracted, she entered the lobby and nearly bumped into Julian, who was pacing back and forth by the reception desk. Because she was on time, Dana didn't comprehend the reason for his agitation until she noticed the chambermaid, who was holding a stack of white towels, her mouth fixed in a firm frown, and the hotel owner, Sandros, who looked equally unhappy.

"*Kalispera*, Sandros." Dana joined him at the main desk.

"*Kalispera*, Dana." He arched a ruffled gray eyebrow at Julian.

Turning to her student, Dana asked him if he had a problem.

Julian rolled his eyes, which produced a snort from the maid. "Service here is very shoddy!" He launched into a diatribe about the linens, the food at breakfast, and the noise coming from the nearby parking lot.

Dana tried her best to calm him, explaining that this was a B-class hotel, and things were run more casually in Greece.

Julian was not to be corrected. "I realize that," he said acidly, "but I expect to have enough towels to take a shower and go to the pool."

"You're supposed to use the towels provided in the pool cabana. Isn't there a sign in your room to that effect?"

"I have absolutely no idea."

"Well, let's see what we can do." Dana turned to the hotel owner. "Sandros?"

The creases on Sandros' face deepened as he glared at Julian. "Okay, okay. We'll put new towels in your room."

Dana herded her prickly student down the hall. "So, Julian, did you have a nice swim?" she asked, wondering if his assignment had been shortchanged.

"Yes, I did, except for the towels." He was determined to be unpleasant. "And I finished four rolls of film. I have thirteen slides in the carousel already."

First in line. "Good, let's go see how all of you did."

Everyone was in the room, as was Luca Alessi, Teresa's boyfriend, who was perched on the arm of the couch. A clear drink was in his hand, probably a vodka and not his first, judging by his red eyes. He gave Dana a smile that bordered on flirtatious, which was odd because Teresa sat on the sofa next to him.

David was loading slides. "Hello, Dana."

"Hi, how did you make out this afternoon?"

"For you to judge," he replied, chuckling.

She chatted with Carolyn while the other students inserted their images in the carousel trays. When Dana was ready to start the critique, Luca came abruptly to his feet and walked to the bar for a refill. As the bartender made the drink, Luca turned to stare at Dana, once again with more than friendly interest.

She began showing the photographs. Many were similar, but David's were noteworthy for his sophisticated handling of shapes. This wasn't surprising because he was an architect and professionally trained to understand dimension and form. Virgil had also produced some fascinating shots, a few taken lying down. The perspective was further skewed by a new 20 mm wide-angle lens that Émile had ordered from Athens. Everyone was complimentary about his work, and Virgil's eyes shone with gratification. Luca, on the other hand, appeared to dislike Virgil or his photographs, if the dark glances he was shooting at Virgil were an indication.

Mike's photographs were sharp, properly exposed, but too symmetrical. Dana praised him and suggested he try more extreme, off-center compositions.

Facing the class, she said, "A photographer's personality often comes through in his or her work. Mike is a strong, solid guy, who makes strong, solid photographs. What I'm asking him to do is akin to a football player being made to take ballet lessons to improve his footwork." Everyone laughed, Mike most of all.

Teresa's slides were projected next. They were fresh and charismatic, which Dana told her. To the class, she said, "It's fascinating to view these two photographers' work in relationship to each other. You can see how style varies from person to person." She paused on an image of Teresa's. "However, this one isn't technically executed on the same level as the concept." She delivered the depth-of-field lecture again and reminded everyone to use a tripod. "This will allow you to set a slow shutter speed —if the subject is stationary—and to use a smaller aperture, which will increase sharpness in more focal planes. A tripod will also slow you down and reduce camera movement."

As Dana spoke, Luca touched his girlfriend's cheek. At first, Dana thought he was offering her congratulations on her work, but Teresa winced and moved closer to Carolyn, who sat beside her.

Julian, whose slides had been reviewed first—somewhat critically—was looking twitchy and had lit a cigarette, taking nervous puffs as if he didn't want to inhale. Dana refused to be hurried and took time with Carolyn's images. At the end, she told her students to meet at the harbor in the morning to photograph the brightly colored caïques and some local merchants.

"There's this one guy who sells fruit," Virgil began. "He's a hunk! He'll have to let me take his photo if I'm in a class."

Dana smiled. As she did so, she caught a glimpse of Luca staring icily at Virgil.

—

CYBELE AND MYRON returned to the police station to file their report before going off duty. There wasn't much to write, though Cybele—whose task it was to type their notes—thought it was obvious that there was a connection between the theft of the photographs and the murder, an opinion that coincided with her captain's belief, which was why pertinent areas of Dana's apartment had been dusted for fingerprints: around the door, on the stair railing, and a few other locations. If the killer was a foreigner or a Greek whose prints weren't on record, these would only be useful if a match was found near the area of Malcolm Hall's death. Cybele hadn't heard any details about the crime scene, however.

Although stealing the photographs was likely the object of the break-in, Cybele was also concerned for Dana's safety—one reason for her eagerness to return to Dana's. She paused in her typing and laughed at herself. "You know why you want to see Dana," she muttered in Greek. "Ah, those blue eyes!"

With two reasons to hurry, Cybele's fingers flew. She cursed every error, every small impediment to her departure. When the forms were completed and on Myron's desk, she fled the building and rushed toward her apartment on Agiou Efthimiou, a cramped place she had been forced to take because the better rentals had been reserved by tourists through October. Cybele had already decided to move as soon as possible, especially since the owner was planning to renovate the interior, and there would be a lot of dust, tools, ladders, noise, and no privacy.

In the bedroom, she undressed and was astonished to see that her hands were shaking. She sat on a chair and took several deep breaths, trying to calm herself, all the while pondering her reaction. No date with a man had ever produced such a response. Her few experiences with women, though more enticing, had been brief, yet sufficient to convince her that dating men wasn't what she wanted to do. As Cybele stepped into the shower, her hands ran along her flanks, feeling their smoothness. She imagined how Dana's body would feel under hers and pictured every detail: the tall physique, strong shoulders, firm breasts, long hands. Dana was so beautiful that Cybele wondered why Dana would be attracted to her when she could choose any woman on the island.

Sighing, she finished shampooing her hair and stepped out to towel herself briskly. Blow-drying her hair back over her forehead, holding strands with her fingers, she remembered Dana's blush and smiled. A few minutes later, in a black sleeveless sweater and white slacks, she stood before her mirror. Eyeliner, mascara, and lipstick applied, she was ready.

With unshakable certainty Cybele knew they would become lovers, if not this evening, then soon.

—

AFTER DIVVYING up the slides to their owners, Dana left the hotel. Her body felt alive, urgent with exhilaration. In response to her burgeoning impatience, she quickened her pace. As she did, she speculated about Cybele's reasons for moving to Mykonos. Many Greeks came from Athens because they were exhausted from the transportation nightmares—constant taxi and bus strikes, car access to the city on odd or even days depending on the license plate number, and the oppressive pollution. The city was overcrowded yet also familial and conservative, so that a lesbian, or a woman who was trying to determine her sexual orientation, would find it difficult to hide her secret from her family and neighbors. Even though Greeks—and Athenians in particular—were relaxed about the issue with tourists, it was another matter for a family member to commit to living an openly gay life. Most gay men and women eventually married heterosexuals, unhappily succumbing to social pressure; many chose clandestine relationships to resolve their needs. Mykonos, however, attracted an international population of artists, musicians, and writers and was a beacon of acceptance. Had that been the attraction for Cybele?

In a small market, Dana bought feta cheese and black olives to offer with the wine. A block away, she came upon an old man and his gray donkey. The animal's tether was a colorful braid as was the rope that held two burlap pouches divided over the donkey's back. The bags were filled with pistachios, the chartreuse nuts peeking out from their tan shells. She bought a generous amount and then walked hastily to Nikos' jewelry shop, where she listened to a tirade about safety all the while Nikos was tending to three customers. Finally, greed got the better of concern, and Dana was able to procure two new keys to her apartment. In a hurry, Dana turned the corner of her building and started down the stone path by the sea. One long leg crossed over the other, Cybele was sitting in a café chair and observing the fading sunset; its orange light made her skin glow. Hearing Dana arrive, she turned and smiled.

"Time for cocktails, as you Americans say?" she asked, picking up a green string bag.

"Yes." Dana used the new brass key to unlock the door and gestured for Cybele to enter first. As she passed near her, Dana once again caught the fragrance of sandalwood. They climbed the spiral staircase into the living room.

"This is the most beautiful part of town," Cybele said, walking to the open doors by the balcony.

"I think so too. I was very lucky to find this place. My lease extends from April through October, though the arrangement is casual. My landlord owns a jewelry shop on the street side of the building, and he doesn't mind if I'm late leaving or early arriving because the apartment is empty during the winter months."

"So you can keep your things here? That's great!"

"Yes." Dana laid her parcels on the counter and returned for Cybele's bag. "A glass of wine or something stronger?"

"Wine is fine for me."

Dana went into the kitchen, poured two glasses of white Assyritiko from Santorini, and prepared a plate of cheese and bowls of olives and pistachios. Cybele joined her and unpacked a salad, cooked chicken, and a container of brown rice.

"Would you like to sit outside?" Dana asked.

"That would be lovely."

The two women walked onto the balcony, placed the glasses, wine, and appetizers on the square table, and sat in two chairs. In the distance, a white cruise ship was steaming into port, its rigging lights festive against the pink and lavender sky.

"*Stin iya sas,*" Dana toasted.

"*Stin iya sas.*" Cybele clinked her glass against Dana's.

They swallowed their wine and were silent. While Dana observed Cybele, Cybele surveyed the dark blue waves advancing on the narrow beach below.

"That night at Caprice," Cybele began, "it was a shame you were busy."

"Yes, it was. I was with Émile de Szasi—a friend of mine. Do you know him?"

"We haven't met. But he owns a large house above town, yes?"

Dana nodded.

"And he is gay." She said this in a neutral voice.

"Yes, he is."

"When you didn't follow me into the bar, I thought that you weren't interested in women." She directed her gaze toward Dana. "I hoped I was wrong."

"There was a time when I wasn't sure. No longer."

Cybele smiled. "I'm very glad of that."

"And you?"

"I came to Mykonos because I wanted to meet someone or at least to be with gay men and women, away from my family. Although my mother and I have never discussed homosexuality, she wouldn't be happy with me. Perhaps one day she'll understand. For many years, I've dated men, but this summer, I couldn't pretend any longer and came here." Cybele ate some cheese. "Now, tell me about your life...why you chose Mykonos."

"I fell in love with the island several years ago. Every spring, I return to teach workshops and photograph until I leave for New York in October."

"And your parents? Where do they live?"

"They're both dead." Dana sliced several chunks of feta.

"I'm so sorry to hear that." A frown creased Cybele's forehead. "Do you have brothers and sisters?"

"No."

Cybele looked sympathetic. "So you're all alone?"

Dana glanced at her dark eyes, noting their tender expression. "Yes, except for my grandfather, who lives in Switzerland and New York. My father's parents died when he was young." She paused and then added, "What about your family?"

"I'm the oldest of five. All of my brothers and sisters live in Athens. My two younger sisters are still at home with my mother, in Kolonaki."

Dana had stayed at the Kolonaki Inn on her first visit to Athens and knew this section of the city was wealthy and sophisticated, with fine restaurants and boutiques. "And your mother?"

"My mother creates costume designs for the theater. She wanted me to go into fashion or become a model, but that wasn't what I wanted for a career."

"You certainly could have done so." Cybele possessed the elegant lines and the erect carriage of a model.

"Perhaps." She shrugged as if unconcerned about her looks. "Instead, I studied at university, took some courses in London, where I became interested in criminal psychology."

"Ah, so that explains the British accent."

"Yes. And my English instructors in Athens were all from there," she replied. "After London, I wasn't sure what to do. I also write, but there is no money in that." She shrugged her shoulders again. "I decided police work might be a good choice. My job in Mykonos began three weeks ago. It's too early to tell whether I'll like it." Her finger edged around the rim of the glass, and a shy smile played on her lips. "I do like that I meet interesting people … such as today."

Dana laughed. "Well, as upset as I am about the break-in, I'm very happy that it brought you to my door."

After this admission, Dana's face warmed, and she averted her focus to the beach. She needed to curb her impulses and fight the urge to hurry through this first stage of their relationship. Yet the glint of promise behind Cybele's smile had been thrilling and hinted at what might lie ahead. "Go slow," she told herself, prying a pistachio from its shell.

Cybele sipped some wine and turned the conversation to more mundane subjects, those two new friends might discuss as they navigated social waters. This continued until she sighed, leaned against her chair, and chuckled.

"We are being so careful, aren't we?"

Startled, Dana smiled and then nodded.

"Well, I am a very direct person." Cybele examined her closely. "And I want to learn everything about you."

Dana felt the intensity of the woman's gaze and sat transfixed as Cybele raised her hand and traced the scar on Dana's face.

"Such as this, Dana. How did this happen?"

She caught her breath, stunned by the intimacy of the touch. Pouring more wine for them both, Dana was tempted to make light of the question, but Cybele would detect evasion. "I don't really like to talk about it."

"But you will." Cybele gave her a gentle smile. "Please?"

Dana exhaled, trying to dissipate the sudden tightness in her chest. "It happened in an accident. Just before my thirteenth birthday. We were at a party, coming home. My father was driving and he had too much to drink. He ran the car off the road into the water. My grandmother died immediately, and my mother passed away shortly after."

"Oh, my goodness!" she whispered. "And your father?"

"He died from alcoholism when I was twenty-one."

Cybele's eyes widened. "How sad! And how painful to lose most of your family."

Dana sensed Cybele's reaction was honest and empathetic. At once, she felt a quickening of hope and a stab of perennial anxiety. "That accident altered my life."

"I'm so sorry, Dana."

"I'll tell you more one day…"

Cybele nodded, and they sat quietly, each with her thoughts, until Dana couldn't suppress the emotions coursing through her.

"To be honest, Cybele, I've been thinking about you ever since that night at Caprice. Wondering who you were, where you lived. If we would ever meet."

For a moment, Dana worried she had said too much, but Cybele smiled and laid a cool hand on her arm. "I hoped to see you again too. Something powerful occurred that evening, if only for a few seconds."

Dana nodded. "It did."

Suddenly, the air seemed to compress between them. Dana felt as if she were being pulled forward by an inescapable force, the way the sun pulls the Earth into orbit. A wave of dizziness passed over her which didn't lessen when Cybele withdrew her hand. Was Cybele experiencing the same attraction?

They spoke of other things, yet whenever their eyes met, the speaker hesitated for a second before continuing. Eventually, after a lengthy analysis of Mykonos' best restaurants, Cybele mentioned the burglary.

"We'll find the thief, I promise." She hesitated before continuing. "But I'm concerned your thief is not simply a thief. I don't want to worry you, Dana, but it's possible that Malcom Hall's killer broke into your apartment. If so, you need to be careful."

"I had the same thought."

They fell silent. In front of them, the sky darkened to deep purple as evening became night. Once Cybele finished her wine, Dana suggested they heat the chicken and rice.

—

During dinner, Cybele related more about her family and her difficult decision to leave them in order to come to terms with her sexuality. Then, setting down her knife and fork, she asked Dana about her own history.

"I've never been sure what I wanted," Dana said. "I know what I don't want—a husband and a little house with a white picket fence."

"A picket fence?"

Dana laughed, realizing how foolish this sounded. "Supposedly, it's what conventional American women wish for. They believe they would be happy with a simple life and children—2.5 children."

Cybele wrinkled her nose. "What?"

"We cut them in half. Didn't you know that?" Dana chuckled. "Actually, 2.5 is considered the perfect average. And you? Do you want children? I'm probably too old to have any—I turned forty in July."

"I will be thirty-three in November. No children for me, either, by choice, although this doesn't please my mother. In Greece it's unusual not to have a family. But I'm not always comfortable in my own country."

"I can understand that. I've always been different too."

"Ah, that's because you are an artist. Your work is very beautiful, yet somewhat abstract. So pure and, how can I explain? So clean."

"Thank you. I find Greece inspiring," Dana replied, smiling. "More so now."

"I think you're teasing me!"

"No, not at all. I'm quite serious."

She studied Dana. "Yes, I can see that."

Dana wanted to take Cybele's hand, which rested inches from her own. It was an elegantly shaped hand, with slim fingers, tanned skin. Why did this simple action feel momentous? She didn't recall being so shy before. A generous swallow of wine didn't give her more courage. "And what about your father? You didn't mention him."

"Like yours, he's dead. An accident…a fall." Cybele frowned. "It's a long story. Not for now."

The conversation dwindled into sporadic reminiscences and died altogether. Dana stared into Cybele's brown eyes, noticed her parted lips and quickened breaths. The invitation was clear. Leaning over, she kissed Cybele and then again with more passion. In seconds, they were in each other's arms. The canvas-backed chairs creaked as the two women stretched across the space dividing them.

Finally, drawing a few inches away, Dana whispered, "Is it too soon?"

"Yes, probably," Cybele replied, "but does it matter?"

"Hemingway said if it feels good afterward, what you do now is fine. Well, something like that. I never remember quotations."

"Is that one of your lines?" Cybele laughed. "But I understand what you mean." She kissed Dana on the forehead. "And, yes, I believe it will be good after. Very good."

Together, they rose and walked into the kitchen with their plates. Dana uncorked a second bottle of Assyritiko and tucked it under her arm. Each holding a glass, they went upstairs. Dana placed the bottle next to an emerald-green vase that held two sprays of fuchsia bougainvillea and lit candles on the side table, bureau, and bookcase.

They toasted each other, enjoying the tension. Then Dana placed their wineglasses beside the bed and tossed her photographer's vest on a wicker chair. Cybele unbuttoned Dana's white shirt and played her fingers along the length of Dana's neck, her touch producing flutters of excitement. Dana responded by stroking Cybele's bare arms, causing her to shiver, and slowly eased Cybele's black sweater over her head and unzipped her pants. With her hands sliding down Cybele's hips and thighs,

Dana lowered the white slacks and gold bikini briefs to the floor; as she unhooked Cybele's bra, Dana kissed Cybele's shoulder. With equal adeptness, Cybele removed Dana's clothes until they stood facing each other, the sea air enveloping them. For a second, Dana hesitated, wanting to treasure this precious first time together, but the electricity careening back and forth was too strong. She wrapped Cybele into an embrace, reveled in the sensation of her warm skin, and kissed Cybele deeply. They stood together, murmuring words of passion, hands exploring and caressing, until at last they tumbled onto the bed and into each other's arms. Listening to the lullaby of the sea, they made love.

As the hours fell far away from midnight, Dana had the strangest sense of becoming some new being, more vulnerable but safe, reassured by Cybele. In the end, spent with emotion, physically tired, they fell asleep.

—

DESPITE his annoyance at the poor service, the man had eaten well. The food made him feel stronger, but he knew that his real strength came from fulfilling his desire. He could already sense the power coursing through him like the temblors of an impending earthquake. But it was too early. Keep it under control, he warned himself. Observe the sunset, how the wispy white clouds create flourishes against the pastel-colored sky. Watch the sea unfold waves onto the beach. Forget the slender bodies salty with perspiration from dancing, bodies eager for the ultimate supplication. Forget and be calm. Later, he promised, you shall be supreme.

CHAPTER FIVE

DANA WOKE FIRST, forgetting that Cybele lay beside her. When she remembered, her heart flooded with happiness. Turning, she saw Cybele open her eyes.

"Good morning." Dana leaned over and kissed her lover's cheek.

Cybele gave her a sleepy smile. They came together, already comfortable with how their bodies fit. "So, Dana, is it good after?" Her expression was playful.

"Yes, it is. Hemingway was right … if it was Hemingway."

Cybele laughed. Drawing her arm tighter around Dana, she said, "I think it will always be good between us. That's my opinion on our first morning together. Now, forgive me, but I must check the time."

"Oh, yes! You have work, don't you?"

She glanced over Dana's shoulder at the clock. "In an hour, I'm sorry to say. And I must go home and dress."

Dana gave her a provocative kiss. "I'd rather you stayed home here and remained undressed."

Cybele laughed and rose reluctantly. "Ah, you are clever this morning. Of course, I would rather spend the day in bed with you."

Dana sighed. "But we have responsibilities."

—

Dana made coffee and toast, both of which Cybele dispatched quickly.

"Will I see you tonight?" Cybele asked.

"Yes. May I take you to Avra for dinner?"

"How romantic!" She hugged Dana. "Now, I am late!" And with that, she was gone.

Dana carried her coffee upstairs and sat on the bed, running her hands over the sheets and replaying the night. Would it be the first of many or one of a few? She recognized what her hopes were, but she'd been hopeful before and had always been disappointed, usually in herself, sometimes in her lover. Would this relationship be different? Was her optimism founded on solid ground or produced by island magic?

Finally, Dana forced herself to confront the day. She stepped into the bathroom, amazed at how energized she felt considering the lack of sleep, showered, dried, and dressed in white shorts and a button-down shirt, the tan vest, and leather sandals. With care, she strapped on her father's Hamilton gold watch. It was a rectangular-faced '50s design with an alligator band and required daily winding—an opportunity to be reminded of her father each morning. Then she added eyeliner and sprayed cologne on her neck, though all Dana could smell was sandalwood.

Feeling bewitched, she walked to the harbor. It was another clear day that would be hot. She had as many cares as there were clouds in the empty sky. As Dana rounded the blue-domed church by the quay, she encountered Tassos. The newspaperman was wearing a rumpled green polo shirt with a pack of cigarettes stuffed in its chest pocket. Although Tassos was a friend, when he greeted her, his expression was sober.

"What's the matter?" Dana asked.

He sat down heavily on a bench and gestured for her to sit beside him.

"I have some very bad news, Dana." He shook his head sadly. "One of your students was killed last night."

"Oh, please, no! Who?"

"Virgil Laine," he said quietly. "I am very sorry."

Dana stared at the fishing boats, the glittering aquamarine water, but only saw Virgil's smiling face, his mischievous grin. Such a cheerful, joyful young man, with so many opportunities and adventures ahead of him! She felt as if the sun had suddenly been eclipsed.

"Has anyone told Émile?" Dana asked.

"Yes, of course. Immediately." Tassos lit a cigarette, took a long drag, and exhaled slowly. "We're not positive what happened. His body was found in the park. No clothes. Choked to death. From what we've learned, it seems that Virgil was at a bar last night with Mr. de Szasi, though Mr. de Szasi told the police that he had left Virgil early because he himself was not feeling well."

"Oh, Émile must be so upset!" Dana sighed, remembering Virgil's happiness the evening before as everyone had praised his photographs. "Virgil was a lovely person. How could anyone kill him?"

Tassos flicked the ash from his cigarette. "The police believe the same person killed Malcolm Hall. With their permission, we featured Hall's passport picture in today's paper and asked if anyone had information about Hall's activities on the night he died. I'm sure someone does, but people might not wish to go to the police or to us."

"No," Dana agreed.

"On a related topic, did you print the photos you took yesterday morning?"

"Yes, but I guess you didn't hear about the robbery?"

He straightened up in surprise. "What?"

"I developed the negatives yesterday and printed three eight-by-tens of an Orthodox priest in a hat and a long black cassock. I left everything in my darkroom because I had to meet my class. When I returned, the door had been forced, the place was a wreck, and the three prints and the page of negatives were gone."

"Did you report it?" Tassos asked.

Dana nodded. "No clues, I'm afraid."

"And you said that the photo was of a Greek priest?"

"Yes, but the image wasn't useful for identification. It was taken too far away, and his head was partly covered with an epanokalimavkion. Did I get that right?"

Tassos blew out a stream of smoke and smiled at her careful enunciation. "You did. But a man of God doing this? And a Greek?" He tucked in his chin. "Not likely."

"I know. It doesn't feel right. From what you said about clothes being removed, it sounds as if the murders had a sexual motive." She wondered if Cybele would be informed of crime scene details.

"I think it must be someone else. A tourist," Tassos decided. "Maybe he was in another photograph you took?"

"I don't think so. Only those prints and negatives were taken."

"I guess there's no reason to steal the photos unless they show the killer." Tassos looked at her. "Dana, please accept my sympathy about Virgil Laine. Now, I must go. We're publishing a story on those American protesters. This island has turned crazy!" he muttered, stubbing out his cigarette on the ground.

—

IN THE EARLY HOURS of morning, the man had scoured the blood staining his wrist and shirt cuff, areas which hadn't been protected by the surgical gloves. He slept afterward but awoke after a few hours, still feeling exhilarated, alive, omnipotent. He thought about Virgil and became aroused again, remembering his face, how his lips felt warm even as Virgil's life drained away. The man was pleased with the masterful job he had done on the body: the blue eyes lined with black kohl, the eyelids brushed with lavender shadow, and the pale nipples encircled with scarlet lipstick. This time he had drawn a small red cross on the chest and spider web lines down the young man's abdomen and up his thighs to his cock—a little lipstick there too. After rolling Virgil's clothes tightly together—except the socks and sneakers, which he'd left on—the man hid the garments in his shopping bag. Reveling in his artistic achievement, he had taken his secret treasures: clippings of the fine, sandy hair from Virgil's head, chest, and pubic area. These samples were placed in a box divided into four compartments, one of which held Malcolm Hall's specimens. The box would be with him always, saved with the others. After this collection was complete, he would begin another, though by then a new location might be necessary. The island was small, the townspeople were on alert, and his anonymity would be increasingly difficult to maintain.

After drinking some oolong tea, he washed the black cassock and his socks, meticulously double-checking that he'd removed all the blood. The man hung everything over hangers to dry and blacked the shoes with polish.

—

DANA WALKED to the edge of the harbor in a daze. How she wished she'd brought her cell phone from New York so she could call Cybele! She wanted to hear her melodious voice, to share a quiet moment of connection, but she was also desperate for information about Virgil. As Dana descended the steps to the beach, she pictured Virgil dying in the black of night, a surreal contrast to the excruciatingly bright sun bouncing off the sand.

Several students were photographing the boats and their brilliantly colored bows reflected in the water. Dana took a seat on the red hull of an overturned caïque and waited for everyone to gather around, which, after noticing her somber mood, they did quickly. Choked with emotion, she struggled to compose herself. In a halting voice, Dana told them what had happened to their classmate.

The group absorbed the news in shocked silence. Carolyn was the first to speak.

"He was such a sweet, handsome boy." She fingered a gold cross dangling from a necklace. "Who would want to kill him?"

"I heard the first guy was gay," Julian said. "Maybe someone is trying to reduce the population."

"That's a little offensive," Mike replied.

Julian dipped his head. "Sorry."

Dana wasn't sure whether Julian was exhibiting callousness, prejudice, or blurting out a remark without thinking. She didn't like his attitude in any case. It sounded as if he approved of such violent acts. Dana gave him a stern look but forced herself to avoid an argument. Under different circumstances, she would have scalded him with censure. Then it occurred to her that the newspapers hadn't mentioned anything about Malcolm Hall being gay. While it was true word traveled fast around town, a visitor wouldn't usually be privy to island news. But Julian may have overheard a conversation at one of the restaurants or bars.

"Yes, both men were gay," she said in a low voice. "No one knows whether that's the reason they were murdered."

David ran a weary hand over his head. "Damned shame. Don't know what this world is coming to, all this violence." He surveyed the pretty harbor. "Such an idyllic place. Hate shouldn't be allowed here."

Mike nodded in sympathy. "Virgil was so young. A good guy."

"The whole thing makes me sick! Why can't we live together in peace?" David added.

Teresa sat next to Dana and gave in to tears. The group was quiet except for Julian, whose tolerance for holding still soon evaporated. He began pacing, kicking up small spurts of sand.

Not knowing what else to do, Dana suggested that the class should continue with the assignment. "If you want to take time off—a few hours—whatever—that's fine." She stood and scanned the area, finally pointing to a man selling eggplants, onions, and tomatoes from a wooden cart. Strings of garlic pods hung from a carelessly constructed open frame. "You might want to photograph him. That's Hercules."

Everyone smiled in spite of their sadness. Hercules was a spindly old man with a bent spine and weathered face crowded with wrinkles. Dana caught his eye and waved. Hercules touched a finger to his black fisherman's cap in response. "He'll pose for you for a few drachmas."

"He has a great face," Carolyn commented.

"And a great hat," Mike said.

"When you're finished, photograph the port and the blue-domed church. Lunch is open today. I'll see you at the windmills at two. You can drop off your film afterward."

A few questions were put forward, which Dana answered. Then, without their usual enthusiasm, the group started working, and Dana walked home.

—

ALTHOUGH CYBELE had applied makeup, her face reflected the activities of the night before—her eyes were too bright, her cheeks flushed. She stared into the mirror above the station's coffee percolator and poured a cup of black sludge. The news of Virgil Laine's death was being discussed at every desk, although details were sparse. A group of senior policemen was assigned to the two cases, and, so far, they were still meeting behind closed doors with Captain Yalouris, whom she hoped would bring the staff up to date shortly. New to police procedures, she didn't know what would happen next, though she intended to pump Myron when they were outside. He had been with the force for twenty years and had been included in the conference, despite the fact that Myron was a kind and honest man but no detective. His career rise had been modest, mostly earned by diligence, dependability, and seniority.

Cybele wanted to call Dana, but, to her immense frustration, she hadn't asked for her number, nor had she given Dana the landline number at her apartment—she hadn't bought a cell phone yet to use on the island. When Cybele checked, there were no listings for Dana Fox. She could use her police authority to get the number, but it might be registered to her landlord, whose name she didn't know. Because she and Myron were heading out soon, she wouldn't have a chance to do any research or to go past Dana's apartment. Myron would be at her elbow all day.

Cybele twirled a pen, nervously rapping it on the desk. The robbery at Dana's was probably linked to the murders, which meant the killer knew who Dana was—if the thief and the murderer were the same person. If they weren't, why would someone steal the photographs of a priest walking on the street? However, if Dana *had* photographed the killer, she could still be at risk because she'd seen the enlargements, even if the prints or film were no longer in her possession. Cybele exhaled slowly. She wished she could speak with Captain Yalouris and share her concerns. But here was Myron, ready to go. She laid the pen on her blotter and fastened the heavy police belt around her waist.

—

DANA WENT inside her apartment and called Émile, though she wasn't sure whether he was in any condition to speak with her. A houseboy answered, and then Émile came on, sounding older than his sixty years.

"I am so sad about this and so very sorry," she began tentatively.

"Thank you." His voice was rough with emotion. "I feel like my world has fallen apart."

"He loved you very much, Émile."

"Do you think he did?" he asked, as if he had doubts.

"Yes. I'm positive."

"It's sometimes difficult, you know, when there is such a difference in ages, such a difference in backgrounds. I hoped Virgil stayed with me because of how he felt, rather than…"

"He was there because he wanted to be with you," Dana reassured him.

"I would like to think that's true. He was such a beautiful man. And very talented. You told him that, didn't you? Just yesterday?"

"Yes, I did. He asked me about studying together after the class disbanded. He wanted to photograph some nudes for you, as a surprise."

Émile chuckled quietly. "That sounds like him."

"I know you're probably exhausted and just want to be alone, but would you like to have dinner tonight or a drink later?" she asked, upset about canceling plans with Cybele.

He considered the offer. "I don't know. Maybe. After dinner. I need to get out of the house. Virgil is everywhere I look."

"Gabriel's?" The bar was one of his favorites.

"No. Too many memories. Besides, some Americans are making a fuss in front of the place. Walking up and down with signs and trying to stop people from entering. I can't deal with that right now. Would Orpheus be okay?"

"Sure. And if you change your mind, just let me know. I'll understand."

Faintly ashamed at her relief that he only wanted to have drinks, Dana agreed to meet him at ten. That would give her time for dinner at Avra.

—

After speaking with Émile, Dana telephoned the police station. Cybele wasn't available. She decided to go there to see if anyone knew more about Virgil's death and to leave Cybele a note, asking her to meet at the restaurant at seven, which in Greece was considered early for dinner. Most restaurants didn't open until that hour.

As she neared the station, Dana recognized the unmistakable heart-racing signs. Was she falling for Cybele? Even though she was depressed about Virgil, euphoria was jangling her senses. She had felt excited before, but as trite as it sounded, this time was unlike the others. Before moving to Mykonos, she had devised an informal philosophy: Enjoy life and keep your powder dry. So much for dry powder.

All through her teenage years, Dana had been confused about her feelings for women. In prep school, her confusion increased when she met Frederica Snow, a young woman who taught sophomore English and ran the photography club. Dana soon became her most devoted student. By graduation, Dana was miserably in love with her, but the love went unexpressed except for one cryptic, farewell card which she mailed. In college, Dana had dated men and liked many of them. She fell in love with women. For a long while, she couldn't sort it all out; when she did, the clarity didn't help her find a lasting relationship. In fact, it set her teeth on edge to recount the failures. Should she admit to Cybele how poorly she had done in the past? About a commitment made in her twenties to a woman who then cheated on her? The list of disasters was lengthy, many self-created, though not all.

At the station, Dana was told Cybele was out on duty. She was shown to Cybele's desk and given a piece of paper and an envelope. She wrote:

Dear Cybele,

I know you've heard about Virgil Laine's death. I asked his lover, Émile de Szasi, to have drinks at 10:00 at Orpheus—after you and I have dinner. Can you meet me at Avra at 7:00? I hope so! I look forward to seeing you. Last night was amazing! Soon—

Dana

She could write volumes but merely added her phone number to the bottom of the page and sealed the paper inside the envelope, noticing as she did that a few of the men were staring at her curiously. It had been her experience that blondes caught the roving eye of men in countries where many women were dark. On the other hand, perhaps her sexual orientation was known. In that case, her appearance at Cybele's desk wasn't discreet and might jeopardize Cybele's reputation.

Her mission complete, it was time for lunch. As she stepped outside, she caught a glimpse of a dark figure wearing a baseball cap and sunglasses. When he saw her, he ducked around the trees and hurried toward Ipirou Street. Was her imagination over-sensitized due to the break-in and the murders or was someone spying on her? She rushed across the square and turned right. No one was there—at least no one who was running away. However, the town was a warren of tiny streets, with numerous places to hide. Dana gave up.

—

After eating a messy lamb souvlaki, Dana walked to the famous Mykonos windmills, whose graceful sails were spinning in the breeze. It was unlikely that any scintillating daytime images would be made at this location, but it was a good spot to reconnoiter. Carolyn was sitting on a wall nearby with the contents of her camera bag spread precariously in true Miss Bumble fashion. Dana shuddered to think of the dust that was blowing into her lenses and cameras. Mike was there, too, giving Carolyn a wide berth as if her clumsiness might be contagious. Teresa stood with Luca. They were arguing about something, both gesturing angrily. Hasina Ambrose was coming up the hill from town. She waved and made her way toward Dana.

"David will be here in a minute," she said. "He had a little run-in with some moussaka. He asked me to come ahead and tell you."

Hasina was beautiful. Every inch worthy of a *Glamour* cover, but Dana thought Cybele was more exotic. And, yes, serene even with her intensity. Odd to be both intense and serene, but that was a fitting description.

"Thanks. Sorry he isn't feeling well. Greek food is heavy, particularly in this heat."

Julian arrived, already out of sorts. "Do we really have to photograph these windmills? They've been done so much." He tossed a cigarette butt on the street.

"You may shoot them now, but the primary assignment is for tonight, after dark," Dana replied.

He seemed irritated by her response but kept quiet. David joined the group, out of breath from climbing the long hill and carrying his heavy camera bag and tripod. He looked queasy.

"Sorry to hold you up," he said.

"No problem at all, David. Are you feeling better?"

He nodded uncertainly. "I think so."

Dana faced her students. "Your assignment involves shooting in low light at night. Using a tripod and a slow shutter speed, photograph the windmills so the buildings are sharp, but the bladed arms will be blurred and ghost-like—as will people moving through your image. Set your aperture about f11 or f16 and try different time exposures. Also wander around town for other subjects. It's okay to shoot black-and-white film, but the photo shop will only print contact sheets. Leave your rolls in the after-hours box to give them enough time to develop and print. There will be no session this evening. Your critique will be tomorrow late afternoon and will include tonight's work and images taken for the next problem."

Dana told everyone to enjoy the hotel pool for an hour or so and that she would see them in the morning. She provided directions to several photogenic buildings and reminded them to be careful. "If you can, stay together in pairs or small groups. Please avoid dark areas without anyone around … or being out really late."

Everyone set up tripods around the windmills. Dana stood by, observing and offering helpful comments, though she caught herself yawning several times. After half an hour, the group was finished and ready to return to the Inn and the inviting pool. Dana warned them again to be cautious.

At her apartment, the answering machine held two messages. The first was from Myron Tsoublekas, checking to see if she had noticed anything else missing. The second was from Cybele, who had received the note on her desk. Because of the murders, she had to work an evening shift and was terribly sorry that she couldn't meet for dinner. Dana felt deflated, disappointment crashing into tiredness. The message ended with her apartment phone number and "see you later." Did that mean tonight, Dana wondered?

Dana jotted down the number and called it. "Cybele, I received your message about dinner. I understand, but I'll really miss you. I'm meeting Émile at Orpheus' Lyre at ten. If you're free, please come."

CHAPTER SIX

CYBELE UNDERSTOOD that she was needed as a foot soldier, but the timing was miserable; she felt even more frustrated when Dana didn't answer the telephone. Because Cybele would be on duty all afternoon and evening, it was unlikely she would have an opportunity to speak with her. Instead, the rest of her day would be spent with Myron—a nice guy, but Myron wasn't Dana.

At two, Captain Yalouris convened a staff meeting and requested everyone to work long hours until the killer was caught. The captain was a tall, imposing man, bald-headed, with a quiet demeanor and, on occasion, a sense of humor. Today, however, his face was drawn and serious.

"We've found a hair sample and two black cotton fibers at the scene—possibly in place prior to the attack. These are being analyzed, but otherwise, there aren't any physical clues." He pointed to the group of photographs tacked to the wall behind him. "As you can see, the crime scenes are nearly identical. Both bodies were left naked, with clothes removed from the location except for shoes and socks."

Cybele examined the pictures and noted that Malcolm Hall's face was rouged, his eyes lined, and eyelids shadowed. These images by Yannis were not as extensive as those taken by the police photographer, who had documented more angles of Virgil Laine's body and done so with better lighting. Virgil's face had similar cosmetic painting as Malcolm's, though a cross had been added to his chest, and black spider web lines had been drawn on Virgil's torso and thighs.

Captain Yalouris paused in his presentation. "It's possible that a relevant photograph was taken shortly after Malcolm Hall's murder. An Orthodox priest. Unfortunately, the negative and the enlargements have been stolen, but the black cloth fibers we found lead us to believe the photographs are of the murderer, an opinion reinforced by the theft."

"We should call him The Black Monk," one of the men said.

Captain Yalouris nodded. "Although I'm skeptical that the murderer is local, stop and interview any priests, especially if they are walking during the night and early morning. Please be respectful and discreet." He paused, then asked two officers to visit the monasteries. "Get alibis from all the clergymen and learn who had access to their rooms and their clothes."

The room grew silent. As Cybele surveyed the policemen, everyone looked grim.

Yalouris tapped a file on his desk. "The medical examiner says both deaths were caused by choking the victim from behind, using a wire. Unfortunately, a wire is a simple weapon to make and easy to hide." He consulted his notes. "The two men were raped—probably after death. Spermicide was found during the autopsy of Malcolm Hall, so we believe the killer wore a condom, but both victims were also sexually assaulted, possibly with a blunt, wooden object." He paused, shaking his head. "We may have more information after Laine's body has been thoroughly examined. It is obvious that the killer is methodical and likely that both men were selected because they were homosexual. There is no reason to assume he will stop."

After Yalouris finished, he instructed everyone to be alert, to report anything suspicious, and to refrain from communicating any information to the public. "Including wives, husbands, and friends. If I learn that anyone has leaked details, he or she will no longer work for me."

Re-energized by coffee, Cybele followed Myron out the door.

—

AT SIX, Dana called the Calvin Carnahan Gallery in Manhattan, which had just opened for the day. They represented her in America and handled the workshop bookings. After her passion for photography had bloomed under the tutelage of Frederica Snow, her beloved school instructor, Dana had taken advanced courses in college, built a darkroom, and worked hard developing her skill. Her inheritance was sufficient to allow Dana to pursue her career without worrying about finances, but her connection with the prestigious gallery was lucrative.

During the conversation with the owner, Dana learned that her next workshop was filled. She explained about the two deaths and told him to expect cancellations, though news of the murders hadn't reached New York. After their business was concluded, Dana sat at her desk and paid bills before dressing for the evening. Although she wasn't hungry, she ate some leftover chicken and rice—no comparison to the planned dinner with Cybele.

At 9:30, Dana was bored and decided that a preliminary drink was in order. She left for Orpheus' Lyre, which was a short walk from her apartment. The club's open door was decorated with a large turquoise and black lyre. As she entered, the patrons were gathering, and a chanteuse was spreading her music on the upright piano. The place was painted a soothing blue-green with a mural over the bar rendering the scene of Orpheus' head floating down the river Hebrus after his body had been hacked apart. According to legend, the head sang sweetly all the way to the island of Lesbos, where it was finally buried. This resonated with the gay crowd and also with the scholars of mythology who appreciated that Orpheus was the son of Apollo, the god born on the neighboring island of Delos.

Dana sat at the bar and ordered a vodka martini. She didn't have them often, but today had been a brute. She kept visualizing Virgil lying dead on the street. Then she thought of Cybele roaming around town. Although it seemed that the murderer was targeting gay men, Dana was worried and hoped that Myron was with her. She tossed off the first drink as the singer began a torchy Greek ballad, one she liked. A second martini appeared and so did Émile, in a tan linen sports jacket and black shirt. He was a dapper dresser, his silver hair neatly cut, his mustache trimmed with precision. Dana stood and hugged him long and hard, something she rarely did because she felt awkward towering over him.

"Thank you, Dana. I'm glad you asked me to come. I was going crazy at the house—you know, without Virgil." He sat on the stool beside her and ordered a drink, which arrived immediately.

"I just can't believe it happened," Dana began. "What did the police tell you?"

"Not much. I think they're trying to control information so that it doesn't scare the public. But two murders should scare the public. It scares me."

"Did you know Malcolm Hall?" she asked.

"Not really. I met him briefly at a party. He was here on vacation and to see Delos. An assistant museum curator or something. Nice-looking, bright—and so young! What a terrible, terrible loss." He was silent for a few minutes, sipping his scotch. "I can tell you this. Virgil died from strangulation. I had to identify his body, and there was a bloody line around his throat where a wire had been used."

"A garrote?"

He nodded. "The police wouldn't confirm it, but when I asked about the mark around his neck, they admitted that his trachea had been crushed." He took out a folded white handkerchief from his breast pocket and wiped his eyes. "I'm sorry, Dana, but I miss him."

She put an arm around Émile and let him cry for a few minutes. Finally, he cleared his throat and sighed. "You know the worst thing?"

Dana shook her head.

Émile swallowed hard. "Whoever killed him…whoever that fiend from hell is…he put lipstick on Virgil…and rouge on his cheeks…" His voice cracked. "And eyeliner. He was made up to look like some kind of street tart. I wish I had never seen him like that. I wish, oh, how I wish!"

"I'm so sorry."

The entertainer was now launching into a series of Piaf songs. Émile blew his nose, dried his eyes, and tossed back his head.

"We need another round of drinks." He held up one finger to the bartender, Georges.

"Let me switch to—"

"Nonsense," he said, "you must have another. You need to catch up to me. I had several scotches at home." He asked the bartender for some potato chips in a bowl. Like the drinks, they appeared promptly. Everyone knew about Virgil.

Dana sipped the martini, feeling its warmth fire her blood. Her father always quipped that one martini tasted okay, two tasted better, and three were divine. She hesitated to think what four would be like and vowed she wasn't going to find out.

"Did you call Virgil's parents?" she asked, eating a chip.

"Yes. It was very awkward, as you can imagine. They knew he was on Mykonos, of course. They also knew he was staying with me, but they don't know he was gay. Or at least they won't admit it—that's what Virgil told me. How anyone could be that blind, I'll never understand. They're flying here tomorrow. I really dread meeting them."

"Perhaps you should let the police handle everything."

"I couldn't do that, in good faith."

"No, I suppose not."

"I spent the afternoon packing Virgil's things. He didn't have much, just enough to fill two suitcases."

They talked about Virgil for a while, but when the singer began Noël Coward's "Mad about the Boy," Émile excused himself, ostensibly to go to the men's room, but Dana knew he was overcome. She asked the bartender to hold their places and headed for the ladies' room, which was crowded, as always. By the time she returned to the bar, Émile was talking to a young man named Bryan Kerr, whom he introduced as an American investment advisor.

"And where is Alexander tonight?" Émile asked.

"I'm joining him at Gabriel's in a few minutes."

"Alexander and Bryan met recently," he explained to Dana. The thought seemed to remind him of Virgil, and his eyes filled with tears again. "Listen, I need to go home, and you need to have another drink, Dana. And Bryan needs to be on time for his date." He kissed Dana on the cheek. "I'll talk to you in a day or so. Thanks for coming, *cherie*."

He and Bryan left. Dana looked at her watch, which was beginning to appear a little blurry. Eleven. No Cybele. For some reason, she felt even sadder than she had a few minutes ago. In fact, she felt rotten. Well, Cybele knew where she was. Finish the martini and try to forget her disappointment,

The place was crowded and smoky. The bartender began talking about Virgil. He explained that everyone in town was upset and on edge. A few minutes later, Dana felt someone move behind her. Cybele? Dana turned, hope springing in her heart. No, it was a middle-aged man, average looking. Brown hair brushed back, a beginning tan, deep-set eyes. Cleanly shaved. He reached past her for a drink that Georges had made for him and excused himself when he jostled her elbow.

"That's okay," Dana replied. For some inane reason, she noticed that the man's upper lip was sculpted into two rising, pointed waves. Like an "M" or the top portion of a suspension bridge. She found this mildly fascinating.

"Do you live here or are you visiting?" he asked.

"I rent for several months of the year." She wasn't interested in talking, only thinking about Cybele and wishing she were here.

"Really? I'm considering buying a place. Where do you recommend?" His voice was pitched down a notch lower than Dana thought natural as if he were attempting to sound more virile. She suspected he liked to listen to himself.

"It depends what you're looking for. There are some nice spots above the town, in the hills. Above where the Dolphins come in—"

"The Dolphins?"

"The hydrofoils," she explained. "And some attractive places close to several beaches."

"Super Paradise?" He named a well-known gay beach.

Dana looked at him, trying to ascertain his sexual orientation. A built-in habit. His face suddenly seemed less distinct than it had a moment ago, possibly because he was smoking like everyone else in the room. The long American cigarette loomed like a shaking white finger in front of her eyes. "Yes, and there are others. Several, as a matter of fact."

"Is the cigarette bothering you?" he asked.

"I know there is so much smoke in here, but, yes."

He obliged by crushing it in an ashtray. "Sorry. So, where do you live?"

Dana took a sip and lied. "Over on Rochari."

"I see." He edged a little closer. "By the way, I didn't mean to be rude. My name is Ray. Ray Johnson."

"Marilyn," she replied, uttering the first name that floated into her mind.

"Hi, Marilyn. You're from the States, right?"

"Yeah, New York. How about you?" She was suddenly eager to leave.

"The Midwest."

He had a soft drawl, not southern, not twangy like Texas or Oklahoma. "Say, Ray," she said, trying not to giggle at the rhyme, "sorry, but I have to go … have an early appointment."

But Ray was already signaling for more drinks. He put his arm around the back of the barstool, cupping her within its confines. "The night's young. Come on, have a martini with me, Marilyn. I don't know anybody here."

Dana didn't want a fourth martini. She didn't want his arm around her. Georges, the bartender, as if prepared, poured from a silver shaker and added the olive with a splash. When Ray's drink arrived on the bar, he leaned to reach it. As he did so, he placed his other hand on Dana's neck, beginning a massage that might have been unconscious or might have been deliberate, Dana couldn't tell. She stared unseeing at the triangular martini glass in front of her, dreaming of Cybele. This was all wrong.

"Come on, a little sip," Ray prompted, lifting her drink as encouragement. His voice was still deep, but now it had become a whisper in her ear, a seductive one.

"I'm perfectly able to do it myself," Dana retorted. And to show him she could, she did.

"That's better, Marilyn," he said. "Now, tell me about yourself."

She stared at his eyes. Green, with a strange glitter. Another woman might find him attractive. "I'm here to work. I'm a photographer."

He laughed and moved in closer. "I'd like to see some of your photographs."

That was too much like the old "come up and see my etchings" line. Dana could smell his breath, acrid from the cigarettes. "Look, Ray, I have to use the bathroom. Here, hold my seat." She stood up, thinking it seemed a long way to the ground. As she took a step away, Ray attempted to pull her over to him. She pushed him gently, not wishing to create a scene. "Hang on. Right back."

The place was jammed. After a few steps into the crowd, Dana turned and saw that Ray was speaking with the bartender. With relief, she rushed out the rear door and onto the sea walk that led to her apartment, hoping Ray would think she was waiting in line for the bathroom. When he realized she had left, he probably would assume that she had exited by the front door.

Outside, the tide was up, splashing seawater onto the stones. "Oh, brother, be careful!" she muttered, as she trailed her left hand along the wall for balance and dodged chairs that haphazardly lined the promenade. "Idiot! Really smart to get drunk when there's a killer wandering around!"

After skirting some patrons standing outside Caprice, Dana found her aqua door and managed to line up the key with the lock. Inside, the place felt empty without Cybele. She felt crushed with disappointment and knew she would be hungover in the morning. She rarely drank this much and already wished she hadn't.

The spiral staircase required caution. It was particularly treacherous to negotiate with damp leather shoes. In the kitchen, Dana swallowed some ice water and then climbed to the bedroom. Lying on the bed, she cried because her pillow smelled of sandalwood.

CHAPTER SEVEN

THE NEXT MORNING, Dana swore oath after oath at her stupidity. Her mouth felt parched, and her head ached as if she had been sitting inside of a large, clanging bell all night. In addition to being disgusted by her behavior, she was even more upset that she hadn't heard from Cybele. Had her one-night, perfect lover been a dream?

A glance in the mirror did nothing to improve her downcast mood: red eyes and a complexion that looked like she had been poisoned. Well, she had. This was one day that sunglasses wouldn't come off. Dana took a long shower, dressed, and decided to invigorate herself with Kostas' high-octane coffee and freshly squeezed orange juice.

"*Kalimera*, Miss Fox. Ah, yes, Dana."

"*Ya sas*, Kostas." She smiled at him and asked to sit inside.

Kostas grinned. "Late night?"

"Yes. I am a fool," Dana replied, sitting in one of his swaying chairs.

"Coffee?"

"*Parakalo*. And the usual plus a bottle of water. And if you have enough oranges, some orange juice?"

He laughed. "Not only a late night, no? A lot of ouzo too?"

"Martinis," she admitted, holding her head.

"Ha! Even I have more sense than to drink martinis!"

"This morning, Kostas, everyone has more sense than I do."

At this, he chuckled and took himself off into the kitchen.

As Dana sat looking through the open door, the reporter, Devin Scott, took a seat at the café across the way, scratched his bearded chin, and tossed his baseball hat on the table. He was dressed in wrinkled jeans and a dingy white Henley shirt; aviator sunglasses perched on his nose.

Dana observed him as he ordered breakfast, sensing that he was aware of her presence. Suddenly, she realized that the man near the police station had been wearing similar sunglasses and cap and was about the same physical size as Devin. In fact, she was now fairly sure that it had been the reporter standing behind the trees. But why would he follow her? Dana tried to remember the comment that Tassos had made— something about Devin asking about the photographs she'd taken. Had that just been reporter's curiosity?

Kostas interrupted her thoughts with the three fluids she coveted: coffee, water, and juice. Dana drank everything, and, when the toast arrived with a pot of honey, she asked for more water. As she ate, Devin was doing the same until they exchanged glances. He nodded, twisted his lips into an awkward smile, and she put up a hand in greeting.

After doubles of everything, she used the bathroom. When she came out, Devin was gone. Kostas told her the amount of the bill, and she counted out the appropriate number of drachmas plus a nice tip for the hand-squeezed juice. Because she was near the newspaper office, she decided to stop in for information.

—

CYBELE WAS at work, exhausted from walking the streets for nearly eight hours and from a sleepless night following the shock she'd seen at Orpheus' Lyre. Off-duty just before eleven, she had hurried to the club, her desire to see Dana overcoming her fatigue. As she made her way through the crowd, she spied Dana sitting at the bar and saw a man fondling her neck in a familiar manner. Shaken and stunned, she asked a woman next to her if the man was Émile de Szasi, and the woman said she knew Émile and it wasn't him. Cybele had then turned and fled the smoky club, running most of the way home, tears coursing down her face. Now, this morning, she felt even worse—a dull sadness that flared into anguish whenever she visualized Dana. She was at a loss what to do, but two things seemed clear: Dana was not trustworthy and Dana was not really interested in her.

—

THE MAN YAWNED, covering his mouth as Miss Becker had taught him. He still thought of her as Miss Becker after all this time. She had been his father's secretary, and, since he was eight, his private teacher, who tutored him in math, science, history, English, and French. On Sundays, because he was not allowed to go to church—as he was not allowed to go to school—she also instructed him on the Bible. Thirteen years older than he, Miss Becker often told him how lonely she was in the large house, how much she loved their moments together. Sometimes, after one of his father's beatings, when he shook with fury, she would soothe him, touching the welts on his bare skin until the pain disappeared and the good sensations began. He still remembered her fingers probing his body.

—

WHEN ANNA saw Dana wearing her sunglasses inside the office, she laughed. "A late night?" Dana nodded and reluctantly removed them. "Oh, my! A very late night!" Anna shook her head. "I don't wish to add to your headache, but you should see this." She handed Dana one of the Athenian newspapers, folded to reveal an article. Dana's photograph of the priest was reproduced two columns wide, with a note in brackets that read: "Source Withheld."

Dana looked at the receptionist. "How did this get to Athens?" Bewildered, she asked Anna to translate. While she could converse socially, Dana wanted to understand the story exactly.

"It's by Devin Scott and a reporter who probably fixed Devin's Greek," she began. "The headline reads 'The Killer Monk.' It starts with the two murdered men, Malcolm Hall and Virgil Laine, where they were from, their ages, occupations. He explains that an American photography instructor took a picture as the priest was leaving the scene after strangling Hall with a wire."

"Well, that certainly points the finger at me, doesn't it?" Dana collapsed in a chair and ran a tired hand through her hair. "I can't believe this! Devin Scott broke into my apartment!"

"He knew that you took the photo. I'm responsible for that," Anna apologized. "I'm sure he did it for the money. These articles and the photo probably paid well. The story is also in the *International Herald Tribune*."

"What a bastard!" Dana tossed the newspaper on the desk.

"And, of course, Devin is guessing about the photograph being of the killer. However, the police were very interested in the picture. They called Devin's apartment, but there was no answer, and then they spoke with Tassos, who said he didn't know where Devin was. Devin hasn't come to work this morning." She shrugged. "Though sometimes he doesn't."

"I saw him eating breakfast a few minutes ago." Dana shook her head. "Wow! That takes some nerve. Showing up on Mykonos after what he did and advertising his theft by publishing his name on the article! Then staring at me just now—the person he robbed."

Anna agreed.

"And, though I'm not positive, I think he's been following me."

Anna's forehead furrowed. "Really?" She was silent for a moment. "I hate to say such a thing, but is it possible that Devin is the killer? It would explain why he was so sure that your photographs were of the murderer."

"It would, but since the police might also come that conclusion, I doubt Devin would be walking around town—if he's the killer. No, he stole the photos for the money. He probably didn't care if what he wrote was accurate."

Anna sighed. "The good news is that your name wasn't mentioned."

"So, if it is the killer in my photograph, he may not know who I am, at least not yet? Unless the killer is Devin."

"No, but it's a small island, and you're the only American photography instructor here at the moment."

"I take your point, Anna. Is there anything else in the article?"

She hesitated. "Ah, yes. Devin gives the impression that there might be more photographs."

"What? That's not true! I don't have any others!"

Anna considered. "Perhaps if Devin is not the killer, he's using you. If the murderer thinks you have other photos, maybe he'll try and get them. Maybe Devin is following you to see if he does."

"He's crazy!"

Anna interrupted her, a grim expression on her face. "I think that you must be very, very careful."

"You're right, I suppose." Dana sighed. "By the way, where is Tassos?"

"He's still speaking with the police about the articles and sharing some tips we received about Malcolm Hall—nothing useful." Anna stood, walked closer to Dana, and laid a hand on her arm. "Dana, I don't like this situation. You must go see Captain Yalouris immediately...to tell him everything."

"Okay, I will. Right after my class." Her students were meeting near the police station. A visit to Captain Yalouris might also provide a chance to see Cybele, who, she hoped would provide a reasonable explanation for her absence. Maybe she worked late and went home? Dana fervently hoped this was true.

After accepting a copy of the *Herald Tribune* and *The Pelican,* she said goodbye to Anna. Dana had forgotten her hat, so she decided to swing past her apartment. There, tacked to her door, was an envelope with her first name written on the front. She pulled it off, went upstairs, and opened it.

Dana,

I guess you had second thoughts about us. I must say, I was very upset to see you with that man at Orpheus last night—a man who was not Émile. I don't understand why you did this, but I don't like women who treat me this way.

Cybele

Dana dropped on the sofa and groaned. Cybele had come to Orpheus after all! At exactly the wrong moment. Of all the miserable, rotten luck!

She didn't know what to do except grab her hat, go to class, and then try to find Cybele.

—

As Dana approached the red-domed church, she spotted Teresa and Carolyn. Teresa was fidgeting with a gold scarf that didn't successfully cover a purple bruise on her neck. Concerned, Dana asked what had happened.

"Luca and I had an argument yesterday afternoon. A bad one," she replied quietly.

"At the hotel?"

She nodded. "He'd been drinking…from lunch on…at the bar by the pool. When I returned to the room after we photographed the windmills, he was there…" Her voice broke. "I really don't want to talk about it."

Dana sighed, unsure of what to do. "If he assaulted you, you should make a complaint to the police."

Teresa shook her head. "No, I'm not ready to do that." She massaged her arm where another discoloration wrapped around her elbow.

"Where is Luca?" Carolyn asked Teresa.

She shrugged. "When I left this morning, he was still in bed. He'd been out late—I refused to have dinner with him—and he went off by himself. He's been drinking in the bars every night since we arrived."

"Are you sure you're okay?" Dana asked again.

Teresa nodded, but her eyes were downcast.

David, Mike, and Julian arrived. Mike gave Teresa a concerned glance but was silent. Julian, on the other hand, didn't notice Teresa at all and began asking about the assignment. Unsettled, the last thing Dana wanted to do was deliver a lecture, but everyone was waiting.

"Well, let's begin with today's compositional problem: figure/ground relationships, in which you concentrate on making your negative spaces —the ground—as important as your figure. In our Western culture, we're very subject-oriented, paying little attention to the surrounding area, yet without this area, there is no containment of the figure. In Zen philosophy, the world is seen as complements that are mutually defining. In order to achieve true perfection, both the figure and ground, the positive and negative, should strive for equality. A perfect figure/ground image is one in which the viewer is visually puzzled as to which is figure and which is ground, even for a split second. Making the negative spaces in your image stronger will also empower the figure."

Dana walked to Julian's camera, which was set on a tripod facing the church. Adjusting the zoom lens, she designed a composition so that the dark blue sky became tightly cropped at the left and emphasized the large curve of the red dome. The sky peeking through the bell tower was also accentuated. She asked everyone to look.

"What do you consider the 'ground'—I mean is it just the sky?" Mike asked.

"The ground is the non-subject. It can be the sky or any area that isn't the figure. For example, the church walls might act as the ground. In the image I've just demonstrated, the sky becomes a dynamic player, with a strength of its own because it's been trapped and contained into its own individual shape."

Carolyn, David, and John bombarded her with questions, which she answered. Julian gathered his tripod and camera.

"Where else should we go?" He was trying to hurry everyone as usual.

"Wherever you like, Julian. You might also want to do some shots of the exterior stairways, though they don't necessarily pertain to the assignment."

"Why do they build them like that?" Carolyn asked.

"I've been told they build the stairs outside so there is more room inside."

This amused Mike. "I think it's a great idea. Boy, think of how much extra usable square footage a house would have if we could do that!"

Dana laughed at his enthusiasm. "All right, everyone, back to the assignment. As you know, the Cycladic style is based on the cube mixed with curves such as on church domes. So look for dramatic architectural examples and crop tightly, prioritizing the negative spaces." She rose to her feet. "Anything else? This is the toughest problem I give, so work hard on it." She wasn't confident that they fully understood the lecture, but sometimes the best way to teach this assignment was to point out the successes and failures in the critique and send the students back to solve it again.

Julian came over to her. "Where are you going to be today…if I have a problem or something?"

Surprised by his persistent interest in her schedule, she paused, weighing her response. "If you need to ask me anything…"

He looked a little dazed and shook his head.

"Okay, I'll see you later, Julian." To her students, she said, "The critique will be at 5:30 so shoot this assignment now and bring your color film in by 1:30. However, drop off black-and-white film immediately after we finish here because they need more time. Have fun and please stay together so you can look at each other's setups and discuss your compositions." Dana also thought that with the recent occurrences in town, keeping the group together would be a good idea.

Everyone nodded and scattered in various directions, immediately ignoring her request. Julian stood next to her for a few minutes, but, with one last inscrutable glance, he picked up his camera and left.

Dana began the short walk to the police station, anxious about encountering Cybele.

—

THE MAN was eating dark red grapes, enjoying the sensuous globes, the thick skin popping open between his teeth, the cool liquid coursing slowly down his throat. He ate one grape after the other, prying the seeds out with his fingers.

After wiping his hands on a white napkin, he stared at the red juice that stained the cloth. Not blood red, he thought, or at least not the color of fresh blood. On this subject, he was an expert.

No luck last night. The garrote was regrettably clean. The man looked at the *International Herald Tribune* lying on the table beside his cup of coffee. The article made him feel proud! He clipped it out carefully with a pair of manicure scissors. And the one or two photographs taken in the crowd by the harbor? Where were they?

He folded the napkin and wiped his mouth, considering.

CHAPTER EIGHT

At the station, Dana took a deep breath as she opened the door. Cybele was not at her desk. Myron Tsoublekas walked over. His black hair was plastered to his head, and large half-moons of perspiration circled under the arms of his shirt.

"Good morning, Miss Fox."

"Good morning, Officer." Dana hesitated to ask where his partner was, though she desperately wanted to know. "Would it be possible to speak with Captain Yalouris?"

"Ah, is it about what happened yesterday? The stolen prints?"

"Yes," Dana replied.

"And about the article in the paper?" The policeman waved the Athens' edition in the air.

"Yes, about that too."

"We are looking for Mr. Scott. He wasn't at his apartment."

"I don't know where he is … but about seeing Captain Yalouris?"

Myron dipped his head three times in rapid succession. "Yes, yes, Miss Fox. I will see if he's available. Please excuse me."

A minute later, Dana was led into the office of Basil Yalouris, a distinguished-looking man in his early sixties, with natural authority and alert brown eyes. Dana knew Yalouris' reputation: fair, thoughtful, and competent. He was sitting at a desk amid skyscrapers of papers and folders; a small gold-leaf icon and several framed citations were hung on the wall behind him. As she came in, he laid down his pen and stood, offering his hand.

"Thank you for coming to see me, Miss Fox," he said with a trace of an American accent. Dana had heard that he had lived in New York and spent a year with the NYPD. "I wanted to see you. Please, sit down."

Dana accepted one of the two chairs in front of his desk. With mild embarrassment, she removed her sunglasses.

Captain Yalouris returned to his seat, pushed some papers to the side, and rested his elbows on the cleared area. "I read the report prepared by Officers Karabélias and Tsoublekas about the theft of the negatives and three photographic prints. Have you seen this morning's newspapers?"

"I have."

"It's obvious that the reporter, Devin Scott, was responsible for stealing your negatives and photographs."

"Yes. In fact, before I knew he was the thief, I saw him this morning at the Blue Dolphin. He sat at a table across from me. That took some nerve."

"So, he's walking around town like an innocent man?"

She nodded. "And I also saw him yesterday. I think he's been following me."

The Captain shook his head and then, with a wry smile, said, "Perhaps if we have someone follow you, we will find him!"

Dana returned his smile. She liked his manner. "Perhaps."

"Now the next question we must ask ourselves is whether this Mr. Scott has anything to do with the deaths of Mr. Hall and Mr. Laine."

Dana shrugged. "I have no idea."

"Nor do we, I'm sorry to say. When we locate him, we may understand the situation better. At the moment, we can only assume Mr. Scott took the prints to sell and for no other reason. Before Mr. Scott's article, we thought the thief was the murderer, removing the photos in order to hide his or her identity."

"I did too."

"But with the publication in the papers, the motive for the theft has changed. Possibly the monk in your picture is only an innocent holy man. Even so, Miss Fox, we have a good reason to believe you may have photographed the killer." He leaned back in his chair, making the hinges creak. "I understand one of your prints was more enlarged than the newspaper reproduction. Is there anything you can tell us? Something we should know?"

Dana shook her head. "The detail wasn't good. The man appeared to be of average build. You already know what he was wearing."

"Yes, we do. And that he was bearded."

"Like Devin Scott."

"And like most Orthodox priests," the policeman replied. "He was also holding a bag in his hand. It's a shame we can't see the writing on it." Captain Yalouris observed her with a grave expression. "Miss Fox, I can't tell you much regarding the case. We keep certain things from the public. I'm sure you can appreciate this."

Although Dana was hoping for some specifics, she wasn't surprised by his reluctance to share clues. "Yes, Captain."

He rested his chin on his hand, thinking, then fixed his eyes on hers. "Miss Fox, I must warn you that you might be in some danger. If Devin Scott has something to do with this, he knows where you live. If the killer is someone else, he will soon guess your identity from the article." He paused before adding, "Another unfortunate thing is that the article gives the impression that you took other photographs."

"I didn't. Devin's just trying to entice readers, promising more to come, when he doesn't have anything else."

"I see. But the person responsible for the deaths may believe his article…that you have other pictures. If so, you must be careful, Miss Fox," he said, drumming his fingers lightly on his desk as if considering. "Would you like me to assign someone to watch your apartment?"

Dana instantly thought of Cybele. "No, thanks," she replied slowly, "I don't think that will be necessary. I'll let you know if anything else happens."

Captain Yalouris asked for her telephone number, which she wrote down. He stood and gave her his hand, smiled, and said goodbye.

In the station's main room, she stopped Myron. "Excuse me. Will you see Officer Karabélias this afternoon?"

"No, she's at the airport. Some trouble with more protesters. She won't be off-duty until late—none of us will. We must work extra hours because of the two deaths."

"Would it be possible for you to call and ask her to check her home answering machine? We were supposed to meet this evening." This sounded as lame to Dana's ears as it did to Myron's. His eyes narrowed suspiciously, so she added, "It's important."

Myron looked stubborn. In his ponderous way, he thought over her request and finally picked up his police radio, turning his back to Dana. After some static and chatter, he spoke in Greek, nodded twice and clicked off. "She doesn't know what time she will be home."

Dana thanked Myron. To hide her disappointment, she left the station quickly and rushed to her apartment. Upstairs, out of breath, she sat on the sofa and tried to calm herself before calling Cybele. What should she say? It was critical to get her words exactly right. After exhaling slowly several times, she dialed the number and heard Cybele's melodic voice—the message was in Greek.

She spoke clearly. "Cybele—I received your note. This is a misunderstanding. I was there with Émile and then I had another drink after he left. The guy you saw was bothering me. Nothing happened at all. I went home alone. I miss you. Please come tonight for dinner. I'll be free after 7:45 p.m. Any time you wish, even late."

Dana realized how plaintive she sounded, but that was honest. On the return trip from the King Minos Inn, she would shop for food.

—

CYBELE WAS one of four police officers sent to the airport after the Olympic Airlines manager called Captain Yalouris to report a fresh influx of religious protesters, each carrying a suitcase and a sign. Yalouris had told him to disperse the waiting taxis and hotel vans so that the people would be contained, except for those arrivals who weren't part of the group. This left eight men and women standing in the hot sun, fuming.

They carried signs that read: "Homosexuality Is a Sin," "Gay Is Evil," and "Jesus Loves You—Find Jesus." Another message was: "Rainbows Are the Lord's Work—Not a Sodomite's." Cybele realized the prudent course of action was to let her colleagues do the talking. She didn't trust herself to be diplomatic.

"Americans?" The senior officer asked them.

"Yes, sir!" replied a man who seemed to be the spokesman for the group. He was tall and gaunt, with a long, weak-chinned face that plunged into an open-necked white shirt. A stack of wrinkles pressed the skin over his forehead into rhythmic undulations when he frowned. "Could you tell us where all the taxis are? We just want to get to our hotel."

"I am sorry." The policeman stared at the signs. "We wish to know your purpose for visiting Mykonos."

An older woman elbowed her way to the front. She was wearing nylon stockings and a belted print dress and looked about to expire with indignation and heat. "Good gosh!" she exclaimed, "We're God-fearing folks who've come to pray. Why're you keeping us here?"

The officer was having some trouble understanding her. He turned to Cybele for assistance. Reluctantly, she came forward. "Where are you from?"

"Iowa," said the first man, his pale eyes squinting in the harsh sunlight. "We don't want no trouble."

"Neither do we," Cybele replied in a stern voice.

"Well, we ain't breaking any laws. We're here for some R & R," the lady in the print dress said, grinning at her comrades. "That's Religion and Retreat. Now, we need some transportation pronto."

Cybele glared at her. She spoke in Greek to the senior officer, who told her to write down each person's name, passport number, and hotel. She removed her notebook and followed orders. Despite her fluency in English, Cybele was so annoyed that she made errors. When her task was complete, she informed the group that they would be under observation. "We don't wish to upset our other visitors or residents. Please remember that you are guests on Mykonos, and disruptions in the streets or at businesses will not be tolerated."

The eight men and women were silent as the police confiscated the wooden signs and one large cross. Cybele went inside the airport and called the taxi company, asking for their cars to return. Half an hour later, the Americans began filling the cabs. One policeman said, in a curt voice, "Enjoy your vacation."

"Have a nice day!" A short woman called out. Whether the statement was made in sarcasm or from habit, Cybele couldn't judge.

—

IT WAS mid-afternoon when Dana awoke, frantic to breathe. Sweat slid down her forehead. It was the dream again, the one that returned relentlessly, conjuring itself when she felt alone and depressed. It was always the same: the big, black car hurtling in space, sickeningly airborne. And the crash; the glass shattering; the water, cold, cold water. The only color—red—flowing over her eyes. Crawling out the window, struggling through the suffocating mud and through the sea grasses twining like snakes around her arms and legs.

She sat up, inhaling sharply. When would the nightmares end? Dana fingered the scar on her face and remembered how tenderly Cybele had touched it. She was too sad to be angry with Cybele, although anger would be easier than sadness. Dana knew she was innocent of misbehavior, yet she felt that failure was preordained, as it always had been, whether she had done something wrong or not. Standing, she went to the bathroom to wipe her face with a wet cloth. Maybe Cybele would come. She closed her eyes and shook her head miserably. Or perhaps Cybele wasn't interested and she was using the scene at Orpheus as an excuse?

The telephone rang. Dana paused for a second, hope rising, and then answered. It was Constantine Bouras at the Meltémi Gallery asking her to stop by. She looked at her watch and decided there was time for a visit there and to the photo shop before her critique. Dana ate a sandwich, grabbed the roll of exposed color film from the coffee container in the refrigerator, and left.

The Meltémi Gallery's double doors were jammed open with wooden wedges. The entrance led into a whitewashed courtyard where, in fine weather, paintings and photographs were exhibited on easels. Around the circumference, under a wide overhanging roof, art hung on the walls, protected in rain by plastic sheeting that unscrolled from under the awnings. Off to the left was an interior exhibit space, and to the right of the entrance, two small offices were carved out: one for Constantine and the other for his sister, Maria.

Constantine was attractive, well-dressed in a white shirt cut precisely to emphasize the lines of his trim torso. His hair was black, thick, and cropped close to his head. His sister was equally attractive, but more reserved, as if it had been agreed that there could be only one peacock in the family. She was a brunette like her brother, but her hair was long and gathered with a black ribbon; her dress was fashionable, a floral design in blue, purple, and green. Since they both dated men, there was ongoing patter between them as to who had the more desirable beau. Dana easily fell into their comic exchanges, enjoying the brother and sister act, but also appreciating their professional expertise. The Meltémi Gallery represented Dana's work on Mykonos and handled European sales from their Athens studio.

When Dana stepped inside, brother and sister greeted her. Constantine kissed Dana on both cheeks. Then he observed her hangover pallor. "My dear Dana! What mischief have you been up to? I hope she was worth it!"

"I was with Émile at Orpheus' Lyre."

He became immediately somber. "Say no more. That was very kind of you. How is he?"

"He's really sad. Virgil's parents are arriving today. I don't think that will be easy for Virgil's parents or for Émile."

"No," Maria agreed. "Do they realize their son was gay?"

Dana shook her head. "Émile doesn't think so, but I'm sure they have some awareness."

"Hard to miss in Virgil's case, but parents can be blind about their children." Constantine cast a knowing glance toward his sister. "Ours still believe I will marry and have ten children."

Maria looked askance and sighed. "They know. They just don't want to know." She turned to Dana, her expression growing serious. "We heard your apartment was broken into. What happened?"

"Yes, it was. By that American reporter, Devin Scott. I took some photos near the first murder. He stole the negatives and the enlargements."

"Do the police think he has anything to do with the killings?" Constantine asked.

Dana shrugged. "No one is sure, but they're looking for Devin."

"Well, whatever is going on, we should avoid being out late," Maria observed, casting an apprehensive glance at her brother.

"Yes," Constantine said. "No more wild nights for us gay people." His smile was disingenuous, leaving Dana to surmise he had no intention of changing his habits.

"We all need to be very careful," Maria stressed. "This situation is frightening. Two deaths. Such violence!"

Just then, the phone rang. Constantine stepped away to answer it. Maria took Dana's arm and escorted her into her office.

"He's making me insane!" she whispered. "He's still out past midnight. You'd think he would stay home and wait for this murderer to be caught. I'm so worried!"

"I can imagine. At least Constantine is not likely to leave the clubs by himself. That's what seems to attract the killer."

"You're probably right, but he is so irresponsible!"

Dana squeezed her hand. "He'll be fine, Maria."

"Perhaps." Although she was still distressed, Maria sat at her desk and opened a green ledger. "Okay, enough about my troubles." She flipped a page and explained that two large photographs and six small ones had been sold. "You may have to print some more eight-by-ten black-and-whites for us. I wrote down the titles and sizes that are running low. And here's a check." She handed Dana a white envelope.

"Thank you. You're both doing a terrific job. I'll be happy to reprint and might have a few new images too."

"Bring them by anytime. Oh, and you will be interested to know that three of the photographs were purchased by your students."

"Who?"

Maria ran a finger down her ledger. "Let's see. Michael Garfield and David Ambrose—actually, his wife, Hasina, came in and bought two for him as a surprise."

"That's very nice."

Constantine joined them. "When are you leaving for New York, Dana?"

Dana thought about Cybele. "I'm not sure. I guess I'll see how the weather is. I know you close in a few weeks."

"Yes, time to go back to dreary old Athens," Maria replied.

Looking at her watch, Dana said, "And it's time for me to go. Thanks for the check. You two are great! And Constantine—listen to your sister and behave!"

He laughed and hugged Dana. "I'll be home every night before midnight. Promise!"

Dana gave Maria a quick kiss and walked out of the gallery. Tomorrow morning, she would deposit the check and withdraw some cash. Between this workshop and the next one, there would be enough money to cover expenses without tapping her New York account. After dropping off the film for development at the photo shop, she walked to the port, hoping to run into Cybele. It was a local belief that if one sat long enough in a taverna by the harbor, everyone on the island would eventually pass by. Dana didn't feel optimistic. She ordered an iced tea.

It was a brilliant day with a stiff breeze scuffing the water into whitecaps. Small boats fretted at their anchors, bows and sterns rocking up and down like a herd of restless, brightly colored horses. She listened to the awnings flap, smelled the tang of the nearby sea, and watched the steady promenade of gawking tourists, fresh off the cruise ships, scurrying around town trying to buy every trinket in sight. Usually the cruise lines arranged for sufficient time in port so their passengers could shop, have dinner, and do some dancing before a late-night departure.

Although it was calming to sit by the sea, the angry lines from Cybele's note intruded. Dana hoped that her message would be reassuring and that Cybele would listen to the full explanation. Dana paid for the iced tea and walked slowly home, wondering if the police had caught Devin Scott, wondering if he could kill two men.

CHAPTER NINE

WHEN DANA ENTERED the King Minos Inn for the evening critique, Sandros was walking up and down the lobby, muttering to himself. He quickly took her arm and pulled her into his office.

"Dana—we have a problem! It is this Luca Alessi!" His hands flew to the sides of his head. "Ah, what an unpleasant man!"

"What happened?"

"He and Miss Corso are having big trouble. Did you see what he did to her?"

Dana frowned. "Yes. I suggested she should call the police, but she refused. Maybe it was only a lover's quarrel—a one-time disagreement."

Sandros snorted his disgust. "No, it was worse than that. I think he is hurting her."

Dana considered this, weighing Luca's smiling behavior toward her against Teresa's bruises and displays of antipathy aimed at him. "Perhaps I haven't paid enough attention, Sandros, but I will now. Is Teresa with the other students?"

"Yes, she just came from her room."

"And where's Luca?"

He shrugged. "He left here during the afternoon…after a lot of shouting. And he was out very late yesterday. My bartender was on duty until midnight and didn't see him. Mr. Alessi also missed breakfast."

"How did he look when he came downstairs a few hours ago?"

"Like he had too much to drink the night before."

"And has he been drinking today?"

"Oh, yes, Dana! I had to order more vodka for him. He is an alcohol lover, that one."

"What do you think is going on with him?"

Sandros stroked his chin as if weighing the dislike he felt against his role as a courteous innkeeper. "Shall we say, he has a bad temper?" He came nearer. "Just between us, I think the sex is the problem maybe."

"How do you mean?"

He raised his hand to the heavens. "This is not a good thing that I tell you. I should not talk about the people who come and stay with me. You are a terrible man, Sandros!" he lamented to some god or goddess above. Then he threw Dana a sharp glance. "I think that he doesn't respect women. He likes bad sex with them. Yesterday, in the bar…what I heard! I know I shouldn't listen, but I couldn't help it. Mr. Alessi was saying something about it being better without being able to breathe. Something like that."

"Asphyxiation?"

"Yes, that's what he said. It made me think about this killer we have in town. He likes the same thing, does he not?"

Dana nodded. No doubt half the population of the island knew how the murders were committed. "Why do you believe Luca doesn't respect women?"

"He might like them—if you understand—but he is not courteous to Miss Corso. He talks with a bad mouth." Sandros pinched his face with disgust. "Also, the other day, when I was at the bar, two gay boys from San Francisco came in. Nice gentlemen. Mr. Alessi watched them very strangely. Like he was interested in them somehow, but not in a good way…he looked like he hated them. You must not tell anyone that Sandros said these things, please?"

"I won't," Dana replied, taking in Sandros' second comment and wondering if there was any connection between Luca's anti-gay attitude and the attacks on the two men. "I'll speak to Teresa. Maybe she's changed her mind about making a complaint. And Sandros, I've asked my students to stay in groups. If you see one of them leave alone tonight, will you remind him or her that it isn't a good idea? I don't want anything else to happen."

"It is done." He brought his fingers to his lips, kissed them, and raised them as a pledge.

—

The photographers had loaded the projector trays and were now passing around their contact sheets. Some were drinking cocktails, some sodas.

"How is everyone?" Dana asked.

Carolyn groaned. "Not so good. My pictures are terrible. Particularly the black-and-whites."

"Remember that a contact sheet is exposed for the average tonality from multiple images. For night shots and with the extreme contrast between the bright lights and the black shadows, there will be an enormous range. Look at your negatives to see what you've actually captured," Dana explained.

"Why can't we get four-by-six prints like we can at home?" Julian complained.

"The camera shop is developing your black-and-white film as a favor. They don't have enough demand to justify printing individual black-and-white prints, nor enough time."

Somewhat mollified, Julian took a seat on a chair and sipped a bottle of beer.

"Let's look at the contacts. Please write your name on each sheet," Dana said.

While everyone handed her their work, Mike offered to buy her a drink.

"No, but thanks. Maybe another time, Mike." She smiled at him and sat on the couch, removing a loupe and a pen from her vest pocket and holding the contacts up to the window. She began jotting comments on the backs and then started the critique with Carolyn, who was having trouble with focus.

"I tried," Carolyn said, "but the bright spotlights and dark areas bothered me."

"Check the magnification on the viewfinder's diopters and also see your ophthalmologist when you go home. Perhaps you're suffering from a little night blindness."

After discussions with each student, Dana finally came to Teresa Corso. She had shot only half a roll of black-and-white. When Dana asked her why, she replied that she had returned to the hotel early after an argument with Luca.

"I just didn't feel like being out last night," she said quietly.

Dana noticed that a fresh bruise was forming on Teresa's hand. She told the class to take a five-minute break and beckoned for Teresa to join her in the hall. "Has more happened? Between you and Luca?"

"Another disagreement." Her fingers rose to the scarf around her throat. "I'm all right."

"Teresa, it's none of my business, but what is he doing?"

She wouldn't look at Dana. "Luca has some ideas I don't like. Ever since we arrived here, he's been acting weird, different."

"How long have you been dating him?"

"Two months. It started slowly, then he became serious, and then possessive. At first, I liked his attentiveness … it was nice to be wanted so much. Now I just wish he would leave."

"You said that he has some ideas that you don't like?" Dana asked gently.

Teresa shook her head. "I don't want to talk about it."

"You could get a separate room. Sandros probably has several available."

"Maybe. Thanks." She gave Dana a weak smile and returned to sit beside Mike.

Although what was happening between Teresa and Luca disturbed her, Dana was helpless to intervene without Teresa's cooperation. She closed the drapes and turned off the lights. Standing by the projector, she said, "Let's review your slides."

The photographs were a mix of the figure/ground problem and night scenes. Julian's work was first. Thirteen images that should have been edited to two.

"Julian takes a lot of photographs, and for the most part that's good." Dana paused, trying to think of a diplomatic way to criticize his slides. "For the figure/ground assignment, the emphasis should be on the non-subject or ground, but Julian is still concentrating on his subject first and his ground second." Dana switched through the slides, demonstrating revised cropping by holding a piece of white cardboard in front of the projector.

"Julian, would you please do this problem over again?"

Though she smiled at him, he didn't look pleased. His low-light pictures weren't any better.

Mike's slides were next: a few stellar shots at night and some daylight photos in which the negative shapes popped forward as if they were foreground shapes. She praised Mike even though she knew Julian would be smoldering at the obvious comparison to his own poor performance.

Carolyn had taken a few acceptable images; however, like Julian, she hadn't solved either assignment well. Dana asked her to do another series. David's photographs were considerably better. He had a knack for doing uncluttered work and instinctively understood the figure/ground philosophy. One shot of a red dome against the blue sky was particularly striking and elicited a round of applause from the class.

As Dana was starting with Teresa's images, Luca stepped into the dim room. He inserted himself in the space between Carolyn and Teresa on the sofa, crowding Carolyn against the arm of the couch. He began to whisper to Teresa.

"Luca, could you speak to Teresa after we're finished?" Dana said.

"I'll talk to my girlfriend whenever I want," he growled.

Dana was surprised by his hostility, which he hadn't directed at her before. She gritted her teeth and didn't respond. "We're about to discuss her slides. I would appreciate it if you could wait."

In the reflected light of the projector, she could see his dark eyes glaring at her. He was silent, sat back against the sofa, and crossed his arms over his chest.

Dana reviewed Teresa's work, most of which were very successful solutions. "You have an innate graphic quality," she explained to her. "You see things abstractly, accentuating shapes rather than subjects. That's one purpose of concentrating on Cycladic architecture—the simplicity and geometry of the forms."

After Teresa's photos were finished, David opened the curtains and turned on the lights. Luca stood and pulled Teresa to her feet.

Dana moved toward them. "You had some nice shots today, Teresa. Very impressive."

Luca scowled at Dana and gave his girlfriend a small shove toward the door.

Teresa held her ground in spite of Luca's impatience. "Thank you, Dana."

His eyes narrowed. "Leave us alone. And while you're at it, keep your hands off my girlfriend."

Dana rocked back on her heels, unprepared for the vitriolic attack. "Luca, apologize to Teresa for your behavior and go."

"No!" he retorted. "Come on, Teresa."

"Teresa can stay if she wishes," Dana countered, taking a step forward and looking down at him.

"So, you do have the hots for her. Just like I thought!"

"What is wrong with you, Luca? Stop this!" Teresa cried. She detached his hand and flicked it away. "You're being ridiculous! There is absolutely nothing going on between us, and you know that. What's going on is that you scare me. I wish you would go home." Pushing Luca on the chest, she ran past him and up the stairs to the lobby.

Luca started to follow her, but Mike blocked his path. "I think you better cool off a little, buddy," he said calmly but with authority. Mike was a big man, and Luca was no match for him.

"This has nothing to do with you." He glowered at Mike but retreated to the bar and reached over the counter to pour himself a free drink.

Mike turned to Dana and whispered, "I don't know what's happening here, but I don't like to see any woman frightened like that."

"No, I agree. I have no idea what's going on."

"If you want, I'll get a group together for dinner, including Teresa."

"That would be very helpful, Mike."

Turning to her students, she wasn't surprised to see them staring at her, although Carolyn was watching Luca with obvious dislike. "I'm sorry for the interruption," Dana said, though that hardly covered the situation, but with Luca in the room, there wasn't much else to say. She walked over to the projector, lifted the tray, and handed it to Julian so he could remove his slides.

"As you know, tomorrow you have a boat ride to Delos. Tickets are with Sandros. Be at the old pier at the left of the harbor at 8:30 a.m. Your host and guide, Eleni, is very nice. If you tend to get seasick, take pills before. Even though it's only a half-hour trip, sometimes it's a rough ride. This is also a sight-seeing trip, so it's okay to take a few tourist pictures."

Everyone laughed nervously, still unsettled by Luca.

Dana shot him a glance, but he was talking to the bartender who had been sent in by Sandros. "When you return, drop your film at the photography store so it will be ready before the critique at six. Have a good time, and I'll see you in the evening. And please be careful tonight when you go out."

When Dana entered the lobby, Sandros explained that Teresa had requested another room and was upstairs packing. He smiled slyly. "The maid is assisting Miss Corso."

"Thanks, Sandros. I hope there won't be any more trouble."

—

THE MAN FINISHED his drink and made a decision. He would not wear his monk's clothes tonight, as much as he loved disguises. After the article in the paper, doing so might increase the risk, and nothing could be allowed to imperil his urgent mission. But another evening? Yes, perhaps. The danger added to the excitement.

Folding the wire garrote into a neat coil, he slipped it into his trousers' pocket along with latex gloves and a clean handkerchief. No need to take the lipstick, rouge, and liner. After all, regrettably, this evening was business, not pleasure.

—

SHORTLY BEFORE seven, Cybele walked dejectedly into her apartment. Her feet were swollen, she was hot, and her spirits were low. Plus her landlord had left a note, informing her that renovations would start in two days and suggesting that she should make arrangements to stay elsewhere for a week, which she suspected was not an accurate assessment, considering the amount of work planned. Where was she supposed to reside, and when would she have time to look? Disgusted, Cybele unbuckled her police belt, tossed it on a chair, and checked her answering machine. She played Dana's message twice and collapsed on the couch, bewildered. She was so tired she couldn't think.

Ten minutes passed. Cybele listened to the tape again. There was no doubt that Dana wanted to see her. She sounded sincere. A misunderstanding? Cybele tried to picture what had happened at Orpheus' Lyre. It was possible she had overreacted, but if she hadn't, she would not become involved with an inconstant woman—particularly one who had affected her so profoundly. That was the real agony, Cybele admitted.

She went to the phone and picked up the receiver, dialed. No answer. She didn't leave a message because she didn't know what to say.

—

AS DANA DESCENDED the hill into town, she glanced at her watch—nearly 7:30. No time to visit the market. She picked up speed and arrived breathless at her apartment, where she unlocked the door, ran upstairs, and checked the answering machine. The "zero" messages came as a shock, though it was possible Cybele had been unable to call because of work. Dana decided to freshen up, noting that the mirror still reflected the ravages of too many martinis. She sighed, combed her hair, washed, added perfume, and went down to the living room. Still optimistic, Dana began playing one of her favorite recordings—Respighi's *Ancient Airs and Dances*. Usually the music made her feel elegant and sprightly. Tonight, it would be nearly impossible to accomplish that trick—not unless Cybele arrived. She grabbed a book and tried to read. By nine, Dana doubted that Cybele was coming so she ate an assortment of very leftover leftovers. An hour later, disappointed, she went to bed.

—

THE MAN USED a paper towel to clean the wire, noting that there was more blood than usual. He sniffed at the towel, savored the saline smell, and rinsed the outside of his latex gloves in the sink. Inspecting his clothes, he noticed that a few drops had fallen on his dark blue shirt. With a dampened towel and some soap, he dabbed at the spots until they were gone, balled up the towels, and threw them in his plastic bag. After a methodical search through the dirty three-room apartment, he found the negatives hidden behind a stack of plates in the kitchen cupboard. Two prints were rolled inside empty green wine bottles.

The man was tempted to switch on a desk lamp to examine the photographs, but it was too risky. Someone might see the light. He slipped the prints into his trouser pocket and took a last look at the lifeless body sprawled on the bed. Satisfied, he let himself out through the door, peeled off the gloves, and placed them in the bag. He hurried away into the night.

CHAPTER TEN

DANA AWOKE. It was still night, but she heard noises in the living room below. She jumped off the bed and listened, frightened, when she remembered leaving the door unlocked for Cybele. Then she heard footsteps coming upstairs. Scanning the dark room for a weapon, she saw nothing useful. Quickly, she hid behind the door. A second later, a figure entered the room.

"Okay, where are you?" said a beautiful voice.

"Right here." Dana stepped forward and placed her arms around Cybele.

Accepting the embrace, Cybele leaned into Dana. Silently, they stood together, unwilling to break the spell with words. A cool breeze blew through the window like a benediction. Dana felt intense relief.

"You'll never know how much I missed you," Dana admitted in a whisper.

Cybele pulled away slightly. "Tell me."

Dana kissed her.

"That is no answer, my friend. I was so angry when I saw you with that guy, who was not Émile. I asked."

"I'm sorry. When he came up behind me, I thought he was you. He was just lonely, hoping to find someone to drink with him." Dana led her to the edge of the bed. "I left soon after."

Cybele was quiet for a moment. "Well, I suppose we had a misunderstanding. I'm sorry too. All I saw was his hand on your neck and that did it."

"I would have been as upset." Dana embraced her again. As if gravity was pulling them downward, they fell onto the bed.

Although there was a great deal to be said, silence suited Dana and seemed to allow them to reenter their private sphere, where words were expressed by touch. They kissed and held each other until Cybele rose on her elbow and looked tenderly at Dana. Without speaking, she moved her hand to Dana's nightshirt and unfastened the line of buttons. After laying the shirt open, her fingers caressed Dana's breast. Her mouth soon replaced her fingers, as her tongue teased in rings until at last she reached the nipple. Dana felt a flush of heat spread throughout her body. She began to rise, wanting to reciprocate, but Cybele persuaded her to lie still as she slipped her hand lower. Unable to restrain herself, Dana raised her hips in anticipation, worrying that Cybele would fail her and yet believing in her heart that she wouldn't. Balanced on this keen edge, Dana let Cybele coax her to a higher level of excitement, bringing her to the peak of sensation, and then over it, into shuddering consummation.

When Dana's breathing evened, Cybele laid her head across Dana's chest, and Dana encircled Cybele with her arms, holding her tightly. The moment was so precious, so moving, that Dana felt tears in her eyes.

Cybele raised herself. "Dana, you're crying…"

All she could do was nod.

Cybele brushed the tears away. "Oh, my dear," she whispered, pulling Dana close and saying something in Greek that Dana didn't understand, though the soft cadences of her voice were soothing. As she let herself be comforted, Dana thought of Odysseus returning to his ancestral homeland after years of wandering—safe but weary from all the years away. She dried her face with the sleeve of her nightshirt. "I promise that I don't usually behave like this, but I thought I'd lost you."

Cybele didn't answer. She eased Dana against the pillow and looked down, her dark hair falling around Dana like a protective curtain. "I know you are not usually like this. You are usually strong. I like that in you, but I also like what I see now. You are as you were when you were born. Open and innocent in a way that is beautiful. You must never be afraid to show me this, Dana. Never." She grazed her fingers along the scar on Dana's face. "This line tells me of a physical hurt, but I know the hurt is inside. A girl whose mother died. Whose father, too, is gone. This mark tells me everything about you."

Dana started to speak, but Cybele kissed her. "I want you to go to sleep now. May I stay the night?"

"Of course."

Cybele removed her clothes and returned to the bed. "In the morning, you may make love to me."

Dana smiled at her. "I will. With the greatest pleasure."

—

A light rain was falling—unusual for Mykonos except during the winter months. Dana slipped out of the covers and walked to the middle window to view the gray drizzle. The poor weather wouldn't last, which was a good thing because her students were due to leave for Delos in an hour. Already the sun was struggling to take charge, and the seas were calming after being roused by the squall. She turned to regard Cybele— the graceful curve of her spine, the tangle of dark hair over her shoulder, and the pale blue sheets wrapping her slender waist.

Sensing that she was being observed, Cybele turned over, revealing a sleepy smile. "Come here," she said in a quiet voice. "You made a promise."

"I haven't forgotten," Dana replied, as she appreciated her lover in daylight. She ran her hand over Cybele's long legs, from thigh to toe, sweeping up and down lightly, and stroked Cybele's arms and shoulders, her neck and face. Moving on top, Dana could feel the swell of her breasts meeting hers, the coolness of their skin warming as they came together. They kissed, at first with more emotion than sexual passion, then again. Bringing her lips to the lobe of Cybele's ear, she pulled gently.

Cybele moaned. "So you are a devil, after all! I suspected as much."

"I confess it." Dana replied, pressing her lower body against Cybele's.

Slowly, they rocked up and down. Dana was in no hurry and wanted to use all the skill she possessed to communicate the depth of her feelings. Cybele began panting, and a faint pink tinge colored her cheeks. She gazed at Dana with eyes that said, "don't stop."

She didn't.

As they were about to make love again, the telephone rang.

"Damn!" Dana muttered. But because it might be Sandros calling to say that the trip to Delos was canceled, she had to answer. She lurched off the bed and grabbed the receiver, trying not to sound out of breath.

It was Captain Yalouris. Dana inhaled, in an attempt to calm her racing blood. "Sorry, I just ran upstairs to get the phone."

"Miss Fox, I apologize for calling at this hour, but we have some news. One of our officers went to Devin Scott's apartment early this morning. He hoped to find him there … "

"And?"

"He's dead. Killed with a wire, like the others."

"Oh, no!"

Cybele sat up in bed, alert.

Captain Yalouris continued. "We don't know the time of death yet, but it happened last night. We assume that he was killed because of the newspaper articles."

"Did you find the negatives or any of the photographs?" Dana asked.

"No. We looked very carefully … also at his office at *The Pelican*. We called the Athens' papers and learned that Scott brought one print, which they digitally scanned and shared with each other. They still have it."

"That means two prints and the negatives are still missing."

"Yes, it does. Unless he hid them elsewhere, it's likely that the murderer searched the apartment and found them."

"But if Devin didn't tell him how many there were, the killer couldn't be sure he had them all." Her mind was racing ahead to the implications of that possibility.

"We doubt any conversation occurred between them. Mr. Scott was attacked from behind, and probably killed quickly. There were few signs of a struggle."

"So if Devin stole my prints and the murderer doesn't know if more evidence exists—"

"Exactly," Captain Yalouris said. "He may come looking for you."

Dana glanced at Cybele, whose face was etched with worry. "Captain, do you think there is something in the photograph that might identify the killer? Something I missed?"

"Unfortunately, without the negatives or prints, we only have the newspaper reproduction. We're trying to get your photograph from Athens or a digital scan of the image."

"Let me know what happens," Dana said.

"I will. And please be alert."

Dana said goodbye, hung up the phone, and returned to the bed. With her arm around Cybele, she explained what had occurred.

"Oh, how terrible!" Cybele replied in a hushed voice, shaking her head.

Dana waited for Cybele to take in the information, as she herself was doing. "Cybele, have you been told anything else? I mean, you must have had a department meeting."

"This is very difficult for me. We've been instructed not to talk to anyone about the details, but I don't know much more than you do. Maybe after I return to the station, I'll learn something new." She glanced at her watch and sighed. "But now, dear Dana, I must go to work."

"What about your clothes?" Dana asked, laughing, in spite of the somber mood.

Cybele colored. "I brought my uniform with me. It's in the living room."

Dana put her arms around her. "I like a woman who plans well."

They went downstairs. As she was dressing, Cybele called the station in case her on-duty hours had altered. A grin spread across her face. She began unbuttoning her blouse.

"Are we going back to bed?" Dana asked.

Cybele took her hand. "I have until eleven and then I work only until eight."

They hurried to the bedroom. When Cybele and Dana finally ate breakfast, it was 10:30.

"So, shall we have dinner tonight?" Dana asked. "At Avra?"

"*Enchanté.*" Cybele began to leave and turned. "By the way, this is no time to leave your door unlocked. Even for me."

—

AFTER SLEEPING, the man was still tired from the adrenaline crash after the kill, although the high hadn't been as electrifying as usual because the death had been a necessity rather than a true gratification of desire. Nevertheless, as always, he had become aroused when the wire bit into the white neck. He loved the neat precision of the act—the bulge of the eyes, the fingers clutching to loosen the garrote, and the frantic breathing followed by silence. Visualizing Devin Scott's face made him eager to go hunting again, this time for his preferred prey.

On the table in front of him were the negatives and two black-and-white pictures: a print of the entire image and one larger than the newspaper reproduction. He assumed Scott left the sharper, less enlarged photograph in Athens since the figure in one was small and the other was grainy. To his relief, the store's name on the bag he'd been carrying was almost illegible, even in the biggest enlargement. Regardless, he hoped Dana Fox was the only person who had seen this version, other than the reporter. With a prick of concern, the man wondered whether additional prints had been made but decided it was unlikely. What really worried him were the other pictures. Although he was one man in a crowd, someone might connect the shopping bag in both locations and discover his identity. Initially, he had thought that the photograph—or photographs—from the harbor would be on the same roll as the one taken earlier on the street, but they weren't on the negatives, and no other film was in Scott's apartment. It was possible that the reporter had left something at the newspaper office, but the man believed Scott would hide everything together in a single place, at home. This meant the photographer still possessed the port images. It was essential to locate her apartment, destroy the negatives and prints, and, as he had done with Devin Scott, terminate her.

He smiled to himself. Once, at age seventeen, three years after Miss Becker had been dismissed from service, he had taken a woman as an experiment. He remembered the thrill of stealing the red MG roadster from his family's three-car garage and driving fast until he saw his victim walking along the road dressed like a whore in a short skirt and cheap jewelry, her face pink with blush, her lips painted red. When he had offered a ride, she accepted. When he brought her to a remote spot near a lake, she didn't object to parking. She didn't object when he tightened the orange scarf around her neck. In fact, she loved being conquered until she realized what he intended. Seeing the fear widen her eyes, he nearly fainted with elation. There had been no sex—her breasts and curving hips, her female smell, had nauseated him—but he had become aroused while choking her. The sense of overwhelming power that radiated from his hands and through his body was intoxicating, producing a violent rush of excitement far greater than he'd ever experienced before. Afterward, as he always did, he recounted every detail to Miss Becker, who shared his secret passions. They had continued to meet secretly after her dismissal.

Now, years later, the man acknowledged that this first human strangulation had left an imprint, although he had quickly determined that his quarry would be men, men who were young and slim. However, after their deaths, before he could consummate his desire, he made them look like the woman by the lake, lipsticked and rouged.

Dana Fox was next. She might be more interesting to kill than the reporter and perhaps more of a challenge. She looked strong and was very tall. Plus, it was possible that the woman would be prepared for an attack, having already calculated that the reporter was not responsible for his own death or those of Hall and Laine. But if he surprised her, she couldn't defeat such an accomplished murderer.

He ripped the two photographs into halves, quarters, eighths, smaller and smaller until his fingers could no longer grasp the pieces.

CHAPTER ELEVEN

WHEN CYBELE arrived at the station, it was a maelstrom of activity. The Incidents Room, which displayed the crime scene photos, town maps, and various diagrams, was open to the staff. She stepped inside to review the photographs of Malcolm Hall and Virgil Laine tacked to the walls. A slow anger percolated through her as she examined the pictures. Whoever this murderer was, he was a pathologically disturbed sexual sadist. Although research was being conducted on aberrant individuals, analyzing the effects of brain formation and chemistry and genetic predisposition, Cybele favored psychological profiling and weighing the effects of early childhood abuse. This was an organized offender, an antisocial personality, who was meticulous, leaving few clues and no fingerprints, practiced, intelligent, without guilt. His desire for publicity wasn't a factor because there had been no on-site notes or messages to the newspapers or to the police. His nationality was undetermined, but Cybele didn't believe he was Greek because of his choice of English-speaking victims, although the selection might be based on opportunity.

Cybele hadn't been introduced to the two detectives who had arrived from Athens, but she suspected they were sophisticated investigators. Myron also told her that Captain Yalouris, while in the United States, had been involved with a serial killer case. However, the other staff officers probably had little knowledge on the subject. She herself was better informed because of her studies in criminal psychology, which had been noted on her police application. Whether Captain Yalouris remembered this credential, she had no idea, but as a junior officer, without any field experience, she hesitated to volunteer her textbook expertise. She decided to wait, gather information, and come forward if she felt confident in her conclusions.

Her thoughts drifted to Dana and the perfect night and morning they had shared. There were no adjectives, in Greek or English, that conveyed Cybele's feelings. She sensed a deep sympathy between them, as if, in the larger design of their individual lives, each had grown to complement the other, timed to meet at this exact moment. She mused over Dana's personality and knew that the blend of sureness with vulnerability, sensitivity with strength, and reserve with openness were profoundly affecting, profoundly compelling. The only imperfection Cybele noticed about Dana was her causal attitude about her personal safety. In the present situation, she hoped this wouldn't prove a significant flaw.

Cybele flipped through a police report on Devin Scott, her eyes passing over the words with only the merest comprehension.

—

IT WAS a hot, airless evening. Dana climbed the long hill to the King Minos Inn. By the time she reached the hotel and looked over Korfos Bay, the sun was in the west, preparing for a glorious demise. The sky was striped peach, lilac, and blue, with a few cirrus clouds running parallel to the horizon. The sea was darkening except where the sun splashed a gold wake over the restless waves. Dana would have preferred to stay home on her balcony, observing the show and luxuriating in tender memories of Cybele, but she took her teaching responsibilities seriously.

Sandros greeted her at the hotel entrance and explained that Teresa Corso was in a new room, that Luca had made a ruckus banging on her door at 1:00 a.m., and that he, Sandros, had woken the bartender to assist in putting the drunk man to bed.

"I'm so sorry for your trouble," Dana apologized, shaking her head in frustration. "Is Luca here now?"

"No. Who knows where he is, but I hope he never comes back."

Dana patted the innkeeper on the shoulder and walked to the room below the lobby. Everyone was there. Carolyn, Julian, and Mike were nursing sunburns. David was sitting on the couch with Teresa, who looked as though she hadn't slept in days. Dana asked her if Luca was around.

"I don't know where he is, but I'm worried. He was crazy last night. I thought he would break down the door."

"I heard."

"Thank goodness for Sandros. Since we left early this morning for Delos, I've managed to avoid Luca today. I hope he doesn't start again tonight."

"Go to dinner with other members of the class. And maybe Carolyn would let you sleep in her room if you're frightened."

"I don't want to inconvenience anyone," she replied, when Carolyn nodded assent. "I just wish he'd return to New York."

"I wish he would too," Dana agreed. "Did you have a good time on Delos at least?"

"Yes, I knew he wasn't there!" She gave a short bark of laughter. "It was a beautiful day, after the rain."

"Glad to hear it. Now, let's look at your slides."

The students sat and Dana began the review. Most of the work was documentary, featuring the weather-worn lionesses, the 300 BC theater, the mosaic floors, and the carved phallus that always surprised tourists, but some slides were imaginative. At the end of the critique, Dana announced that the class would meet the next morning at the Archaeological Museum, at ten. "After that, we'll work at the Maritime Museum, and then you'll have a free afternoon to go to the beach, shop, or do whatever you wish. No critique until the following day."

Everyone liked that idea.

The slides were returned, and Sandros entered the room. "Dana, Maria at the Meltémi Gallery called. I have the number."

She followed him to the lobby and dialed.

"*Kalispera*—Meltémi." Maria answered.

"*Kalispera*, Maria. This is Dana."

"Ah, good! We have been trying to reach you this evening."

"Someone is buying my entire portfolio?" she teased.

"No, nothing like that, I am sorry to say. It is, well, a little unusual. This man, he came into the gallery a few hours ago. He knew your name, and he knew you were a photographer. He looked at some of your work but not carefully. Sort of in a hurry." Maria paused, sounding upset. "Dana, he wanted to know where you lived. To have your address and telephone number. I didn't tell him."

"Thank you for not giving him any information. As you know, my number isn't listed. A habit from the States. What was his name?"

"His said his first name only—Robert. But you know what? I'm not sure he was telling the truth. There was something strange about the man. He had too much curiosity."

"What did he look like?"

"Brown hair…I'm not sure how old. Mid-forties. An American. Dressed nicely. I had another client, so I didn't talk with him long."

Dana tried to imagine who it was. Luca? Maria would have mentioned Luca's jet-black hair and Mediterranean complexion. Julian? He had sandy-colored hair and was in his thirties. Still, Julian's curiosity about her had been worrisome.

"And his name was Robert?" Dana asked.

"Yes."

"I don't know anyone called Robert here on Mykonos."

"He said he wanted to take you to dinner. That you knew each other."

"Did he say where he was staying?"

"No."

She wanted to question Maria in more detail, but she needed to return to class. "Okay, well, tell Constantine about him, okay? If he returns, please call me. Thanks, Maria."

Dana hung up the phone feeling anxious. She knew no one named "Robert" except for two people who lived in New York. Possibly one of them was visiting the island.

—

Arriving at the apartment before Cybele, Dana showered and slipped into black slacks and a tunic, adding a gold dolphin necklace. The lipstick could wait.

A few minutes later, Cybele knocked on the door. When Dana opened it, she noticed a travel bag in Cybele's hand.

"Planning on staying long?" Dana asked.

"Who knows?" Cybele replied, smiling coquettishly. "By the way, you look very chic, my dear."

"Thanks. So do you." And she did—in a sleeveless dark green blouse that emphasized the long line of her arms, a black skirt, and a summer sweater tied around her neck. Dana kissed her lightly, then with more intent. She could feel a stirring that might waylay the promised meal. "I made reservations for nine."

Cybele grinned mischievously. "I'm ready."

"Ah, but for what?" Dana laughed and was tempted to lead her upstairs. Instead, she dredged up some self-control, and, after another tantalizing kiss, they applied their lipstick—salmon pink for Dana and dark cherry-red for Cybele. Walking arm in arm in the European fashion, they strolled to the restaurant, encountering a few admiring stares from some of the men who passed by. At Avra, they were seated in the garden near a large tree. The candle on the table flickered like a gigantic firefly, illuminating Cybele's face, making her high cheekbones appear more angled and her eyes more intense.

Dana ordered a bottle of white wine. They agreed on Caesar salads; Dana selected grilled swordfish and Cybele opted for mullet.

"So, what is the news from the station?" Dana placed a slice of bread on her plate.

"The archbishop called. He says the clergy isn't responsible for the murders. He's mad about the publicity. As for the killer, the man has been extremely careful. No prints so far. We think he killed Devin Scott, of course, but we doubt the murderer is a local priest."

"Why?"

"We have our reasons, but I'm not allowed to say. Sorry."

When the wine arrived and was poured, Dana continued the conversation. "You must know something about serial killers…from the classes you took."

Cybele nodded. "Yes, I do. This one is very experienced. Wherever he comes from, he probably killed there…more than once. We're asking cooperation from agencies in Europe, England, and America, but it will take several days for them to provide information."

"Do you think Devin was killed because he saw the enlargements?"

"It's likely." She put her hand on Dana's, and her expression darkened. "And that means you may be in danger as well, my friend, because you're the only other person who saw them."

"But after one of the photos was printed in the newspaper, why would the killer care about me?" Although Dana posed the question, she sensed a reason might exist. "Maybe there's something about the one that was enlarged most, the one no one saw except for me and Devin—"

"And the killer," Cybele finished. "Of course, it's possible that the murderer was provoked by Scott's article and killed him because he was angry." She swallowed some wine.

"Mmm, possible. So, Officer, do I need police protection? Around the clock, every hour, every minute, every second?"

Cybele shook her head. "I wish I could be with you all the time."

Their eyes locked on each other, and everything else fell away: the distant music, the hum of conversation at nearby tables, the clatter of plates being placed and removed. Dana was silent, deserted by her usually quick responses. The salads arrived, the pepper was cracked by the waiter, and still she was quiet, trying to slow the feelings that were racing through her.

"You look very beautiful this evening," Dana said at last.

Cybele greeted this compliment with humor. "Ah, so you are now the flatterer?"

"I only tell the truth. You *are* beautiful."

"Thank you. I think we make a handsome couple, don't you? One light, one dark."

Smiling, Dana agreed. Then, with another attempt at levity, she asked, "So, will we be a couple next month?"

Studying her carefully, she replied, "What do you think?"

"I think so," Dana whispered. "I would like that very much."

"I would also. You know, it makes me a little afraid…how perfect everything is between us. Like a story in a book. Like we've met and will live happily forever."

Dana nodded and speared some lettuce. "In America, it's a joke of sorts. What do lesbians do on their second date? Answer: pack a moving truck."

Cybele threw her head back, laughed, and stared at Dana with an impish gleam in her eye. "Dana, now I'm embarrassed."

"Why?"

"Oh, dear, after what you said, I'm not sure I should ask."

Dana raised an eyebrow. "Ask what?"

"Well, would it be possible for me to stay with you for a week? My landlord is beginning some construction on my apartment tomorrow."

Pleased by the request, Dana smiled. "I would love that. I should warn you, however, that I may not be easy to live with. I mean, I've never shared a place except with my family."

"I don't believe you!" Cybele scoffed.

"It's true. Weekends and occasional vacations, yes, but otherwise, no." She shrugged. "Perhaps I've been involved with women who—"

"Will not come too close?"

Dana sighed. "Maybe."

"Are you afraid that might be true of me?" Cybele asked in a tentative voice.

Dana pondered this. "No. Our relationship feels different. How can I explain? Everything sounds trite." She swallowed some wine and gazed at Cybele. "I do know that if this table wasn't between us, I would…well, I'll show you later."

After the waiter left the main course, they continued to focus on each other, reluctant to end the intimacy of the moment. At last, Dana grasped her fork.

"Our dinner will get cold," she said.

Cybele agreed and began to eat, remarking on the grilled fish, which had been traditionally marinated in lemon, olive oil, and herbs. They ate and talked about their lives as if everything needed to be communicated at once. Cybele offered childhood anecdotes and asked about living in New York, how it must be difficult to afford a place in Manhattan. After briefly describing her neighborhood near Lincoln Center, Dana diverted the discussion to the art scene because she was reticent about discussing her financial situation. She wasn't concerned that Cybele was attracted to her because of money, but past experiences had made her cautious.

"New York sounds like an exciting place," Cybele said. "I would love to visit sometime."

"I'm sure you will." Dana was tempted to offer an invitation but fought the impulse.

Cybele poured more wine and studied her. "You know, I didn't expect to feel this way about someone. I was searching—yes—it was why I took the job on Mykonos." She leaned forward, candlelight illuminating her face. "Dana, I feel like we have known each other for many years."

"I feel the same way." Dana squeezed Cybele's hand. "Let's use this week together as an experiment. To see how we get on."

"I want to give you money for rent."

"Not necessary," Dana replied. "We can split the cost of food."

Cybele raised her glass. "And wine."

"Yes, and wine. Later, if things work out, we can discuss the details."

—

After coffees and a shared snifter of Metaxa, the two women walked toward home. As eager as they were to return to the privacy of Dana's apartment, they strolled slowly, prolonging the moment. Finally, laughing, Cybele pulled Dana into the shadows and kissed her.

"There! I couldn't wait any longer," she said.

Dana laughed, sharing her high spirits. They pressed together and kissed again, feeling the heat rise between them.

Just then, a man's voice cut the air. "So, here you are. I've been looking for you … and it's just like I thought … a lesbian. No, wait, two lesbians."

They turned to see Luca Alessi. A trail of cigarette smoke rose from his thin lips. He resembled a slick hood, the type with a switchblade tucked in a boot. Undoubtedly, he had witnessed them kissing.

"So where's Teresa?" he asked, moving closer.

"I have no idea," Dana replied.

"You haven't got her stashed some place … some den of lesbians? No, I guess not, you're already busy with one, aren't you?" he sneered, pointing to Cybele.

"Luca, I don't know where Teresa is. I do know she doesn't want to be with you. Leave her alone and go back to New York."

He stopped a few feet away, weaving slightly, obviously under the influence, mad, and out to cause trouble. "I'll do as I please. She's my girlfriend. I came to this miserable island with her, and I'm returning with her. Do you understand?"

The implied threat roused the professional in Cybele. Without hesitation, she stepped in front of Dana and thrust her police I.D. in his face. "That is enough! You will treat my friend with respect, and you will not disturb us or anyone else." Her voice was even, but there was anger underneath. "Go to your hotel and sober up."

Surprised, Luca withdrew a pace, squared his shoulders, and set his jaw. "I'll do what I damned well like."

Cybele held her ground. "I will tell you to go one more time. Or I will arrest you."

Luca's eyes shifted toward Dana, assessing the situation. "Well, Dana, you got yourself one hell of a little lady. Got more balls than half the guys I know." He inhaled on his cigarette and blew the smoke in Cybele's face. "I'll see you around." With this, he turned and sauntered down the narrow lane.

Dana took Cybele's arm, which was rigid. "Let's go home."

Cybele's eyes flashed as she stared at Luca's back. She cursed under her breath in Greek. "What's the matter with him? He's a horrible man!"

"He is," Dana agreed.

Cybele shook her head as if to clear it of negativity. "I hope I never see him again! Something unfortunate will happen if I do."

Dana rubbed Cybele's shoulder until she relaxed. "You were really wonderful."

She shrugged and exhaled a long breath. "We shouldn't let that guy upset us. He's just a little man with a hurt male ego."

"I hope that's all he is," Dana replied, thinking that Luca's arrival on the island coincided with the first murder.

They headed down Solomou and veered toward the sea. When they stepped onto the promenade, the wind hit, blowing Cybele's dark hair and flicking Dana's in her eyes. The water was nipping at the edge of the wall, puddling the stones on the walkway. The temperature had dropped, and the two women shivered. Dana withdrew a key from her pocketbook and handed it to Cybele.

"Here. This is for you."

"Thank you." Cybele kissed her and opened the door.

Inside, Dana threw the new bolt, in no mood for unwanted visitors. After climbing the stairs, she uncapped a bottle of seven-star Metaxa and poured the brandy into two snifters.

"To us," she toasted.

They sipped the liquor, looking steadily at each other. Dana knew that drinking the Metaxa was stalling their move to the bedroom, compressing their desire minute by minute. Finally, she took a large swallow and set down her glass. Cybele grinned and did the same. Hand in hand, they ascended the stairs, laughing. After lighting three candles, Dana inserted a CD of one of her favorite singers, Angélique Ionatos, into a portable CD player.

"I love her! 'O Erotas,'" Cybele exclaimed.

The windows were open, and damp sea air was blowing in, causing the candles to flicker. Dana closed the wooden shutters. The room became still and intimate.

"It looks like a church." Cybele chuckled. "Am I tonight's offering?"

"Yes."

After an embrace, Dana gently guided Cybele's blouse over her head. They undressed, reveling in each other's touch, and with the moody voice of Ionatos as accompaniment, they made love, at first with abandon and then with care.

At some time during the night, Dana awoke. One of the candles near the bed was still burning. She studied Cybele, her dark hair covering the pillow. In many ways, she looked young, but as Dana examined her face more closely, she could see the beginning of a line on the side of her eye, the faintest crease. Dana could imagine how she would look in ten years or twenty and thought she would grow to love Cybele more as time passed.

—

THE MAN buttoned the cuffs on his black, long-sleeved shirt and tucked in its tails. When he slipped the wooden ruler into the small of his back, inside his belt, the man's fingers trembled as he remembered his father using the ruler on him. Over and over. He pressed his lips together, still incensed by the cruel treatment, which had continued for years. Donning a lightweight black jacket, he took a large swallow of vodka, snuffed out a cigarette, selected a pair of latex gloves from a box, and placed them in the slash pockets of his coat along with two condoms, two folded paper towels, a plastic bag, manicure scissors, and the wire. He was now ready for the hunt. A powerful shot of anticipation surged through him, but he sternly reminded himself to stay in control, a mantra he repeated whenever he felt his impulses overcoming the cold precision of his mind.

The man loved darkness and instinctively understood how to woo its mystery: following shadows down the streets, crossing into more shadows to avoid the light of a streetlamp. He knew the town's alleys and byways by heart, knew each gay bar and when the boys left, drunk and flushed from dancing, and where they went afterward.

Malcolm Hall had been a fortuitous find. Alone, he had left a club that closed very late. Staggering and carrying two bottles of beer, he had walked along a deserted street, wobbling slightly until he came upon a low wall. He placed a hand on it to steady himself and then decided to sit on top to drink the beer. Because the man didn't want to risk a frontal assault and was afraid the bottles might serve as weapons, he waited for a long time, growing concerned when the sky began to brighten. When Malcolm spun around, possibly because he was about to be sick, he exposed his back to the man, thus beckoning his fate. The man obliged with only a brief hesitation, enjoying the twist of the wire in his hands. His only regret was that he couldn't see Malcolm's eyes and witness the first moment of panic. He had punished the boy's body for not giving him that last look.

CHAPTER TWELVE

IN THE MORNING, Dana felt Cybele's hand on her back, playfully circling around her shoulder blades, tracing the line of her spine, tugging at a lock of hair.

"I have to go to work," Cybele murmured, easing out of bed.

A moment later, Dana heard the shower running. Though she was tempted to join Cybele, she drifted into memories of the night before. When she awoke, the room was empty. A note lay on the chest of drawers.

My dear Dana,

You are so innocent when you sleep. I didn't wish to wake you. Forgive me! I will see you tonight about 5:00. It is my turn to bring dinner—and, unless you change your mind—a suitcase. I miss you already.

Yours, Cybele

—

Shortly before ten, while walking to her class, Dana arrived at the edge of Akti Kambani and was surprised to see another cluster of protesters parading along the seafront esplanade. Hand-made signs and wooden crosses bristled above the tightly knit group: "Homosexuality Is a Sin!"

"Gay Is Evil!" "God Forgives!" The scene reminded her about the roll of film she'd taken of the previous gathering. There wasn't time to pick it up at the photo shop now because she was due to meet her class at the Archaeological Museum. Dana slipped past a taverna, behind the group and the arriving tourist police, and made her way around the curving harbor to Manto Square.

As Dana glanced back at the port, she noticed that a cruise ship was expelling passengers who would soon head toward the protesters, maximizing the confusion. The tourist police were attempting to disperse the sign-carrying men and women while the Mykonians gaped on the sidelines, always eager to watch foreigners acting foolishly. Meanwhile, word had apparently spread through the members of the gay community, many of whom were flooding the area, some festooned in makeshift rainbow flags and ribbons, others in dresses and outlandish hats, probably vestiges from drag costume contests. A group of lesbians was getting into the act, shouting suggestive curses and pushing some of the people holding the most offensive signs. A tinderbox was about to explode.

Dana hurried toward the museum, where her students were gathered outside. "What's going on, Dana?" asked Carolyn.

"A clash of beliefs." Dana stared at the distant mêlée.

"I hope it doesn't turn violent."

"It looks like it already has." David pointed to a fight in the square.

Dana was dismayed by what was happening, but there was nothing she could do. She noted that all of her students were present except Teresa and asked Mike where she was.

"I have no idea. She wasn't at breakfast." Mike sighed. "I should've knocked on her door before I left the hotel."

"Julian? Did you notice Teresa this morning?"

Julian shook his head, his eyes anxiously glued to the protest.

"Did any of you see her?"

No one had.

Dana was concerned, remembering Luca's drunken, hostile state the night before. "Who saw her last?"

"I was with her at dinner," Mike offered.

"And Hasina and I bought her a drink at a bar in the Little Venice section," David said.

Near her apartment, Dana thought, and not far from where she and Cybele had encountered Luca. "Did you walk her home afterward?"

David hung his head. "Well, no. Teresa left about eleven. She had been talking to a man and may have left with him. Hasina and I were dancing, so I'm not sure."

"What did he look like?"

"I don't know. American, I think. Brown hair, medium height. A beard. I didn't get a good look because the bar was really crowded."

Dana excused herself and rushed into the museum. She knew the manager and asked to use his telephone.

On the third ring, Sandros answered. He hadn't seen Teresa that morning or last night. Worried, he asked the chambermaid to look in her room while Dana stayed on the line. A few minutes later, he told her that Teresa's bed had not been slept in, but her clothes were still in the closet.

"Sandros, my students don't know where she is."

"Ah, that is not good," he muttered.

"What about Luca Alessi? Did he come back to the hotel?"

"Last night? It is possible Mr. Alessi returned, and no one saw him. He didn't eat breakfast today."

"Would you check if he's in his room? If he doesn't answer, could you open it to see if his things are there?"

"Okay," he agreed. "Should I call the police?"

Dana thought for just a second. "Yes, if he isn't around. Let them know about Teresa and whether Luca slept in his bed last night. By the way, I ran into him after dinner, and he was very drunk and angry," she said. "Sandros, I'm really concerned. After I finish my talk here at the Archaeological Museum, I'll go to the station. If the police need to speak with me, tell them where I am and that I'll be there soon. Again, I am so sorry for the trouble." Dana hung up, feeling overwhelmed with anxiety.

She turned to find David standing nearby. Her other students were also entering the museum. "I don't know if you saw this, Dana." He showed her a clipping of the two-day-old *Herald Tribune* article.

"Yes, I did."

He shook his head, frowning with concern. "How many photography instructors are there in town? That pretty much nails you, doesn't it?"

Dana nodded. "It does, but there's really no reason for him to come after me."

"Don't you have other photographs of the killer?" Julian asked.

"Yeah, that's what the article said," Carolyn added.

"No, they were all stolen from my darkroom. Besides, the prints were really grainy and didn't show much detail."

David looked surprised. "Stolen?"

"Yes." Dana explained about Devin Scott's murder. "Now, we need to begin class because we only have the museum for an hour."

When the students were gathered, Dana described their assignment. "I would like you to try minimalist portraits of the statues. Select a part of the sculpture and use it to tell about the whole. Avoid background material that distracts and try different perspectives by getting down low and shooting up. Experiment with depth-of-field. And remember the negative spaces."

They asked a few technical questions, which Dana answered patiently even though she felt a growing urgency to rush to the police station. After helping Carolyn with a jammed lens filter, she told everyone where she was going and that they should meet her at the Maritime Museum unless she made it to lunch at the Sesame Kitchen. On Mike's map, she indicated how to get there, avoiding the port. Julian, who suddenly seemed interested in her safety, offered to escort her. Dana thanked him but said she would be fine.

As she stepped out the door, police whistles pierced the air. Dana walked to the taxi stand and saw that the protest was breaking into physical altercations, mostly between the men, but some women were going at it too—the lesbians throwing signs onto the beach below, and the

Christian women whacking gay men with their heavy wooden crosses. A man in a sequined evening dress was using a sharp stiletto-heeled shoe to axe the head of one of the burlier male picketers whose face was turning bloody. One lesbian was doing serious damage to a spectacled man who was shouting "Jesus gave you AIDS so you will die!" Everyone else was yelling and throwing anything they could grab from the cafés and tavernas, which was provoking the outrage of the restaurant owners. Bible raised high, at the edge of the crowd, was the minister standing precariously on a chair. With his right hand holding onto a vertical awning support, he was exhorting his flock to re-group, presumably into their parade formation.

The tourist police had lost control of the situation. Over the din of screams, wails of emergency and police vehicles could now be heard. There was nothing useful Dana could do so she hurried to the police station. When she arrived, the building was nearly empty. The two men left behind were busy answering phones and scribbling notes. Dana went up to one, introduced herself, and asked if Sandros from the King Minos Inn had called to report a missing person, Teresa Corso. He nodded his head and, after resolving an incoming call, turned toward Dana.

"I'm sorry, Miss, what was your name?"

"Fox."

"Yes, we did learn of the disappearance of one of the guests at the King Minos. Unfortunately, we haven't found her. As you can see, all of our men are dealing with the problem at the port. Ah…" he mumbled a curse as ringing started again.

Dana waited until he finished the call. "Did Sandros say if Luca Alessi had slept in his bed last night? Whether his clothes were still there?"

"Mr. Alessi's things were in the room. His bed was unmade, but the housekeeper hasn't cleaned for two days. No one knows where he is."

"I guess we should assume they're both missing—Teresa and Luca."

"Yes. When this matter at the harbor is settled, we will investigate."

"These people seem really organized," Dana remarked, referring to the protesters.

He looked disgusted. "They caused problems in Athens first. Picketing in front of the gay clubs. The group that came here have been doing the same thing—annoying the patrons at the discos. They are led by a minister, Paul Owens Merrill, and a couple, Mary Lou and Walter Schatze."

"I saw the minister just now."

The policeman shook his head sadly. "Captain Yalouris will probably arrest him…at least for a few hours."

"Why did they come to Greece?"

He shrugged and made an empty gesture with his hands. "Something about Greece being where it all started. You know the ancient Greeks—boys with boys—that sort of thing. They are all crazy, if you ask me. We do not bother them, why should they bother us?"

"You're right," Dana agreed. "Will you tell Captain Yalouris that I was here and why? I'd appreciate it very much."

"I will."

Dana left him, walked outside, and sat on a nearby wall, unsure what to do about Teresa and wondering where she was. She was also upset about Cybele and hoped she was all right. Why couldn't they spend a peaceful week without dealing with bigotry and murder on their carefree island? Frustrated, Dana laid her head down on her arms, too tired to move out of the hot sun.

A few minutes later, she felt a hand on her shoulder. Startled, she looked up. Cybele stood beside her with a bruise on her chin and dirt smudged on her shirt.

She gave Dana a tired smile. "What are you doing here?"

"Oh, Cybele! Are you okay?" Dana blurted out.

"I'm fine. Just one confrontation with a cross," she said, feeling the bruise. "I bet I look a mess."

"You do." Dana was tempted to touch Cybele's face but refrained because they were in public. In a lower voice, she said, "I wanted to see you. And to check about my student, Teresa Corso, who seems to have disappeared."

"I heard about her. No one knows where she is."

"And what about Luca Alessi? Has anyone seen him?"

"No, but we've been busy."

Dana frowned and shaded her eyes from the sun. "I don't like the sound of this, Cybele. You saw Luca last night. He was furious because Teresa's rejecting him." She explained that he might be using asphyxiation as a sexual turn-on.

Cybele shook her head. "I don't understand things like that. When love can be so gentle, why must some people make it violent? I think it is too much TV and too many films."

"I know."

"Listen, my friend, I'm sorry, but I must go. If I hear anything about your student, I'll call and leave a message. And when Captain Yalouris returns, I'll speak with him."

"I'm glad you're safe." Dana fought the urge to kiss her, but a police van full of troublemakers was pulling into the station parking area. "See you later."

Cybele raised her bruised chin in acknowledgment and went inside. Relieved that Cybele was okay, Dana detoured to the post office to buy stamps so she could send her grandfather a letter.

He already knew about Dana's sexual orientation. Though he was somewhat unhappy about it, he loved her and probably would be pleased to hear about Cybele. During Dana's recent visit to Switzerland, her grandfather had commented he would die easier if he knew someone was taking care of her. Of course, he was still envisioning a man. Even so, this came as a surprise because she thought of herself as self-sufficient. But Dana knew what her grandfather meant. She had been emotionally adrift since the death of her parents. It was too facile to say she had commitment issues. In fact, the honest truth was she was desperately afraid of losing anyone she loved. Her reactions to Cybele's withdrawal after the misunderstanding had been disturbing, igniting old fears and the recurring nightmare.

She paid for the stamps and went to meet her students for lunch.

—

CYBELE TUCKED a strand of hair behind her ear and kept typing. Sitting beside her was the minister, Paul Owens Merrill, his red shirt dark with sweat and his white collar drenched. At first, he had stiffly refused to remove his jacket but had finally done so. The man spoke with the rounded tones of someone who loved to hear his voice. When she requested his name, he spelled it out letter by letter, enunciating each, ignoring the fluency of her English. This irked Cybele. His perspiring presence annoyed her even more.

"Iowa," he was saying in response to his address, his grayish-green eyes staring at her with contempt.

"And why are you here on Mykonos?" she asked, trying to tamp down the irritation that was vying with her professionalism.

"We are here to pray for the souls lost to homosexuality," Merrill intoned. "We have a ministerial clinic that endeavors to transform misguided men and women, to show them God's love and the way to a virtuous life. We have had great success."

Cybele's fingers came off the keyboard and clenched in momentary anger. She swallowed and continued. "What is the name of the clinic, please?"

"The Rainbow Center. We selected that name because it represents hope and salvation and, needless to say, will attract homosexuals. We do Christian work, hard work, but it's very rewarding." He smoothed his damp brown hair against the top of his head.

"How are you funded?" She was curious, despite her dislike of Merrill and her dislike of what he represented.

"Privately. We do not discuss our benefactor…benefactors."

"It must be very expensive to pay for all these people," she commented, observing the sweat streaming unimpeded down his jowls.

"Money is not an issue for those who are in service to God." He shrugged. "But some pay their own way; some are supported through my ministry. We have a radio program, you see, and receive donations. Soon we will begin television appeals. I'm looking forward to that."

Cybele noted that Merrill had dropped the plural "we" on the last sentence. A huge ego, she thought. "When do you plan to leave Mykonos?"

The minister studied the ceiling as if the answer might fly down from on high. "When our task is completed."

She frowned, and was about to make a sarcastic remark, when Captain Yalouris came out of his office and walked to her desk. In Greek, he instructed her to jail the minister in a non-air-conditioned cell for two hours before releasing him. Stifling a smile, Cybele agreed. Yalouris gave her a reprimanding glance, but his eyes twinkled.

CHAPTER THIRTEEN

HER STUDENTS WERE examining the restaurant's menu, with its idiosyncratic English spellings. They greeted Dana with the news that Yalouris' force had arrived at the harbor and been a more demonstrative presence than the tourist police. Protesters and some of the gay men and women had been stowed in vans, separately, for transportation to the station.

After lunch, Dana accompanied the class to the Maritime Museum, where she gave an assignment. The lure of a free afternoon, however, was affecting the students' concentration. Miss Bumble was especially dangerous, nearly toppling a model of an ancient ship.

"As you know, tomorrow is the last day of our workshop," Dana told them. "Drop off your film this afternoon and pick up the slides in the morning. We'll meet at the hotel promptly at 9:30. Your flight leaves in the afternoon, so you should have your suitcases packed before our critique."

"What about Teresa?" Mike asked.

"No one knows where she is. The police have been dealing with the mess in town, but they're aware of the situation."

"We can't leave without her," protested Carolyn.

"I appreciate your concern. I admit that I'm very worried too," Dana said. "I'll call the police in a little while. If I hear anything, I'll tell Sandros so he can relay the news."

"Do you think Luca did something to her?" David wanted to know.

"It's possible."

"Or could it be The Monk?" Carolyn ventured.

"I have no idea."

Dana asked the group about their plans for the afternoon and evening and learned that Hasina, David, and Carolyn were going to the beach, Mike was taking more photos, and Julian hadn't decided. Most were meeting at Katrine's for dinner.

"Enjoy yourselves and be safe. I'll see you tomorrow."

—

Two and a half hours before Cybele came home. Dana liked the sound of that and smiled as she walked toward her apartment. Nikos was out in front of his shop, whistling tunelessly and surveying potential customers. Every once in a while, he would spot someone who looked rich and would intercept them, starting a conversation. He thought this behavior was engaging; Dana had mentioned to him that most Americans would be put off except the ones who didn't realize they were being hustled. He grinned and replied, "If they do not know I am hustling them, then they are just the people I want in my store." It was a small joke between them.

Dana greeted Nikos, who drew her inside his shop. "Dana, I would like to ask you a question. Very seriously." He leaned forward in a conspiratorial manner. "This story in the newspapers, the one about the photography instructor. That is you, no?"

"Yes, it is."

"Ah, good God!" he cried. "Everyone will realize it is you. And the people in town, when they read this, they will believe you know who the murderer is." He threw his hand in the air. "So, the person who is responsible, he will also know who this instructor is."

"If it's someone who lives here."

Nikos shook his head. "I hope nothing bad comes of this, Dana. You must be very careful. I am old enough to be your father, and I tell you to be, how you say? Vigilant." He liked this word so much that he repeated it, wagging a thick finger at the same time.

"I'm always vigilant," she replied, using his favorite new word. "And I have company."

"Oh, that is good." Narrowing his eyes and leaning forward again, he asked, "And who is this company. A handsome man or a beautiful woman, eh?"

Dana laughed. "A very beautiful woman."

He punched her on the shoulder. "Ha! You are in love! I can see it! Nikos knows all the signs. *Sinharitiria*! So, tell me, what is her name, this beauty of yours?"

"Cybele," Dana answered, chuckling at his exuberance.

"The mother of the gods, no?"

She laughed. "I think that's a fine description, Nikos."

"That is not all! Cybele is the goddess of nature, mother of man, giver to the arts—she should be a great benefit for you." In a whisper, he added, "And great, great orgies were celebrated in her honor!" He reared back and laughed and laughed.

His hilarity was contagious. "And this is my duty?" she gasped. "To celebrate her with orgies?" Tears of laughter began to fall down her face.

"Yes, on your honor. It is your duty! No kidding!" Nikos swiped a big hand over his own streaming red cheeks.

"No kidding! How do you know all this?"

He threw out his robust chest. "I am Greek! We know these things! And besides, we sometimes say that Cybele is one form of Aphrodite, the goddess of love and beauty."

"That describes her very well," Dana replied, drying her eyes.

"You are a lucky one. I, Nikos, am sure of it."

"Thank you. Now, I suppose it's time for me to go plan this evening's revelry."

"Ah, yes! Absolutely. Lots of wine, beautiful music…the sea! I am envious!" He clapped her on the shoulder and began laughing again as she waved goodbye.

—

On the answering machine, there was a message that Myron Tsoublekas had called. Dana dialed the number and was placed on hold until he came on the line.

"Miss Fox, we have learned nothing about Miss Corso. She hasn't been seen since last night. Mr. Alessi is also missing. Perhaps they are together? I'm sorry. We don't know."

"Teresa was trying to avoid Luca. She was afraid of him. Did you check the other hotels in town? Maybe she's hiding until her plane leaves tomorrow."

"We haven't, but I will call the hotels and see if she is staying at one of them. Today has been very busy. I apologize for our department."

"You might also ask about Luca Alessi. He has black hair and a dark complexion. Thin, not very tall. Thirties."

Myron was silent while he wrote down the information. "We have their passport numbers already."

"Good. By the way, whatever happened to all those protesters?"

Myron giggled. "Ah, they will lose their lunches, I think. Captain Yalouris sent some of them to Athens on the Dolphin. The sea is very rough today."

Dana laughed. Even on a bright sunny day the Aegean could be turbulent.

"Oh, and before they left, we fed them well, Miss Fox," he said with a chuckle. "Moussaka, pastitsio, dolmades, and lots of retsina. That was the Captain's idea. Even the ladies who do not drink, we told them it was only polite. A custom in our country."

Some of the richest Greek fare. "What a mess that'll be! Your Captain is a brilliant man."

"He is indeed. Now, let me telephone the hotels. If I learn anything, I will call you."

"That would be very kind. *Ya sas.*"

After hanging up, Dana sat on the balcony, pen and paper in hand, to write the letter to her grandfather even though she had no idea when it would reach him; he followed the opera circuit, attending the first performances of the new season in various cities. She could telephone, but Dana wasn't ready to discuss Cybele yet, or at least not in conversation. She began with news of her workshops and the brisk gallery sales and then mentioned that a woman, an Athenian, was living with her temporarily. She didn't elaborate on the nature of their relationship. By the time her grandfather arrived home in New York, perhaps the situation would be clearer, and she could report exciting news.

After pasting on sufficient postage for the United States, Dana left to mail the letter, deposit the gallery check, and walk to her favorite purveyor of French bubbly.

—

THE MAN BEGAN to search for Dana Fox in the late afternoon. Although she couldn't identify him from the first photo, the ones taken by the harbor concerned him. After an hour, he stopped at a café and ordered a vodka tonic, emphasizing to the waiter that he wanted no ice. He preferred his drinks at room temperature or warmer. After squeezing the slice of lime into the cocktail, he sipped the tepid, clear liquid, enjoying its acid sweetness. Idly, he watched a dark Greek youth lift cartons of soda onto the top step by the door, his muscles rippling the stripes on his shirt. The man raised his glass a few inches from the table in an unseen toast.

—

BY FIVE, Dana was dressed in an aqua-and-white Greek blouse and slacks. Two bottles of Veuve Clicquot chilled in the freezer, and a bouquet of pink roses brightened the balcony table, which was set with yellow plates and matching cloth napkins. Three white candles were set in blue bottles. Dana had the romantic trappings down well, but this time it felt special. Strangely, despite her trust in Cybele, she was apprehensive that Cybele wouldn't come, as if a person so wonderful would prove to be a fantasy. Dana sat on the balcony, unable to read because she was too distracted. Twenty minutes later, she heard her name and saw Cybele below, opening the door. Relieved, Dana sprang to her feet and went to help.

"I thought I would never leave that place!" Cybele cried, kissing Dana. "Oh, have to be careful!" She rubbed her bruised face lightly, then kissed Dana again and laughed.

"Welcome home!"

"Ah, that sounds wonderful!" She handed Dana a paper bag. "See, I didn't forget dinner even with all those crazy people today!" Cybele wheeled a large black suitcase inside.

"Myron said they were shipped out on the hydrofoil after a big Greek lunch."

"Yes, one of our better ideas," Cybele said as she lugged her suitcase up the spiral stairs.

In the living room, she gave Dana an appraising look. "You look nice and clean. Do I have time to shower?"

"Go ahead. I'll carry this upstairs for you."

In the bedroom, Dana showed Cybele where to hang her clothes, provided a set of towels, gave Cybele a lengthy kiss, and then returned to the kitchen. In Cybele's shopping bag, she found a container of taramousalata, calamari cooked in lemon and herbs, rice pilaf, and a six-inch square of spanakopita. She laid some crackers on a plate with the fish roe salad and brought it out to the balcony. In a few minutes, Cybele appeared, her black hair wet and sleek, combed back on her head. She wore a flimsy white blouse with no bra. Getting a precarious grip on her impulses, Dana went to the refrigerator and removed a bottle of French Champagne, popped the cork quietly, and filled two Waterford crystal glasses.

Cybele read the label and examined the dance of bubbles breaking for the surface. After a toast, she took a swallow. "This is perfection! And these glasses are so beautiful."

They took seats outside and sat in companionable silence, savoring their drinks until Cybele turned her chair to look at Dana and said, "I want to talk about something."

"What?" Dana was instantly worried.

Cybele applied a reassuring hand on her arm and smiled. "No, it's not a problem between us." She paused before continuing. "I'm concerned about the articles in the Athens papers and the *Herald Tribune*."

Dana began to make light of the subject, but Cybele persisted. "It's very likely the killer has identified you. If not, he will soon. The television and the newspapers are running the story constantly. The town is talking of nothing else except the murders. This is such a small place, Dana. It would be easy for him to find out your name and where you live. You walk around town with your cameras and your students. You are noticed—with your height, your blond hair."

Dana sighed. "I really don't think he's after me."

Frowning, Cybele disagreed. "You can't assume that."

"Okay, I know. I promise to be cautious. My landlord made the same point a little while ago. The irony is that I couldn't recognize the person I photographed that morning. When I took the shot, my head was behind the camera, and I was focusing on the architecture when the man walked into the composition. And the image of the priest wasn't sharp and was only a profile."

"So perhaps the killer didn't see you, either?"

Dana hadn't thought of that possibility. "I don't know. The person was out of sight by the time I straightened up. With a camera in front of my face, I'm not sure I was recognizable. Wearing my photographer's vest, I look similar to my students."

"Maybe that's why Virgil Laine was killed. Because the murderer thought he was you."

"He did wear the same vest and had light-colored hair."

"But by now, the killer knows Virgil wasn't an instructor."

Dana nodded in reluctant agreement. She spread two crackers with taramousalata and handed one to Cybele and ate the other.

"We believe the murderer will probably stop dressing as a monk, if he hasn't already, because there are so few Orthodox priests on the island, which was mentioned in the newspaper," Cybele said. "And we believe he's after gay men, so they are still at risk. As are you."

"Do you think the situation with Teresa and Luca is related? They were both here when the murders began. And, as you witnessed, Luca doesn't like lesbians."

"Yes, but does he hate gay men as well?" Cybele asked. "And as for being the killer, he doesn't have a beard like the man in your photograph."

"Easy enough to fake." She then thought about how Luca had glared at Virgil during class. "Most likely Luca dislikes all gay people, but I think he's more obsessed with Teresa than in killing off our community on Mykonos."

Cybele ate another cracker. "Dana, that may be true, but he's still a threat. He may blame you for Teresa rejecting him. I think he's dangerous."

"If Luca is the murderer, where did he get the cassock and hat?"

"It's possible to buy religious clothes in Athens. He was there before flying here."

"Then I hope someone will read Devin's article in the newspaper and report an American man purchasing Greek Orthodox clothes." She shook her head. "Kind of hard to pack a stovepipe hat, though. You'd think Teresa would have noticed. And where does the man change into his disguise? If he's staying at a hotel or pension, he couldn't do it in his room and walk out through the lobby."

Cybele conceded the point. "It would be difficult, yes. I'll mention this idea about the clothes to Captain Yalouris. But, Dana, please. I'm concerned about you."

"So what can I do? The workshop finishes tomorrow. I need to go to the hotel for a last critique and to say goodbye to everyone."

"Then you'll come home and stay here. Maybe the police can find the murderer, and everything will be okay again."

"Can't you get assigned to protect me?" Dana teased, taking her hand and smiling.

"My dear, I would like nothing better!"

CHAPTER FOURTEEN

AFTER THEY FINISHED eating dinner and were halfway through the second bottle of Champagne, Cybele began to talk about her family. Dana asked what her father had done for a living. She set down her glass and studied Dana carefully.

"I think it is time to tell you. Please don't be alarmed by what I say." She retreated to the back of her chair; her eyes seemed troubled. "My father was a thief." She let the admission settle. "He was a very good thief. And very charming with women."

"As is his daughter."

Cybele acknowledged the comment with a sad smile. "My father worked the big hotels in Cannes and Nice and St. Tropez. He was clever, skillful, stealing only jewelry and cash. Over the years, he made a lot of money. The strange thing is that he didn't need to be a thief because my father's family has money. My mother's family too. Not rich, not by American standards, but well off. He liked it … the excitement, the danger."

"What happened to him?"

"Ah, that's a tragic story. One night, after he'd taken a diamond necklace from a hotel suite, he was climbing a rope to the roof, where he planned to change clothes and escape down the stairs, pretending he was a guest. My father was handsome, sophisticated. This trick he had done often, but this time he was seen from below, and a detective was sent to catch him. When my father tried to get away, he slipped and fell six floors. A horrible ending," she whispered.

"I'm very sorry." Dana took both of her hands. "How old were you?"

"I was seventeen." She shrugged and looked out to sea. "He wasn't a bad man. He never hurt anyone—not physically. He was just addicted to stealing. Even so, I loved him. He was full of life and told amazing stories. But his death changed everything. I was older then, of course, but I had come to realize what he was doing was not a game, that he harmed people by stealing from them."

"And that he could hurt you and your family by putting himself at risk," Dana suggested.

"Yes. I suppose I'm angry at him in some ways. Because he cared more about being a thief than being a father and a husband."

Dana considered for a moment. "Did this influence your choice of career?"

"Maybe." Cybele furrowed her forehead. "I felt ashamed about what he did, yet I ate the food he provided and went to university because of his criminal life. I never told him to stop."

"He was your father. You don't have to atone for what your father did."

"I know." She paused, deep in thought. "Even my mother never insisted he take a real job—not that I ever heard anyway. I guess I blame her a little, too, for not preventing what happened. But we all loved him and the presents he gave us, and now we feel guilty. My brother, he's also a policeman, and my sister is a social worker, working with juvenile delinquents. Another sister is at university, but she's having problems. My mother and I are concerned that she's like my father. She's been caught shoplifting twice."

"I'm sorry to hear that, Cybele."

She nodded in acknowledgment. "Because I wanted to understand my father, I studied sociopathy." She poured some Champagne and considered for a moment. "So, yes, his death influenced me greatly. And though the situations are different, you probably were changed by your father's death."

"Yes, I was. Instead of being addicted to stealing, Dad's addiction was to liquor. It wasn't so noticeable until after the accident and my mother's and grandmother's deaths, which were his fault—a fact he never forgot, nor did I, as much as I tried." Dana shook her head. "I wish he and I could talk…to ease his pain and erase my anger toward him. You probably also wish you had a chance to speak with your father."

"I do. And I wish he could meet you."

They watched the sea and didn't speak. Dana placed her arm around Cybele's shoulders and pulled her close. "I don't mean to be inquisitive, but a little while ago you said your parents had money?"

She turned to face Dana. "Yes. I have some inheritance already. From my grandparents."

"That's good. I'm glad to hear it." When Cybele gave her a puzzled look, Dana smiled. "It's not what you think. I need to explain more about myself—something I usually avoid doing."

Cybele put a hand on her arm. "Why?"

"Unfortunately, I've learned that it isn't wise to talk about this subject." Dana sighed. "People become interested for the wrong reasons."

"And you've experienced this before?"

"Several times," Dana replied. "But I want you to know about my situation. After Dad died, my inheritance was substantial. My grandfather's financial advisor helped arrange a stock portfolio and buy my condo in New York City. In fact, to be honest, I don't need to work for a living, but I would feel purposeless if I didn't, like I wasn't contributing. Even my photography career is doing well…at least in the last few years as I've become better known here and in New York. I'm very grateful for my good fortune." Dana glanced at Cybele, worrying how she was digesting the information. "I know I shouldn't apologize for who I am, but sometimes I feel like I should."

Cybele was silent, attentive. Then she leaned over and kissed Dana. "Thank you for giving me your trust," she said softly. "And, yes, you're correct. There is no need to regret anything."

Dana nodded and studied her hands. "I was afraid to tell you."

"So much worry." Cybele stroked Dana's cheek and laughed lightly. "Let it go."

Dana didn't know what to say.

"You are quiet, eh? Well, we should speak of other things."

"Like what?"

"Well, which of your parents do you take after? Your mother or your father?"

"My mother."

"She must have been very beautiful. Did she have the same eyes? They are so blue—like the Mediterranean Sea far away, on the horizon." She traced Dana's eyebrow with her finger. "Tell me more about her."

"Her name was Astrid. She came to America from Sweden with her parents when she was three. Later, she studied at Wellesley—mostly literature, but drama was her passion. Several film producers asked her to be in their movies. She never accepted because she had married my father by then—they met in Boston during their junior years—Dad was attending Harvard. His family didn't approve of such a career."

"What do you remember most about her?"

"She loved to play the piano and sing—opera and Broadway—but the memory I cherish is reading with her on the veranda of our Nantucket house during the summer. It was a wonderful old place built high above the dunes. With gray weathered wood, a fireplace where we burned beach plum branches in the early fall. Such a sweet smell!"

"Do you still own it?"

"No. After my mother died, my father was too upset to be there. He felt her presence in the rooms, on the road where the accident occurred."

"And your father? What was he like?"

"A very kind and caring man, with a good head for business until his drinking interfered. His death was a great shock even though I knew that he was killing himself."

Cybele mused on their situation. "We've lost our fathers. Only your grandfather is alive. I feel separate from my family. Perhaps we can do what we please, yes?"

Dana nodded and smiled at her. "I know what I would be pleased to do right now."

She returned Dana's grin. "First, we have to clean the dishes. I must be strict with you!"

—

IT AMUSED HIM to improvise. Tonight, the man wore black, added talcum powder to gray his hair, and affected a limp, which would make him seem like an elderly man. Although it was tiring, he liked small changes in his performance. His was an art form, after all, requiring nuance.

About 2:00 a.m., he rounded a corner, keeping close to the building walls, and saw two policemen and they saw him. He ducked into the shadows and ran into an alley between two houses, turned at the end, and followed a second passageway to the left, in the direction of the police. The man hoped that traveling toward them would be unexpected. When the passage opened onto a small square, he entered it warily, scurried across the space and down two more lanes, and found a dark area to hide between a closed shop and a house. Silently, he waited, his heart beating with excitement. In the distance, he heard police radios. Pressing into the shadows behind a white trellis, the man kept out of sight until all was still, then crept down the walk, thwarted in his quest, shaking with rage.

—

THE NIGHT SEEMED at once endless and brief. Cybele was an adept and generous lover; Dana fervently hoped to match her sensitivity. Near dawn, after a few hours of sleep, Dana woke. As she lay in bed, it suddenly seemed that her life was coming together. She listened to the shallow breathing of the woman beside her and felt happy, the exhilaration sharpened by the edgy thrust of anxiety. There was so much to lose with Cybele. The stakes were high and heady. Did she trust herself enough to make this relationship work? Somehow, Dana trusted Cybele more. She was more centered, more giving, more in touch with her emotions. Then, although it hadn't occurred to her during dinner, she wondered if Cybele had only moved in because she was worried about Dana's safety. That thought deserved to be chased away, yet its remnant floated stubbornly in her mind as did a trace of fear. The combination of feeling afraid and in love was quite unsettling, but she had to admit that both emotions existed, because as much as she wished to ignore her foreboding, Dana sensed a malevolent presence close by, as if someone was watching or obsessively thinking about her. She shivered, but not from cold.

—

CYBELE LEFT early for work after eliciting a promise from Dana that she would return home once her students were on the van to the airport. With half an hour to spare before her class, Dana called Captain Yalouris for news of Teresa and Luca.

"Good morning, Miss Fox," he said pleasantly. "Yes, I have some information on Mr. Alessi. Sometime late last night he returned to the hotel. This morning, when the maid opened his room, she found him asleep. Sandros called us, and we went to the King Minos to question him. Mr. Alessi states that he doesn't know where Teresa Corso is and that he hasn't seen her since Sunday night."

"Do you believe him?"

"I'm not sure. I think he lies easily."

"Is Luca free or is he in jail?"

"We had no reason to hold him, but until Miss Corso is found, we told Mr. Alessi to stay at the King Minos and not leave the island. I understand your workshop is finished?"

"Yes, Captain, in a few hours. But how can you keep Luca from walking out of the hotel?"

The policeman chuckled. "We have two men watching the front of the building. As you know, the back is surrounded by a high wall around the pool. The only way he can get out is past my men. If he leaves, they will stop him."

"I'm relieved to hear it. And the killer? Do you have any more information?"

"Not really. It was quiet last night. Two of my officers saw an older man out late, but they were unable to find where he went."

"Too bad. Well, I have a class. I'll let you know if I hear anything about Teresa."

—

After donning her straw hat and locking the outside door, Dana checked to see if anyone was taking notice. A few people were aligning the café chairs on the walkway and swabbing the flagstones—no one suspicious. At the hotel, she noted one policeman across the street and another leaning against a dilapidated cart.

Sandros was sitting at the desk, reading the morning paper, smoking. He offered coffee and a pastry. Dana accepted with pleasure.

"So, any news this morning?" she asked, sipping the hot liquid.

"No," he said. "Perhaps the killer has left the island, and fortune will smile again."

"I hope so."

"Only one thing. There is a couple staying at the Hotel Moros. They caused trouble last night at one of the bars over on Matoyiánni Street."

"What happened?"

"They wrapped large wooden crosses in newspaper and set them on fire by the door so no one could go in or out. A lot of smoke. Everyone was very angry. The police came and fined them for the damage. Mikis —you know him, right?"

"Yes, he's the owner of Gabriel's."

Sandros nodded vigorously. "It was his disco. He was so mad he poured a pitcher of beer on Walter Schatze—that's the husband."

Dana chuckled. "And he probably doesn't drink!"

Sandros laughed and Dana ate her pastry.

A minute later, Mike came upstairs from the dining room.

"Good morning," he said. "Any news about Teresa?"

"No, none," Dana replied, "but Luca came in sometime last night."

"How did you know that?" Sandros' eyes opened wide.

"I have my sources." She enjoyed surprising him.

"Well, Luca better stay away from me," Mike said, his sunburned face turning a shade darker. "By the way, Julian and I canceled our flight to Athens."

"Really?"

"Yeah. Actually, it was Julian's idea. He wants to do more black-and-white photography, trying out red, yellow, and orange filters. He plans to create a portfolio to sell at home in New Jersey." Mike shook his head. "I doubt he'll do very well, but Julian is really gung-ho about the idea. For myself, I just want to do some more shooting…and shopping and tourist stuff."

"Your decision doesn't have anything to do with Teresa's disappearance, does it?"

He gave Dana a broad smile. "Well, maybe a little. But, hey, I like Mykonos."

Carolyn and David joined them at the desk. Miss Bumble was sporting a strawberry jam stain on her yellow gingham blouse. As Dana was explaining about Teresa, the telephone rang.

"*Kalimera,*" Sandros said and then looked at Dana and pointed to the receiver. "Yes. Miss Fox is here now." He moved the phone into his office and beckoned for her to come in. He handed over the receiver.

"Dana, this is Teresa Corso."

CHAPTER FIFTEEN

DANA QUICKLY asked Teresa where she was and if she was safe.

Teresa hesitated before answering. "I'm in Athens, but please, don't tell anyone. Especially not Luca."

"What happened?"

"On Monday night, I was having some drinks with David and his wife. I wasn't having much fun. I was worried that Luca would find me—you know, if he made the rounds of all the clubs."

"He *was* looking for you."

"Yeah, I bet he was. Anyhow, as I was leaving, I ran into this nice guy, Todd, that I met on the boat to Delos. We started talking. I told him what was going on, and he offered to take me to his hotel. It's not what you think. Todd is gay. He was alone here but hadn't had any luck with the guys in town. So, that's where I was Monday night. Yesterday, since I had my purse and my camera gear, Todd took me to the airport. I was hoping that Sandros or you could mail my clothes to the Electra Palace Hotel. I know it's a lot to ask, but Sandros can add the expense to my hotel bill. There's an open charge there on my credit card."

"We can do that."

"Look, I don't want to make a complaint or anything, but Luca, well, he practically raped me. I'm a little bruised and sore, but at least I'm on the pill so that's not a problem. I don't know what happened to make him change so much. He didn't behave like this in New York."

"Sometimes people disguise who they are to get what they want," Dana told her.

"Well, he certainly fooled me. Anyway, I'm extremely embarrassed that I put all of you to so much trouble. Please tell the class I'm sorry. Just don't mention that I'm in Athens. I'll stay here until my clothes arrive."

"We'll say you flew home."

"Would you? Oh, thank you!" She dictated the address of the Electra Palace to Dana.

After she hung up, Dana explained the situation to Sandros, who offered to have the maid pack Teresa's things and to hide the suitcase behind the desk, whereupon he would take it to the post office himself.

She clapped him on the back affectionately. "You're the best, Sandros!"

He gave her a half-bow.

Julian and Hasina had joined the cluster in the lobby. Dana led the group to the room where the projector was set up and closed the door.

"I have some news about Teresa. She called from the airport in Athens. She's about to board a plane for New York."

"What happened?" Mike asked.

"I don't want to go into the details, but as you know, she had trouble with Luca. Late Monday, she ran into someone she knew who put her up for the night. Yesterday, she left Mykonos—I guess no one at the airport realized she was a missing person. The police probably didn't notify them because of all the confusion in town," Dana said. "She asked me to thank everyone for being so kind and to apologize for causing you concern."

"Boy, Luca is going to be furious!" David exclaimed.

"He's here?" Carolyn asked.

"Yes," Dana replied. "The police interrogated him but couldn't charge him with anything because Teresa refused to make a complaint and then went missing. All they could do was confine him to the hotel. And now that she is no longer here, he'll be free to go."

"That bastard shouldn't get away with this," Mike growled. "The way he mistreated her."

"I understand your feelings, Mike."

"He scares me," Carolyn said. "Is he leaving with us today?"

"I don't know his plans, but please don't mention anything to him about Teresa. Now, let's load the first carousel with the museum slides and set up a second with your best photos from the course. I'll be back in a minute."

Sandros nodded when Dana asked to use the phone. In his office, she closed the door.

At the police station, Myron answered. Dana explained that Teresa Corso was in Athens. "That means that Luca Alessi is free to leave the hotel."

"And he caused her no problem?"

"He did but she chose to get away from him. Don't mention where Teresa is—just tell Luca that she has flown home to New York."

"Okay, we'll call Mr. Alessi and give him that information."

"Fine, thanks. If you want, I can notify your two men outside that they can go."

"That would be very helpful, Miss Fox."

Dana hung up the receiver and stepped through the hotel's front door. She walked to the nearest policeman and apprised him of the situation. He whistled to the second officer and they left.

When she returned, everyone was sharing their favorite images, trying to decide on their "best shots" selections, and loading slides in the carousels. Dana sat in an armchair and waited, wondering what Luca would do. With any luck, he would catch the afternoon flight to Athens. She would rest easier knowing he was off the island. Cybele would too. And maybe his departure would mean the killer was gone.

Carolyn was the last to insert her slides. Julian had been the first—true to form. Dana darkened the room and began analyzing the images taken at the two museums. The low light at both locations and the clutter had proved to be tough problems for everyone. Only David had done well, with some very interesting minimalist cropping.

After reviewing the last carousel of favorites, she opened the curtains and began her standard end-of-workshop lecture. "Every one of you has taken hundreds of photographs—"

"Thousands!" Mike called out, causing chuckles.

"Thousands, yes. What's nice about a workshop is that it gives you an opportunity to do just that, without having to worry about a job or other obligations. For that reason alone, I hope you had a good time," she said. "What I'd like you to take away from this week is a better understanding of figure/ground relationships. If you can keep that idea on your mental clothesline, it will strengthen your work." She spoke about the assignments and praised each class member. "I think you've all improved greatly."

When her summation was complete, the students pulled their slides from the carousels. Sandros came in, as if on cue, and announced that everyone should bring their suitcases to the lobby. Dana waited until her students were gathered by the desk and then thanked each of them and said goodbye.

"It was so much fun!" Carolyn said.

"I've enjoyed having you in the class."

Julian even sounded appreciative. He then asked Dana if she would be available if he or Mike had questions.

"I'll be around, Julian. Ask Sandros to give me a call."

"Can't you give me your phone number? I promise I won't bother you."

Dana smiled, though she was uncomfortable about his persistence. "I know you wouldn't abuse it, Julian, but I don't give it out. I'd be happy to discuss anything with either of you, but please go through Sandros."

Julian's face tightened. "What's the deal? Is it the money? I mean, all I want is a few minutes—maybe to drop some slides at your place? You could call me when it's convenient, and I could bring them by."

Dana sensed an undercurrent of tension within him. She tried to convince herself that it was Julian's impatient manner that was putting her off rather than something more ominous. All the warnings from Cybele and the police were making her uncharacteristically suspicious. "I'm sorry. I'll do my best to be available."

David interrupted their conversation. "Thanks for everything. I had a great time. By the way, are you teaching in New York?"

"As a matter of fact, yes. I'm scheduled to do three seminars at the Calvin Carnahan Gallery in February."

"Perfect! I'll come."

He shook her hand, as did his wife. Dana complimented him again on his work. Hasina beamed proudly, taking his arm and squeezing it.

"See, I told you your photographs are excellent!"

Dana smiled at her and agreed. She bade David, Hasina, and Carolyn a safe trip and asked them to bring their suitcases down to the lobby. After she stored the projector and neatened the room, she walked upstairs and collided with Luca Alessi, who was descending from the floor above.

He gave her a purposeful shove that sent her flying into the wall. "Get out of my way!"

Dana gripped the railing hard, righting herself. She had never been physically threatened before, and her response shocked her. All she wanted to do was punch Luca's snarling face.

"Listen, you touch me again and I'll—"

"You'll do what? Huh? Get your pretty girlfriend? You're the reason the police came after me! You made up some stupid story about Teresa."

Incensed, Dana took a step closer. "Don't blame me for your sick behavior! You're lucky she didn't press charges of rape!"

Luca laughed without amusement. In a taunting voice, he retorted, "She wanted it, just like your girlfriend probably wants it."

She felt her hands crunching into fists. Sandros rushed over. "Now, I don't want no problems!" he shouted. "Please! Mr. Alessi. I let you stay here, but if you cause trouble, you must leave."

Luca glared at Sandros and snapped, "Fine! I'm going!" With that, he turned sharply and ran up the stairs.

Sandros muttered some words in Greek and faced Dana. "Are you okay?"

Dana refolded the long sleeves of her blouse and shot a smoldering glance at Luca's back. "Yeah, I'm okay," she replied, although she wasn't.

Seeing Dana's expression, Sandros took her arm and steered her to a chair in his office. He poured her another cup of coffee. "You should know Mr. Alessi is not going to Athens today. After the police told him he was free, he asked me to call the airlines to cancel this afternoon's flight. He didn't reserve another one."

Dana lifted the mug and noticed her hand was shaking. She tried to calm her voice. "That's not good news."

"No. He might be a problem for you."

"For some reason he blames me for what happened with Teresa."

"He has a hot temper. Those Italians, you know."

Dana laughed, in spite of her agitation. "And Greeks are all pussycats?"

"Ah, but of course!" He grinned at her. "We are a reasonable people!"

—

CYBELE OVERHEARD Myron's phone conversation and asked if he had been speaking with Dana Fox. He explained that Teresa Corso was in Athens, and Luca Alessi was no longer under surveillance. Pleased about the first report, distressed by the second, and worried that Luca might hurt Dana, Cybele felt a surge of protectiveness and frustration that they didn't own cell phones. She would buy two as soon as she had time.

Other than a late-night sighting of an older man in black, Cybele had heard nothing new. Everyone at the station was short-tempered from working long hours, discovering no leads, and dealing with the tourist organizations, archbishop's office, mayor, and angry shop owners anxious about business. Then there was the matter that had occupied her this morning: the incident at Gabriel's with the two cross-burning fanatics,

Mary Lou and Walter Schatze. Although she hadn't interviewed them, Cybele knew that Captain Yalouris had fined both for damages and for creating a public nuisance. She and Myron had escorted the couple to their hotel; however, they were not restricted to its premises.

Myron finished writing some notes and signaled that she should join him outside. After yesterday's protests and the killings, they had been assigned to protect the gay-owned establishments during mid-day, which meant a lot of walking around town. Cybele jammed the notebook in her back pocket and followed him.

—

IT TOOK DANA an hour to work off the rush of anger from her run-in with Luca. She had promised to remain at her apartment and should be doing some darkroom printing, but the thought of being trapped inside an airless room wasn't appealing. As she approached her door, she veered off to the jewelry shop, but Nikos wasn't there—only his daughter, Sophia. She was as quiet as Nikos was boisterous.

"Any mail?" Dana asked.

She reached behind the counter and handed Dana a cream-colored envelope. The name and address were written in a stylish hand. Émile de Szasi. Inside was an invitation for a memorial service for Virgil: tomorrow evening at eight. Dana supposed that Virgil's parents had left Mykonos, and that Émile was now able to hold a gathering. She thanked Sophia and placed the envelope in her pocket.

The afternoon lay before her. She called the photo shop to see if her film was developed and printed. Helen, the owner, said it wouldn't be ready until Friday because the printer was broken. She apologized but Dana assured her there was no rush.

Hanging up, Dana thought of Cybele and wondered about buying her a gift. What would she like? She left the apartment and began walking toward the harbor, relieved to see the area was peaceful again. Even the sea was calm, with only a faint ripple of white marking the waterline.

Her meanderings soon came to an end at Lalaounis. Grandly elegant, the store specialized in reproductions of Greek jewelry inspired by different historical styles. Dana realized she was being impetuous, acting like a hormone-infused adolescent, but perhaps the anxiety and fear about the murders had heightened her feelings.

She entered the showroom and was greeted graciously. Unsure what she had in mind, Dana examined the cases. There were several rings she liked, but a ring was premature, though it warmed her to consider such a purchase. Finally, she settled on a gold, Hellenistic-inspired, braided bracelet, which the saleswoman gift-wrapped.

Dana slipped the package in her pocket and left, happy and excited. She stopped at the Blue Dolphin Café, ordered a coffee, and received some teasing from Kostas. Afterward, she went to the market and purchased a half leg of lamb, three onions, a bag of lentils, and a ripe tomato. Coming out of the grocery, she checked to see if anyone was following her: no one. Near her street, she slowed to stare at a shop window to use its reflection to see behind her. Again, all clear. Dana cut around to the stone walkway and unlocked her door. Upstairs, she began cooking the lentils—a Syrian recipe made with rice and onions, simmered slowly, and served thick. Once the lentils were on the stove, Dana concentrated on the lamb. From a terracotta pot on the balcony, she clipped several redolent sprigs of rosemary. Slivering four cloves of garlic, she inserted tufts of rosemary and thin wedges of garlic into cuts in the meat, made a red wine marinade in a plastic bag, and placed the lamb inside. After storing the meat in the refrigerator, Dana set the table and lay down on the couch with a book.

—

A while later, she heard the door open and Cybele's footsteps on the stairs. When Cybele leaned over the couch to give her a kiss, Dana pulled her down. Cybele tried to get loose, but Dana grasped her firmly around the waist.

"You are very, very strong!" Cybele giggled, trying to get free.

Dana laughed. "I am, aren't I?"

Cybele stopped struggling. "There! You win … this time! I let you."

"You did, did you?"

"Yes. I should use karate on my beloved?" Cybele worked herself on top of Dana. "Eh? Would you like that?"

Dana shook her head. "Please, no!"

She tickled her. "So, dear, what is for dinner?"

"Hey!" Dana said, squirming. "Roast lamb and lentils—if you can spare me for a minute."

Cybele moved down to Dana's neck, produced the response she desired, then stood abruptly. "Ah, it is nice to have a wife!" She took Dana's arm and hauled her upright. "Dinner!"

Dana shook her head and went into the kitchen to preheat the oven. After stirring the lentils, she set the lamb in a pan and slipped it in the oven. "There! Now, what should we do?"

Cybele came up close and whispered. "How long do we have?"

"Two hours."

She studiously considered this before breaking into a smile. "I think that's enough time. Enough for you, anyway."

—

IT WAS TWILIGHT, the time the man had loved best as a child, when the bats flew out of the eaves of the house, and he pretended he was a vampire, like in the movies. Secretly, he had always yearned to sink his teeth deep into flesh, tasting the salt of blood. He remembered confiding this once to Miss Becker, who had smiled strangely. But now, with AIDS, it was too dangerous. It was also dangerous in other ways: His saliva could be sampled from the body, and imprints of his bite could be taken. He had studied forensic techniques carefully, and, though he assumed the detectives on Mykonos were no match for those in the States, he knew caution was essential while practicing his favorite activity.

CHAPTER SIXTEEN

THE HOUSE was perfumed with the scent of garlic, lemon, and rosemary. When they finally came downstairs, the meat was ready. Cybele opened a bottle of Beaujolais, and Dana sliced the lamb and the tomato and ladled out the lentils.

"What music do you want with our fine dinner and to celebrate the end of your workshop?" Cybele asked, flipping through the music collection. "How about Vangelis' 'El Greco'?" Dana approved, and Cybele inserted the CD, poured the wine, and carried the bottle and wine glasses to the table, while Dana brought two heaping plates outside and lit the candles.

They sat in the captain's chairs, and Cybele spread her hands across her stomach. "Yes, it is nice to have a wife. My wife, Dana." She took a large bite of lentils. "Oh, these are delicious! It's a good thing I walk a lot during the day, otherwise I would get fat."

"It's hard to gain weight on Mykonos—with all the hills."

"And what about New York? I know there is an uptown and a downtown so there must be hills there, too, yes?"

"Yes, there are. You'll love the city…it's so vibrant. Something going on all the time. Lots of tall skyscrapers."

"I've seen photos."

Dana stopped eating, aware that she had implied an invitation to Cybele. "Usually, I stay on Mykonos until the end of next month and then return to New York. My schedule isn't fixed, but that's what I usually do."

Cybele laid down her fork and looked at Dana. "And this year?"

Dana shrugged. "I'm not sure. What about you?"

"When I accepted the job here, Captain Yalouris suggested I try it through October. He said I could continue during the winter or start again next spring."

"Would you jeopardize your job by leaving?"

"No, I don't think so. The force is reduced a little after the tourist season."

"Were you planning to go home to Athens?"

"I hadn't decided yet." Cybele's eyes focused on her plate. "But I couldn't live with my family again." She considered. "Not after this. Not after meeting you."

Dana placed her hand on top of Cybele's. "We've only known each other for five days, but if everything is still going well between us, I'd be overjoyed if you came with me to New York."

Cybele searched her face closely. "For a visit or…"

"Whatever you want."

She swallowed some Beaujolais. "I would love to see America. Perhaps we can decide in a week or two?"

Dana was disappointed—irrationally. Cybele was being sensible, and she was being impulsive. "Okay." Her voice was tighter than she intended.

Cybele tousled Dana's hair. "Do you think that I won't come? When it's been in my thoughts? Things will work out. You must learn to trust in how we feel."

"I do. I'm sorry. I sound ridiculous." Dana reached over and hugged her.

"Ah, we would have great fun in the city, you and I!" Cybele said, smiling. "Tell me, do you have a room with such a splendid view?" She swept her arm at the sea in front of them.

"Only a glimpse of the Hudson River, but my condo is on the top floor. Glass all around the living room and kitchen. A rooftop deck."

"And the bedroom?" Her eyes were bright with amusement.

"I have a very large bedroom with a very large bed."

"In that case, we would be very happy!" Cybele announced.

They finished dinner and the wine. It was growing chilly on the balcony, so Dana suggested they go upstairs. There, they lit candles and opened the windows wide.

Cybele sighed, observing a ship, its lights glowing faintly a mile away. "It's sad to see them leave." The breeze flicked her hair and the hem of her long blouse. "But always, always there is another one. Tomorrow or the next day. They will come for another two months, and then the sea will be one long blue line."

"You sound like a poet," Dana told her, straightening the pillows on the bed.

Cybele smiled at her. "All Greeks are poets. But, yes, I write a little."

"Really?" Dana stopped, sheet in hand.

"Poetry mostly and a few stories. I had two poems published last year in a small magazine and one story. I have an idea for a novel."

"That's very exciting! What's it about?"

"I'll tell you after I start, if I start."

"You have such a beautiful speaking voice," Dana said, moving beside her at the window. "Some night you should read something you've written to me."

"In Greek?" Cybele laughed. "Okay, I will. Perhaps in your large bed in New York City. When it snows."

She embraced Cybele. "Absolutely. Now, come here. I have a surprise." She led Cybele to the bed.

"A surprise?"

"Yes." Dana set the box on the bedspread and placed an arm around Cybele. There was so much she wanted to say, but words had flown.

Cybele opened the package with deliberation. When she saw the Lalaounis logo, she stared at Dana with amazement. "What have you done, eh? I know it will be so beautiful that it will break my heart."

"Open it. A five-day anniversary present."

After untying the velvet pouch, Cybele withdrew the bracelet. "Oh, Dana, it is magnificent! Please, will you put it on me, for luck?"

She did as Cybele asked.

"I love it so much. I don't know what to say." She buried her face in the curve of Dana's shoulder. "This is like a magic story," Cybele whispered. "Will I wake up tomorrow and you'll be gone?"

"I've wondered the same thing myself."

Cybele backed away a few inches and gazed at Dana with such deep affection that Dana was again silenced. Kissing her passionately, Cybele began a prelude to the most intense seduction Dana had ever experienced. The night was not long enough for either of them.

⸻

THE MAN HID the garrote and the tools of his trade in the pockets of his black pants and jacket. After weighing the risk, he had concluded that wearing the priest's clothes again would increase attention instead of providing anonymity. To add some concealment, he sported a blue 2004 Athens Olympics cap—Greece was already selling products to advertise this event.

Strolling through town like a tourist, he came to his chosen hunting ground, a gay bar, but didn't venture inside. Instead, the man sat at a secluded table on the patio and ordered a vodka tonic. As the music pulsed and the scent of smoke and provocative male lust wafted through the open doors and windows, he felt the powerful heat of desire spread through his body. An artery in his neck throbbed. He pressed his forefinger against it, massaging slowly until his control returned, though all he could think about was the warm, muscled necks of the young men dancing in the disco with their heads thrown back in ecstasy. They seemed to taunt him with their thrusting hips and raw sexuality. In spite of his firm will, he was growing hard within the confines of his trousers. He began to caress the garrote in his pocket, pushing it against himself.

The man finished his drink and was about to order a second, when a pair of policemen stopped in front of the bar. He paid the waiter and, once the two men walked away, fled into the darkness, furious and frustrated.

—

THEY WERE both exhausted in the morning, but Cybele had to leave. She removed the bracelet, saying it was too beautiful to risk wearing at work, and then closed and locked the door below. Dana returned to bed and slept soundly. Just after ten, she roused herself and stumbled downstairs to eat cold lentils and rice. Afterward, darkroom duties called. Because the chemical solutions were still in the trays, it took no time to print one of the small images for the Meltémi Gallery—only a few minor adjustments were required to perfectly match the edition print that she used as a standard. By late afternoon, Dana had made fifteen copies and also completed a partial series of three additional photographs. Leaving a batch to dry in the racks, Dana went to shower and dress for Émile's event. She selected a white blouse and black cocktail pants. Cybele arrived an hour later and dressed in a purple skirt and V-neck top. She added the bracelet, remarking again on its beauty, and began brushing her straight hair so carefully that Dana began to laugh.

"What's so funny?" she asked her.

"You might want to wait and comb it just before we go into the house."

"Why?"

"Because we're taking my Suzuki, and the top is off."

"Oh, no! I'll be a mess!"

"Bring your brush. Come on, we'll be late."

They walked to the garage where Dana parked the blue 4 x 4. She removed the dusty tarp and stored it behind the back seat. When she turned the key, the engine coughed uncertainly.

"Hold on to your teeth," she laughed, as she put the Suzuki in gear.

A nearly full moon was rising, slicking the sea with gold light. The island, barren and rocky and nearly treeless, provided an unearthly landscape as they wound their way up the hill. The town below was charm itself—the curving harbor, the white cubist buildings stacked like a tumble of child's blocks. After passing a whitewashed wall, Dana turned right into a driveway crowded with cars. She parked off-road and rotated the tiny rearview mirror so Cybele could comb her windblown hair. Then, hand in hand, they strolled to Émile's villa. "I Will Survive" was blasting its triumphant cry over and over—probably Émile's anthem for the night.

The carved entrance doors were open. Cybele and Dana passed into the dramatic living room, decorated in black-and-white, with a large collection of art on the walls, including many of Dana's photographs. Through a sliding door, they stepped outside onto a wide patio where the guests gathered around a rectangular turquoise pool, its water fragmented with the reflections of the spotlights from the house and dozens of white candles of all sizes that were placed everywhere: in the garden amid chest-high bushes of aromatic lavender and cascades of pink bougainvillea, on the tables, and in silver buckets set several feet from the pool's perimeter. Even some of the young branches of arbutus and olive trees, which grew in front of the high fence that enclosed the rear property, were pressed into candle-holding service. A long cocktail bar flanked the left of the patio and was doing an active business, gauging from the constant pop of corks and the rustle of ice into drinks. On the right was a buffet table replete with Greek mezes and French canapés. Men outnumbered women ten to one, but there were some ladies Dana knew, a few intimately. Dana noted with pride that most of the women were admiring Cybele, who appeared incandescent in the soft light. Émile, handsome in a white dinner jacket, greeted them and hugged Dana.

"Émile de Szasi, Cybele Karabélias," Dana said.

Émile took Cybele's hand, kissed it, and winked slyly at Dana. "I think, my dear, that you are living up to your name—the fox. Where have you found this lovely lady?"

"She came and investigated in my apartment." Dana returned his sly manner.

"Well, aren't you the lucky one, Dana! She is absolutely, marvelously stunning!" To Cybele, he whispered loudly, "And of course Dana is pretty stunning herself, but we must not tell her. Part of her charm is her lack of vanity, *n'est-ce pas*?" Émile smiled and procured two flutes of Champagne for Dana and Cybele. Cybele tried to express her condolences to the host, but he waved her comments away and said he was determined to celebrate Virgil's life rather than grieve his death. Raising his glass, he toasted, "To Virgil!" Then, observing Dana closely, he said to the crowd, "and to Cybele and Dana!"

Dana was unprepared for this public anointing of their relationship and felt her cheeks redden. Cybele, by contrast, beamed with pleasure and gave Émile a brilliant smile before turning to Dana and kissing her, which caused some amused titters.

As Émile left, a woman—Djuna something-or-other—cruised by for a closer examination and requested an introduction. Dana knew little about her except that she had changed her name to emulate the writer Djuna Barnes. The woman was short and broad, garbed in a purple silk cravat and a man's white guayabera shirt, and was affecting a kind of retro sophistication by smoking a cigarette in a black holder. She chatted with them for a few minutes, probably to get the goods on the new couple for the gossip mill. After her departure, Rhea strolled over, smiling seductively at Dana. They had been involved briefly three years ago when Dana first arrived, though Rhea had been involved briefly with every woman on the island, or so it seemed. She was the self-elected matron of the lesbian community, partly because she had been on intimate terms with most members, partly because she was a woman of a certain age, style, and confidence. With unabashed curiosity, she surveyed

Cybele's physical attributes, took in the gold bracelet, and nodded approval. To her, as with everyone, Cybele was easy and smooth in conversation. From Rhea, they migrated to a male couple. Dana listened with only half an ear, preferring to study her lover as she worked the floor, noting how she graciously steered attention to others.

When "I Will Survive" was on its fourth repetition and they were on their third glass of Champagne, Dana saw Bryan Kerr, whom she had met briefly at Orpheus. She introduced Cybele, and Bryan presented his boyfriend, Alexander Stavros, who had been an alternate on the Greek national diving team. With his thick dark hair and beard, wide shoulders, broad chest, and tapered legs, Alexander was the envy of a number of partygoers. Next to him, Bryan looked slight and boyish, with a sprinkle of pale freckles on his nose and neatly combed ginger-colored hair. Their arms were wrapped around each other; both wore matching white polo shirts and shorts. Bryan explained that they'd met several years ago in Athens, had been reacquainted at a party on Super Paradise Beach twelve days ago, and had fallen in love.

"Émile sent us to look at your portfolio at the Meltémi Gallery," Alexander said. "Depending on how things go," he gave Bryan a smoldering glance, "we would love to have some of your Mykonos images in our house."

"To remind us of where we met," Bryan chimed in.

"I'd be honored," Dana replied. "Where are you going to live?"

"Oh, dear, it is so difficult to decide! Alexander loves his homeland, which I do, but New York is where my office is located. And because Alexander could study with a diving coach in Montclair, he says he'd like to live in America."

"Dana has an apartment in New York," Cybele added.

"Are you two going to winter in the city?" Bryan asked.

"We're talking about it," Cybele replied, placing her hand in Dana's. "It would be my first trip there."

"You'll love it," Bryan gushed. "The city that never sleeps and is never, ever boring. Winters in New York, summers in Greece. That sounds fabulous! Maybe we can get together? Dana, where do you live? Upper East or West Side? Or the Village?"

"West Side." She told him the address.

"Oh, my! Cybele, you are moving to a very posh neighborhood, you lucky girl!" Bryan said. "You can go to the opera every night and frolic in the fountain after."

"We know something about Dana, but Cybele, tell us about you," Alexander inquired.

"I work for the police department and I'm interested in criminal psychology." She smiled at Dana. "Right now, my life is changing. It's all very exciting, very new."

"I Am What I Am" now blared on the stereo system, the bass throbbing. Everyone broke into twos, threes, or fours to dance.

Cybele gave Dana a tentative look. "Do you dance?"

Dana grinned, took Cybele's glass and placed it next to hers on a table. Quickly, Dana whirled her in a circular spin, improvising a series of moves, which Cybele followed with ease.

"Oh, you're a wonderful dancer!" Dana whispered in Cybele's ear.

"I am, aren't I?" Cybele laughed.

At the end of the song, Dana pulled her close and hugged her. "There, our first time."

Cybele was a little out of breath. "You are very good," she said. "And not just on the dance floor!"

Another popular song came on, and they found themselves in the midst of a throng of dancing young men, who, as they became hotter, began removing their shirts. Before long, several had slipped into the pool.

At 1:00 a.m., Émile, who was still standing but with effort, made a last toast to Virgil. Tears sprang to his eyes. In this show of emotion, he wasn't alone. Some of the men had also known Malcolm Hall, and there was renewed conversation about his death as well as Virgil's. Dana and Cybele were speaking with Farley and Martin, a couple from Philadelphia who had been together many years. They were very concerned that the police weren't taking the murders seriously enough. When they learned that Cybele was on the force, they grilled her for information. She told them everything that was openly known and apologized for her inability to reveal more.

"I think it's those Christian types," Farley said with an air of disgust. "Why can't they stay on the other side of the pond? Don't they know they are so *passé*? They might as well be wearing chastity belts and suits of armor."

Martin picked up the theme. "I wouldn't be surprised if the people that set fire to the crosses at Gabriel's had a hand in all of this."

"We've interviewed Mr. and Mrs. Schatze," Cybele offered. "They had no alibi for the time of either killing. They told us they were together asleep in their room. Unfortunately, we can't prove where they were."

"Very suspicious," Martin replied, laughing. "Imagine! Sleeping on Mykonos. It just isn't done! I hope the police keep an eye on them along with the other bigots still in town—you know, the ones who got away from the police during the protests."

"There were quite a few gay people who got away too," Cybele said, with a mischievous glint in her eye.

"*Touché.*" Farley clinked her glass.

"Well, nothing has happened for a few days. Maybe our killer left," Dana suggested.

This comment was greeted with uneasy silence.

CHAPTER SEVENTEEN

AN HOUR LATER, Émile said goodnight and went to bed. The music was turned off, and slowly everyone drifted into various rooms or departed.

"I think we're the end of the party," Dana told Cybele.

"Yes, it appears so."

They embraced. Cybele slid her hands down Dana's back, under her blouse, and around to her breasts. "I think we need a little more privacy," Cybele whispered.

She took Dana's arm and headed to the cabana, where, with amazing dexterity considering the alcohol she'd imbibed, Cybele unwrapped Dana's blouse, removed her bra, and unzipped her trousers. Shivering with excitement, Dana began undressing Cybele, eager for that moment of warm union when their bodies came together. Finally, they stood against each other, smelling the sweet lavender surrounding them, listening to the scuff and moan of the olive branches blowing in the breeze.

"So, do foxes swim like they can dance?" Cybele asked.

"Like otters," Dana exclaimed cheerfully.

"What is this 'otter'—a fish?"

Her serious look made Dana chuckle. "No, it's an animal. Very sleek, like you."

Laughing, Cybele led Dana to the pool's edge and down the curving steps into the water. "Oh, you get me into so much trouble!"

"I love trouble! Besides, who is leading whom?" Dana gently turned Cybele around so that Cybele's head rested on her shoulder and snugged an arm under Cybele's breast. Easing Cybele off of her feet, Dana began to float. Above, a fleet of silver stars sailed in the clear night sky.

"Make a wish," Cybele told her solemnly. "But you mustn't tell me what it is."

"You too," Dana replied, as she began a leisurely, one-handed stroke, gliding them in the still water.

They were silent with their thoughts, each probably wishing the same thing. At the end of the pool, Dana negotiated a curve and turned toward the shallow end.

"Dana?"

"Yes?"

"Will it always be this way? Between us?"

"I'm not sure that I'll be able to dance like that when I'm eighty, but I'll certainly try."

With a flip of her hand, Cybele splashed water on Dana's face. "I didn't mean that!"

Dana placed her feet on the bottom, held Cybele on the surface, and caressed her body, prompting shivers of anticipation. Between the sensuality of the water, the moonlight, and Cybele's graceful acquiescence, Dana was overcome by the beauty of the moment. She listened to her lover murmur with pleasure and then slipped her fingers inside Cybele, exploring the soft, billowy warmth. As Cybele's breaths quickened, Dana matched them with her own respirations, all the while moving her hand faster to bring on a climax. Finally, Cybele shuddered and cried out. After Dana leaned over and kissed her, she started again, even though Cybele protested that it was Dana's turn.

That happened in the cabana a few minutes later. They moved two chaise lounges together. It wasn't the most comfortable arrangement, but Dana soon forgot her discomfort. When they finished, the faintest blush of dawn was rounding the scrubby, close-cropped hill to the east.

"Should we go home?" Dana asked, once she had recovered her voice.

"I don't think we were invited for breakfast."

They rose and found towels. After rubbing each other dry, they dressed, walked around the pool, and left the house. The Suzuki started with a cranky sputter. Dana made a left onto the road but, instead of heading toward town, she drove to the top of a deserted hillock and cut the motor. After placing her arm around Cybele, she asked more about her childhood and life in Athens, and then they sat in silence as the sky intensified into brilliant pink.

"This has been an amazing night, Dana. How could it have been more perfect? We will remember this forever, yes?"

Dana kissed the tips of her fingers one by one. "Yes. We will."

—

After parking the jeep in the lot, they strolled hand in hand down the steep hill to the sea walk, sad to end the magic. At the corner of Dana's building, they stopped short. Propped against the wall was a man's body, naked except for sandals. Bryan Kerr. Blood ringed his neck and stained his chest. The murderer had rouged two circles on his cheeks and drawn a bull's eye around each nipple. A large smear of crimson lipstick turned his gaping mouth into a contorted smile. But the most horrible sight to behold were his eyes—wide with shock from the last horror he had seen before death.

Cybele kneeled and felt for a pulse. "No heartbeat!" She turned, distress clouding her face. "Oh, my God, Dana! He's dead!"

Dana pulled Cybele away and held her, shielding both of them from the sickening vision, but, even with her eyes tightly pressed closed, Dana saw the lurid details chased by a second image of Bryan and Alexander laughing, so in love, so hopeful. She was certain that Cybele was beset by the same indelible pictures. Finally, knowing that they had to face reality, Dana separated from Cybele and offered to call the police.

"No, I'll do it," Cybele said in a hushed voice. "You wait here with Bryan."

She stroked Dana's hair, as if to say, "let nothing happen to you," and hurried down the walk to the apartment door.

Dana stood by the body, aching with sadness over the loss of such a bright and gentle man, yet also chilled by the presence of evil. It almost seemed that the killer's scent was floating in the early morning air, elusive but nearly detectable. She shivered and crossed her arms and thought how strange it was that Bryan had abandoned Alexander, if, in fact, he had. A few hours before they had seemed inseparable. Dana tried to remember when the two men departed the house and recalled them saying goodbye about 1:30 a.m.

As she stared at Bryan, she noticed his wallet lying on the ground; just past it were faint drag marks, most likely made by his sandals where the leather had scuffed the whitewash outlining the flagstones. Dana followed the marks to the street. The trail ended in dark stains of blood. She didn't know whether Bryan had been attacked here and moved to where his body presently lay or whether he had been killed elsewhere and carried to this spot. In either case, the proximity to her apartment was unnerving. Dana retraced her steps to the promenade, collapsed in a café chair, and gazed at Bryan's face. She had no idea whether Bryan had been sexually molested, but she prayed that he'd been spared that additional torture.

When Cybele returned, Dana indicated the blood and the marks, which Cybele examined carefully. At the street, she looked up and bit her lip. "The placement seems deliberate."

Dana nodded; her eyes locked on Cybele's.

In a quiet voice, Cybele asked, "Where do you think Alexander is? It doesn't make sense that he left him last night."

"No, it doesn't. They didn't mention a hotel, did they?"

"No."

"I don't want to call Émile to find out, either. Émile will be absolutely devastated."

"I wonder if Alexander had anything to do with this," Cybele said.

"I doubt it, but Captain Yalouris might think so. Alexander is strong enough to kill, and he's been here since before the murders began—they told us they both arrived several weeks ago. But why would he murder other gay men, especially his lover?"

Cybele shook her head, exhaled a long breath, sat next to Dana, wearily rested her head on her hand, and closed her eyes.

Fifteen minutes later, two of Cybele's colleagues arrived. She introduced Theo Mintzas and Detective Pakis Pantazakis to Dana and drew them aside to go over the details. Dana was surprised that Cybele admitted to being at the party, but when Dana thought about it, that would be her way—to be honest, even though she could have devised a fabrication. Mykonos was very gay-accepting, but Dana wondered if Cybele's truthfulness was going to cause problems for her at work.

Theo asked Dana if she could photograph the body. It was so early, he explained, it would be easier if she did it. Dana agreed and went to get her camera, a flash, and her 50 mm lens. Returning, she detailed the scene and the drag marks. After shooting a roll, she placed the film in its canister, wrote the time and date on its label, and gave the film to Theo.

"I'm off today," Cybele told the policemen, "but the captain can call me if he needs to ask any questions." As she dictated Dana's telephone number to them, a doctor came down the street accompanied by two more policemen and a man pushing a handcart lined with plastic. Cybele said goodbye, took Dana's arm, and together they walked to the apartment. After a few moments of stunned silence, they climbed the stairs to bed.

—

IT HAD TAKEN only seconds for the trachea to break like a snapping stalk of bamboo, hissing a gentle stream of air and spraying blood across the young man's pristine white shirt. Such a pretty sight!

He had checked the driver's license. Bryan. He liked the name. From New York. Probably full of disease, he thought. It was okay. He had used a condom and latex gloves. He had been careful. Safe sex.

The man laughed, remembering his triumphant night: how he had burst through the shadows and surprised his prey, pulling Bryan into an alley, tightening the garrote, and taking his sexual reward. Then he had placed Bryan's arm over his shoulder and carried him across several deserted streets before lowering him to the ground and staining the white pavement with blood. Since no one was nearby and it was still dark, he had removed Bryan's clothes, painted the body, and dragged his kill to a final resting place on the promenade. The clothes would be treasured for a while before being destroyed.

—

IT WAS mid-morning when Dana and Cybele rejoined the living, abandoning happy dreams for the dense gravity of Earth and the harsh memory of Bryan's death. Dana noticed that Cybele's face was gray with fatigue—she had slept little over the last several days. For that matter, she herself was exhausted, rent apart by the emotional friction between the high-octane bliss of love and the ever-present anxiety.

Though they weren't hungry, they ate breakfast. Then Cybele called Captain Yalouris to tell him when Bryan and Alexander had left Émile's party and to ask if there was any new information. As she recounted to Dana, the policeman explained that Alexander and Bryan had argued on the way home—according to Alexander, who had been located at his hotel and rigorously questioned at the station. He reported that Bryan wanted to have another drink in town, but he had refused. In an inebriated condition, Bryan staggered off, and Alexander went to bed alone. The police were now awakening bartenders, trying to ascertain where

Bryan had gone and to substantiate that Alexander hadn't accompanied him. So far, no one remembered serving Bryan, but more calls were being made. Similar to the practice at the King Minos Inn, Alexander's hotel offered late-night arrangements for its patrons, so no one had been at the desk to witness his return. Captain Yalouris said that Alexander was now there, in his room.

After they had discussed the news, Cybele sighed. "How terrible Alexander must feel."

"I keep thinking the same thing."

A few minutes later, Sandros phoned and put Mike Garfield on the line. Mike wanted to know if Dana had seen Julian. "We were supposed to meet for coffee and then go take some pictures. He hasn't been around, and Sandros doesn't know where he is, either."

Dana's mind began to spin. What was going on? "Mike, please ask Sandros to open Julian's room. And, by the way, you may not have heard the news, but there's been another murder."

"No! I can't believe it!"

Dana described what had happened. "This probably has nothing to do with Julian, but under the circumstances, will you have Sandros let me know if Julian is there?"

Mike agreed to do so.

While she waited for his call, Dana once again worried that the murderer had left Bryan's body for her to find. A forty-foot proximity to her door seemed intentional—and on a relatively exposed walkway, though at the time of the murder, the area was mostly empty. She hadn't discussed this with Cybele because she didn't want to consider the implications herself. She suspected Cybele hadn't mentioned it to her for the same reason.

The phone rang. "Julian Witten is not there," Sandros told her, "but he slept in the bed after the maid cleaned his room yesterday. Maybe he left early this morning to take photos?"

"Perhaps," she said, doubting it. "Will you let me know when he turns up?"

"Okay," Sandros replied. "What about the murder last night?"

Once again, news flew through the community with astonishing speed. Though Dana didn't want to review the story, she gave Sandros a condensed version. After hanging up, she informed Cybele that Julian was absent, trying to downplay her apprehension. But was she more worried that Julian was hurt or that Julian was responsible for the deaths of Malcolm, Virgil, Devin, and Bryan? She recalled how curious he'd been about her apartment. It would have been easy for him to follow her home after class, to learn where she lived and thus know where to leave Bryan's body. With reluctance, Dana related Julian's odd behavior but also expressed concern that he shouldn't be implicated solely because of it.

Cybele frowned and asked one of several obvious questions. "Dana, what was Julian's attitude toward the murders?"

"I don't know…he seemed homophobic, but I doubt that he had anything to do with what's going on." She didn't sound convinced, even to herself.

"He's been here since the first death, yes? And he decided to stay a few days longer?"

Dana agreed that it had been Julian's suggestion to remain on the island, not Mike's.

Cybele gave her a knowing look. "Tell me about him, Dana."

"He's in his thirties. Impatient and easily annoyed. Rather antisocial, but I really don't know much about him except that he's not married. He manages a business of some kind."

"How big is he?"

Dana could see where she was heading. "About an inch shorter than I am. Maybe five feet nine."

"Would he be strong enough to carry Bryan?"

Dana gave her a long look. "Yes, I suppose so."

"He should be on the list of suspects. And this Mike—is he friendly with Julian?"

"What do you mean?" Dana asked. "Oh, no, they're not involved. That I know for sure. Actually, I'm surprised they decided to stay here together. Other than a shared interest in photography, Mike and Julian have nothing in common."

Cybele took this in. "There's probably a good explanation for his absence, Dana, but we should report that he is missing."

"No, not yet. Let's wait. Sandros will call if he sees him."

Cybele bit her lip, as if about to argue, then she ceded to Dana's request. "Now, I hate to leave, but Captain Yalouris asked me to return to duty. We never have enough time, do we?"

—

After Cybele departed, Dana was in a quandary. Should she search for Julian? And, for that matter, where was Luca? Although their disappearances were unnerving, the shocking thing was that four people had died. She felt deeply upset about Bryan. He'd been so alive and sparkling last night! It was difficult to believe the inert body had been his. She also worried about Alexander, who must be grief-stricken. And she was apprehensive about Cybele's safety. The thought of something happening to her made Dana shudder with horror.

She lay on the couch, drinking coffee and thinking. Finally, she decided to be productive and began to catalogue and number the new photographs, recording their sequences in her edition books and signing the backs of the prints in pencil. After doing so, Dana ate a late lunch, donned her straw hat and sunglasses and, feeling wary and exposed on the street, walked to the Meltémi Gallery.

Maria was alone in the shop. She was surprised to see Dana, having heard about Bryan Kerr's death from Constantine, who had heard it from a friend. She rose and gave Dana a hug, holding her longer than usual. "I am very sorry."

Dana sighed. "I just met him a few days ago and again at Émile's last night. A very nice guy. In a new relationship and so happy."

Maria shook her head. "Constantine and I hoped that the murderer was a tourist or even a visiting priest, who would leave after a few days."

"I was hoping that too." Dana sat on the chair near the desk and removed her sunglasses.

"Well, whoever the person is, he doesn't seem to be going anywhere."

"No. This is an easy spot for hunting. I hate to use the metaphor, but killing gay people in Mykonos is like shooting fish in a barrel."

Maria frowned, obviously trying to picture the image, and then let out a long, anxious breath. "I'm so worried something will happen to Constantine. I told him not to stay out late, but he is extremely stubborn."

"He needs to be sensible," Dana replied. "At the moment, it seems as if the island is being punished for its enlightened and welcoming atmosphere and is attracting the wrong kinds of people. It's terrible that one sick individual can create so much fear in such a peaceful place."

"I know. Everyone is suspicious. Many clubs are closing early. People go home in groups. Yet the cruise ships keep coming, which, I suppose, is a good thing, although two are leaving port at ten. Staying just late enough for their passengers to have dinner in town."

"It won't be long before they re-schedule altogether," Dana said, "and the island's reputation will be ruined for years."

Maria sighed. "This nightmare can't go on forever."

"You're right. He'll get caught." Dana laid a box of photos on Maria's desk.

"More prints?"

" Yes. Additions to the series and three recent images."

Maria carried the photographs to two gray museum boxes, one housing eight-by-tens and the other holding eleven-by-fourteens. "We'll need to restock your oversized work next spring—once you return to New York and can make ink-jet reproductions." She examined the new photos, offered compliments, and suggested that two should be enlarged more. After inserting the new prints, Maria closed the boxes and added, "And by the way, we sold a few more prints. Would you like a check now or shall we wait?"

"Thanks. No need."

Maria returned to her desk and poured Dana a cup of tea. "So, I heard some interesting rumors…" she began, a slow smile spreading across her face.

Dana laughed. "Whatever you heard…they're probably true."

She tucked in her chin. "A beautiful policewoman? How did you manage that?"

"Dumb luck, as we say in America," Dana replied. "Cybele has moved in. We're seeing how it goes."

"And what will happen when you leave for New York?"

"That's under discussion."

"I see. You aren't rushing this? You just met her." Maria studied Dana with concern. "Does anyone know anything about Cybele? I mean, she's new on the island, isn't she?"

Dana sipped some tea. "She began with the police in August."

"Just before the first murder."

"Yes, which is a good thing because Cybele studied criminal psychology and might be very useful on the case." Dana felt a little deflated by Maria's cautionary attitude. "As for our relationship, by the calendar it may seem like rushing, but, strangely, it doesn't feel hurried."

"Love happens like that." Maria renewed her smile. "Bring Cybele to meet us soon."

Reassured by Maria's friendliness, Dana agreed and started to leave, then turned. "That guy who was asking after me, did he ever return?"

"No, he hasn't. He's probably left the island."

CHAPTER EIGHTEEN

CAPTAIN YALOURIS asked Cybele to go to the photo shop to pick up the pictures that Dana had taken of the Bryan Kerr crime scene. Unfortunately, they were sealed in a brown manila envelope so she couldn't see them. When she handed the packet to the captain, however, he invited her to participate in the senior staff meeting and told her she was now privy to all details regarding the police investigation.

Inside the Incidents Room, Pakis Pantazakis and Athanasios Pyrgos, the two Athenian detectives, were sitting on wooden swivel chairs. Cybele watched as Pantazakis lit one cigarette after another, nearly setting fire to his graying frizzle of hair. His pale eyes were alert, flitting around the room over objects, photos, and faces as if clues might be present, awaiting discovery. Pyrgos, his partner of many years, was calmer, almost lethargic, or perhaps it was his heavy, square-shouldered build that gave that impression. He seemed uncomfortable in a jacket that gaped several inches in the middle and that had sleeves that rode his wrists.

Captain Yalouris opened the envelope and spread the enlarged photos of Bryan Kerr on the table. After everyone had examined them, Cybele stepped forward to look. In the glossy prints, the horror of death was slightly removed and clinical, yet she knew that these last sickening images of Bryan would be what she would remember of him.

She stepped back and found a chair, wishing she could go outside in the bright sun and escape the disturbing pathology contained in the airless, smoky room. Instead, she read the report by Pantazakis that included her statement about finding Bryan. When she finished, Captain Yalouris asked if she recalled anything else. Cybele shook her head.

"Captain, do you have other clues?" she asked him.

"Not many. The attack was typical—using a garrote. The victim had a high level of alcohol in his system and may have been unable to defend himself, though we found latex under three of Mr. Kerr's fingernails, most likely from a glove, so the victim struggled. No relevant fingerprints. No new cloth fibers. One strand of brown hair was bagged, which may or may not belong to the killer. You may not know this, but the single hair we found at Malcolm Hall's crime scene was synthetic. We doubt it was from a wig because the hair was short and a tiny bit of adhesive was attached to the end."

"So the beard was fake?"

"Probably," Captain Yalouris agreed.

Cybele realized this information enlarged the field of suspects. "Was he sexually abused?"

Pyrgos nodded in the affirmative. "The perpetrator used a condom like he did before. And some kind of tool like he did before."

Cybele gritted her teeth and was silent.

"We understand that one of Miss Fox's students, Julian Witten, has been acting oddly." Pyrgos read from his notebook. "This was reported by the owner of the King Minos Inn."

Looking at him in alarm, Cybele asked if Julian had been located.

The detective shook his head. "No, not today, but he was seen the night of Bryan Kerr's death…at one of the gay discos, the Pink Sphinx. We learned about him by accident when we interviewed several bartenders this morning. One remembered an American who was similar in appearance to Mr. Kerr. When he checked the charge card receipt, it was Witten's."

Cybele took this in with mild surprise. "A lot of people go to the clubs."

"Perhaps," Pyrgos said, "but we're interested in his arrival here as well as his activities."

"He came on September sixth for Dana Fox's photography class," Cybele replied.

"It was the day before," corrected Captain Yalouris. "We confirmed with the airport and the King Minos Inn. This might have no meaning, or it might mean he came to familiarize himself with the town before the first murder."

"We're looking for Mr. Witten now," explained Pyrgos. "He's under suspicion."

Cybele didn't dispute his conclusion and wondered if Dana's assessment of her student's innocence was accurate. She would ask her more questions tonight.

—

IT WAS late afternoon when Dana entered the photo shop, exhausted and dispirited. Helen helped a customer and came over, a worried expression on her face.

"Are you all right, Dana? You found the body, didn't you?"

"Yes, I did. And I had just seen Bryan at Émile's."

"That's what I heard. How horrible!"

Dana felt suddenly overcome, as if her emotions had been postponed earlier and were now bursting through. Tears rimmed her eyes. She swiped at them. "Yes, it was."

Helen was silent and then, to allow Dana time to compose herself, went to ask the printer for Dana's color prints. Emerging from the back room, she laid the bag on the counter. "Steve said these were good. And the ones you took of the murder scene came out fine."

"How did he know I was the photographer?"

Helen smiled. "Steve says he can identify your work when he sees it. We also printed enlargements for the police."

After making arrangements with Helen for her next workshop, Dana left. Outside the store, she glanced at the prints taken several days ago. Satisfied they were okay, she slipped the packet into her vest's back pocket. Although she had no idea whether Cybele would return for dinner, Dana walked to the market to purchase vegetables for a stir-fry with the leftover lamb. She paid, stepped into the street, and cut through a narrow lane. As she did, Dana heard the fast slap of rubber-soled shoes. Spinning around, she saw Luca Alessi hurrying toward her. He came to an abrupt halt and stared at her with focused dislike. His hands were clenched into fists.

"What do you want?" Dana demanded, making no effort to be pleasant.

His expression changed into a sexual leer. "Oh, I don't know. I guess I'm just curious."

"Well, I'm late."

She began to turn from him, hoping that he wouldn't strike like the snake he resembled, but Luca caught the sleeve of her blouse. Furious, she ripped his hand away. He stumbled and then attacked, dashing her bag of groceries to the ground and flattening her against the wall, tipping off her hat and slamming her head against the stone. With surprising violence, he thrust a stiff arm across her throat.

"You didn't ask me what I'm curious about, Dana."

She curled her fingers around his forearm, trying to pry his hold loose. With the force against her neck, she wasn't able to speak.

"You liked my little Teresa, didn't you? Huh?" he sneered. "That's why she left. Because of you and what you did to her." His mouth was so close that she could smell the stench of cigarettes and alcohol. His face, dark with an unshaven growth of whiskers, prickled with menace. "What happened? Maybe you shared her with your girlfriend? Hey, I think your girlfriend needs the real thing."

The threat to Cybele detonated what was left of Dana's control. She shoved her right knee into his groin, causing him to double over. Dana started to run, but only managed a short distance before Luca grabbed her. For his size, he was unexpectedly strong. Before she could prevent him, he jerked her around and threw her onto the pavement, fell on top, and pinned her hands. Ominously signaling his intentions, he plunged his body into hers.

"Teresa told you what I like, didn't she?" he grunted. "You know… how I like it."

Dana wanted to smash his face in, to destroy his mean eyes. Adrenaline pulsed through her, fear and fury fighting for supremacy. She twisted hard and tossed him aside. His forehead scuffed the rough whitewashed stones, and blood spurted jets of red. With rage propelling her fist, Dana cuffed him on the jaw. He slumped sideways, then turned and stared at her, looking surprised. Blood streamed down his face, but Luca wasn't finished. As Dana came to her knees, he threw a punch, connecting to Dana's chin. Reeling and dazed, she managed to parry his next blow and to strike upward with the heel of her hand. She heard a satisfying crunch as his nose broke. Blood poured from his nostrils.

"You bitch!" he screamed, his fingers cupping his nose.

Dana started to rise to again, but Luca lunged forward and tackled her. She fell backward and hit her head.

Red was everywhere. Dana's shirt and vest were saturated with it as were Luca's clothes and the whitewashed walls and street.

"I'll show you what I like!" In a frenzy, he began tearing at her blouse.

Dana tried to fend off his attack, but that only made him angrier. She should scream, call for help, but she could hardly breathe. With the last of her fading strength, Dana caught his left hand in both of hers and snapped it violently backward. He cried out in anguish and cradled his wrist against his chest, glaring at her with hatred. Then, as if in slow motion, she saw him draw back his other fist. The pain exploded as her vision went black.

—

Dana awoke. Her head felt as if a bomb had detonated inside. She didn't want to move, just to sleep on and on, but from far off, her name was being called. She opened her eyes and tried to focus on who was speaking until finally Cybele's tearstained face became clear. Beyond her, other people were gathered around, murmuring in Greek.

"Dana—talk to me!" Cybele pleaded.

The question seemed to pass through an endless series of passageways before it made any sense. She tried to sit up but collapsed. On the second attempt, with Cybele's help, Dana propped herself against the wall.

"Is anything broken?"

Dana tried to get her tongue to work and tasted fresh blood. She shook her head and closed her eyes to fight off dizziness. "Home" was all she could say.

A bystander provided a towel which Cybele used to staunch the blood. When the wound stopped bleeding, she and a man from the crowd lifted Dana onto a handcart similar to the one that had taken Bryan away.

"Dana, you need a doctor," Cybele insisted.

"No, please," she whispered. "I can't…really…not necessary…"

Sighing, Cybele asked one of the men if he could bring a doctor to Dana's apartment. He ran to do so, and, as the wagon creaked down the street, Cybele walked alongside, holding Dana's hand and whispering words of reassurance, forgetting to speak in English. When they arrived at the apartment, Cybele unlocked the door and she and the cart owner eased Dana upright and inside.

"Can you climb the steps?" Cybele eyed the staircase with concern.

"Yes." She grasped the rails in her swollen hands.

Cybele thanked the man, who left. With Cybele supporting her from below, Dana carefully mounted the steps. In the living room, all Dana wanted was to lie down on the sofa but realized she needed to continue upstairs before her energy was depleted. With her arm around Cybele's shoulders, every muscle aching, she managed. In the bedroom, Cybele removed Dana's bloody vest and threw a towel on the bed, and Dana fell on top, exhausted.

After rummaging around in the bathroom, Cybele returned with a basin of water, a cloth, a bag of cotton balls, a bottle of alcohol, and two towels. She washed Dana's face, clearing off the caked blood, and then unbuttoned what was left of Dana's tattered blouse. When she saw the bruises, she exhaled slowly and tears welled up.

"It was Luca," Dana said.

"I know. We'll talk about him later."

She placed a warm hand on Dana's chest and held it there until it seemed to be making an imprint on her heart. Dana had never felt such love, such kindness, such caring. When the doctor knocked on the outside door, Cybele rose, covered Dana with the sheet, and ran downstairs. A conversation in Greek ensued, which Dana couldn't hear well.

When Cybele and the doctor entered the room, he introduced himself. "Miss Fox, can you tell me where it hurts?"

"I was hit on my chin and banged my head against the pavement."

He pulled down the sheet, examined her thoroughly, and checked her eyes with a penlight. After looking in her ears and testing her reflexes and arm strength, he listened to her heart and lungs.

"Miss Fox, rest tonight. I think you are okay for now. Tomorrow, you must go to the hospital to be sure you don't have a concussion. I don't think you do, but you must do as I say."

With one quick glance at Cybele, who was standing, arms folded, behind the doctor, Dana knew there were no options and promised to follow instructions.

The doctor dressed the torn knuckles on her right hand, closed the small cut on her cheek with adhesive strips, and took out a bottle of pills from his bag. "Painkillers," he told her. "They will make you sleepy, but your body needs to rest." He handed her a glass of water and a pill. "In about four to six hours, you may take one or two of these if the pain is bad. Do not hesitate to call me if anything changes."

Dana thanked the doctor, and Cybele ushered him out. Dana closed her eyes, waiting for the aches and soreness to ease, and drifted off. When Cybele reappeared, Dana woke and tried to sit up, but her arms trembled with the effort.

"Hey, where are you going?" Cybele asked, placing her hands on Dana's shoulders.

"Nowhere," Dana said. "Could you please turn off the lights? They're hurting my eyes."

Cybele did so—except the bathroom light. "Now, let me help you with your clothes."

She unfastened Dana's pants. When she saw more bruises, her eyes clouded. After shedding a few tears and muttering to herself, Cybele walked into the bathroom for Dana's nightshirt, ran fresh water, and returned to finish removing dirt and blood. With her help, Dana sat, her head spinning in an unpleasant fashion. Cybele guided her arms through the shirt's sleeves and eased her against the pillow. With a steadfast look, she laid her hand on Dana's cheek. Her touch seemed like warm, vibrating energy. After a moment of silence, she buttoned the nightshirt and covered Dana with the sheet.

"I'll make you some soup."

With this, she disappeared. Dana slept until she heard crockery being set on the end table. Cybele sat beside her on the bed.

"Can you manage this?"

Dana wasn't sure but said "yes;" however, the effects of the opiate and the clumsy bandage on her hand impaired her coordination. She spilled on the napkin.

Cybele snorted with laughter. "Ah, my graceful lover! It's a good thing that we're not dining at Avra!"

The second attempt was more successful, though she could only eat a small amount because her stomach was rising unsteadily. Cybele wiped Dana's mouth with the towel and chided her.

"How do you say in English, eh? A slob?" She gave Dana a teasing look.

After bringing the tray downstairs and returning, Cybele changed into a nightgown and assisted Dana to the bathroom. A few minutes later, they were both in bed.

"How did you find me, Cybele?"

"Go to sleep. We'll talk in the morning." She rested her head on her hand and looked down at Dana with affection.

"Did—"

She covered Dana's lips with her fingers. "You don't listen very well, do you? Sleep."

—

THE MAN slept fitfully. Thoughts of Bryan Kerr haunted his dreams. He was sorry that he hadn't kept Bryan's wallet as a souvenir, but footsteps had startled him, causing him to leave the wallet on the ground after reading the man's name. He remembered the feel of its leather, supple from Bryan's warm body. Unconsciously, he rubbed his fingers together. He was also distressed he knew so little about Bryan. Like a lover, the man was hungry for details: where he was from, his age, the credit cards he carried, photographs of loved ones, and names to call in case of an emergency. Some biographical information would be printed in the newspapers, but he was disappointed that no photograph of Bryan had been published yet. It was a special gift whenever one was reproduced, a gift he saved with locks of hair. Last night in bed, he had smelled Bryan's shirt, becoming aroused, but today he would need to burn all of the clothes, as he had done with Malcolm's and Virgil's garments.

The man lay back, replaying each exquisite moment he had spent with Bryan. Then he began plotting his next outing. Should he apply the mustache and beard again? While they were a nuisance to attach with spirit gum and took time to remove, the fake facial hair greatly changed his appearance, though he would need to avoid meeting anyone who might recognize him. This wasn't likely late at night when he was hunting. Sadly, wearing the priest's garb on the streets was no longer possible because he now knew only a few monks lived on the island, and the outfit would shine a spotlight on him rather than serve as camouflage. Even so, the man could not bring himself to burn the cassock and hat.

CHAPTER NINETEEN

SHORTLY AFTER DAWN, Dana awoke, her head pounding. Quickly, she reached for the codeine tablets and took one. Cybele bolted upright and looked at her in alarm.

"Are you okay?"

She nodded. "Just a headache. Actually, a tremendous headache."

"I'm not surprised. You should see yourself."

Dana swiveled her legs to the side of the bed, and pain broke out in a dozen places—knees, back, ribs—and with it, mild vertigo. Cybele was by her side immediately, supporting her arm. They went into the bathroom, where Dana was appalled by the apparition she saw in the mirror: swollen bruises on her chin, cheek, jaw, neck, and the top of her chest as far as the nightshirt was opened. Feeling faint and nauseous, she leaned against the sink.

"Are you going to be all right in here by yourself?"

She said that she was, but all Dana wanted was to hold still. After Cybele closed the door, she forced herself to freshen up. Returning to bed, she was grateful to lie down again.

"Hungry?" Cybele asked.

"Not sure. Maybe some toast."

Cybele gave her a professional examination. "No, you do not look well, my friend." She smoothed Dana's forehead and ran fingers through her hair. "Let me see what I can find."

Dana drifted to sleep until Cybele brought a cup of tea and lightly buttered toast on a tray. She managed to eat everything and keep it down.

"That's better," Cybele said, smiling. "Now, while I get dressed, tell me what happened."

"First, how did you find me?"

"Ah, well. We received a call that a man was wandering in the street, drunk, with blood on his shirt. When two officers found him, it was Luca Alessi. He wasn't making much sense except to mention your name. They drove him to the hospital, and several of us began checking near your apartment. When I saw you in the alley, you will never believe how I felt! I thought you were dead," she said. "It was a terrible moment. I was so afraid!"

"Luca attacked me with no warning. How is he?"

"Oh, he's not so fine! He has a broken nose and wrist and some cuts on his face."

"That makes me feel a little better."

"Now, I'm your official policewoman. Tell me everything." She buckled her belt, withdrew a small notebook from her pocket, and sat on the bed.

Dana explained about returning home from the market and described as much of the fight as she could remember, adding that Luca had pushed her at the Inn three days before.

Cybele looked up suddenly. "What do you mean?"

"I didn't mention it because I didn't want to upset you. I'm sorry."

"Dana, always be honest with me." She sighed. "So, why is Luca angry with you?"

"I don't know. He has some lunatic idea that I'm to blame for his failure with Teresa—that I came on to her. And he blames me for his trouble with the police."

Cybele wrote down the information, anxiety tightening her face. "And he did nothing else? I mean…"

Dana knew what she meant. "He tried. I think that was his plan. But no."

"Oh, I'm so relieved!" She hesitated before adding, "I would kill him if he had…"

—

The journey to the hospital was an exhausting process. Cybele arranged for a taxi to meet them as close to the apartment as possible, but even the short walk was difficult for Dana. At the medical center, a doctor undertook an examination of her eyes and reflexes, checked the range of motion in her neck and jaw, and asked numerous questions. He confirmed that she was very mildly concussed but allowed her to go home as long as she promised to stay in bed for a day or two. Cybele assured the doctor that she would keep Dana under house arrest, though, as they were leaving, Dana and Cybele agreed it was tempting to find Luca's hospital room so they could give him a few well-placed kicks.

Captain Yalouris came by an hour after their return. Cybele showed him upstairs into the living room where Dana was lying on the couch, recovering from the morning's ordeal. After apologizing for disturbing her, he took a seat and asked about Luca Alessi and what charges should be brought against him. "Besides the attack." Then, clearing his throat, he added, "Forgive me, but was this…an attempted rape?"

"Yes." Cybele was quick to say.

Dana nodded. "I was lucky that he didn't succeed. Mostly, Luca was drunk and angry." She laid her head against a pillow. "Captain, I trust your judgment as to the indictments."

Cybele was not so accommodating. "He should be sentenced to prison!" she cried with indignation. She proceeded to give him an earful of Greek, concluding with a brisk slap on the table.

Yalouris listened, leaning against the chair and resting his chin in his hand. When she had finished, he said, "Miss Fox, we'll charge Mr. Alessi with physical and sexual assault. He has already been transferred from the hospital to jail, where he will remain until trial. And, Officer, will you please take some photographs of Miss Fox's bruises and bag her clothes? As proof?"

Cybele agreed to do so, using Dana's camera. When Yalouris stood, she did, too, but immediately her upset spilled over once again, and she started a second exchange with her superior, who was attentive, often nodding his head in agreement. After a few minutes of conversation, he turned to Dana.

"There is another matter I should mention. While it's possible Mr. Alessi is the murderer of the four men, there isn't evidence to support this theory, except we know he's capable of violence. We checked his hotel room and found nothing—no priest's clothes or the wire."

"Luca didn't have a garrote with him," Dana replied, "but he tried to choke me with his arm." She explained that Luca used asphyxiation to enhance his sexual pleasure with Teresa.

The policeman bowed his head solemnly. "Thank you for your help." Crossing the room, he touched her shoulder. "Be well, Miss Fox." To Cybele, he said, "Keep her safe."

An acknowledgment of their relationship? It seemed so.

—

They took the requested photographs and spent the remainder of the day in bed. Cybele was tired, and Dana was sleepy from the pain medication. After eating dinner, Dana was surprised to see Cybele sit beside her with a volume of Byron's poetry in hand. Cybele began to read, perfectly catching the poet's cadence. Listening, Dana found that the memories of Luca faded much as her childhood nightmares had evaporated when her mother had read stories aloud. Unaccustomed as Dana was to receiving comfort, she found the evening intoxicating. Their feelings deepened, though little was said. The sea air was warm and soft, floating in the room like a delicate presence, mixing with the smell of Cybele's sandalwood. Except for the headache and soreness, Dana felt as if she were riding on white clouds.

—

The next morning, Sunday, Cybele was off from work. After she finished cleaning the breakfast dishes, there was a knock on the door. She went down to see who it was and returned with an enormous bouquet. The note read:

Dear Dana,

I was very distressed to hear what happened. Are you feeling better? This has been a horrible time, hasn't it? I will call in a few days to see how you are, although I know your darling Cybele is taking fine care of you. When you are well, we must have dinner—the three of us. À bientôt!

Love, Émile

"That was very kind of him," Dana said.

Cybele placed the flowers on the end table. "They will cheer you up."

Dana laid a bandaged hand on Cybele's arm. "You cheer me up."

She laughed lightly. "Thank you."

"I wonder if Julian Witten had dinner with Mike?" Dana reached for the phone and dialed the King Minos. Sandros answered after a few rings.

"Ah, Dana! How are you? We were so upset to hear what Luca did! What a terrible man!"

"I'm getting better."

"He is in jail?"

"Yes."

"That is good. I never want to see him again!"

"Nor do I," she agreed and then asked if Julian was in his room.

"Oh, that is another story." He sighed. "Mr. Witten came back to the hotel on Friday night, but he didn't speak to anyone."

"Did he talk with Mike?"

"No, but he left him a note to say he was not feeling well and would see Mr. Garfield this evening for dinner. What he did yesterday, I have no idea. Maybe he was sick. He didn't order room service or take any meals. The maid hasn't seen him, and there is a "Do Not Disturb" sign on his door. However, it's possible he left sometime during the afternoon because the pump in the pool broke, and I was not always at the desk. And, of course, Mr. Witten could use his key after midnight." Sandros paused, then asked, "Is something wrong with Mr. Witten?"

"He's acting oddly, don't you think? There must be a reason."

Sandros agreed. "I'll look in his room when he goes to dinner with Mr. Garfield."

"That's a good idea, Sandros."

"Now, do not worry about anything. Rest. I will talk to you soon."

After she hung up, Dana related the conversation to Cybele, who wondered why Julian was avoiding Mike, particularly when they had decided to stay on together to do photography.

"This man is not normal," Cybele pronounced. "Is he up to something?"

Dana shrugged. "Maybe, but I think he's just immature and self-centered. He's probably involved with creating his portfolio and doesn't realize how his behavior affects other people. Or he might really be ill."

Cybele sat on the bed beside her. "Dana, did you know that Julian Witten arrived on Mykonos the day before your class?"

"No, I didn't." She stared at Cybele, puzzled. "Maybe Julian wanted to come early to scout out the island before the workshop."

"Or to scout out his killing territory. And, according to Captain Yalouris, Julian Witten was at a gay bar the night Bryan was killed."

Dana was surprised. "What? I can't imagine Julian in a gay bar. I had the impression that he almost approved of the murders. I mean, not that he would have committed them."

"Captain Yalouris considers him a suspect."

"Really? Well, maybe Sandros will find something when he checks Julian's room—to prove his innocence." She thought for a moment. "I was also curious about those protesters."

"All I know is that they're walking around with signs in front of the bars. Walter and Mary Lou Schatze are there, too, even though we told them to stop." Cybele examined Dana closely. "You don't look so good, you know?"

"Thanks. A nice thing to tell your lover."

She wagged a finger at her. "You need some sleep. For just a while, eh? I'll bring the film and your bloody clothes to the station, then I'll shop for us. What would you like?"

"I'll leave it to you." Dana took her hand. "But be careful, Cybele. Going to the market can be dangerous." She tried to make it sound like a joke to disguise her concern.

"Anyone who bothers me—I'll take care of him. Don't worry!"

—

Dana started awake when she heard the downstairs door slam. It was a habit of Cybele's that was discordant, her tendency to close doors loudly. If that was the total sum of her annoying traits, however, Dana could live with a little noise. A few minutes later, Cybele entered the bedroom, carrying two cups of tea and a stack of white church candles.

When she saw Dana staring at the candles, she laughed. "I paid for them! The market didn't have any, so what was I to do? We must have candles."

"You took them from a chapel?" Dana was amused.

"Yes," she replied without a hint of guilt. "For me, this is a shrine. As holy as some place with a Jesus on a cross."

—

About eight, Sandros called to report that he had searched Julian's room. In one of the drawers, in the back, were pants and a shirt that had been washed by hand. "Not a good job. There was blood on the clothes," he explained.

Dana covered the receiver so that she could relay the information to Cybele. "What should Sandros do?" she asked her. "In Greece, is it okay to conduct a search without a legal document—a search warrant?"

She shrugged. "I'm not sure about a hotel."

Dana returned to Sandros. "Do you have the right to enter a room?"

"Ha! This is my place!" he boomed. "I can go anywhere I wish."

"Sandros, call Captain Yalouris and tell him what you found. Let him decide how to handle this. If Julian is guilty of something, everything needs to be done correctly."

"Okay, okay," he muttered.

"Good. I'll talk to you tomorrow." She hung up the phone and looked at Cybele. "Maybe he fell and hurt himself."

"Maybe."

"But you don't think so."

Cybele shook her head.

—

The two sat on the balcony, though Dana felt shaky and admitted to a small headache and muscular pain. She accepted two aspirin but refused the codeine tablets. They ate a supper of couscous and chicken with a salad of cucumbers, tomatoes, olives, and feta cheese. She was pleased to note that Cybele was a fine cook. When she asked Cybele about her favorite dishes, Cybele reeled off some French recipes, much to Dana's surprise.

"What do you think, eh? That I have never traveled?" she teased.

"Where have you been?"

"Most of Europe. The best food is in France and northern Italy, but I even like American hamburgers," she announced with a grin. "McDonald's."

Dana chuckled.

"And you?" Cybele asked.

"I like anything you cook for me!" Dana replied with a grin.

"Wait a minute! Who is the wife here, eh? I thought you were going to shop and clean during the day and make dinner every night!"

They laughed together like old friends.

CHAPTER TWENTY

CYBELE LEFT for work. Dana ate a light breakfast and walked to the doctor's office. He checked her eyes, re-dressed her right hand and her cheek, and concluded she was on the mend, though he warned her to report any coordination difficulties, increased pain, irritability, fatigue, or memory lapses.

After stopping to replace her sunglasses that had been shattered in the fight with Luca, Dana had nothing to do. The sun was triggering a headache, so she returned to her apartment, did laundry for both Cybele and herself, and hung the wash outside to dry on the balcony. She made a cup of coffee and sat behind the dripping clothes, exhausted from her modest labors.

A few minutes later, she saw a man standing near the end of the building. He was facing away and wore a cap pulled low. Although his posture seemed vaguely familiar, Dana couldn't place him. Probably a client or acquaintance from New York, she thought, trying to ignore her anxiety. She lowered herself in the captain's chair to partly hide behind the railing and was relieved when he disappeared.

Dana returned inside and tidied the kitchen. After a short nap, cabin fever set in. She reapplied liquid makeup to the bruises, which were darkening by the minute, but couldn't disguise the bandage strips on her cheek. Dana placed her wallet in her photographer's vest, grateful to Cybele for scouring the bloodstains from its front, and set off for lunch at Sesame Kitchen.

The popular restaurant was in the Three Wells area near several gay discos and served seafood and vegetarian fare. After eating a salad, Dana paid the bill, and was just leaving when she heard a fuss coming from the vicinity of the Pink Sphinx. She walked over to investigate. In front of the bar, a noisy crowd had gathered. A man and a woman, who were immediately recognizable as Americans, were standing on the street, bibles in hand, and carrying signs: "Jesus Loves You—Repent!" and "We Love the Sinner, Not the Sin." From the scowling looks of the nearby clientele, it was clear no one was interested in being loved or in repenting.

Dana surmised that they were the infamous Walter and Mary Lou Schatze. Looking like a matched salt and pepper set, they wore sun hats and outfits in pastel shades of green and yellow—polyester being the dominant material—presumably chosen for its resistance to wear. The Schatzes seemed as tough as their clothes and were unfazed by the catcalls and remarks made around them. Although Dana didn't like what they were doing—in fact she detested their activities—the situation was getting out of hand much as at the port several days earlier. She decided to intervene, which would also give her a chance to satisfy her curiosity about the couple's possible connections to the murders. Dana made her way through the crowd and said "good afternoon" in a determinedly pleasant voice.

Up close and personal, the Schatzes appeared to be in their fifties, of sturdy stock, with Midwestern accents that spoke of the heartland. Mrs. Schatze had a slight squint as if what was before her eyes was too painful to behold, a squint that narrowed when two gay men walked past, dolled up as if for an evening at Moulin Rouge, with crimson lipstick and blush. Their heels were higher than anything Dana had ever dared to wear— dangerous on these uneven streets.

Mary Lou Schatze glanced disdainfully at the pair and turned to Dana. Although Mary Lou was young to have false teeth, she possessed a pearly white set. The smile she fixed on Dana was supernaturally bright but didn't extend to her eyes.

"Are you an American, dear?" she wanted to know.

"Yes, from New York."

"Oh, my. There." Obviously, she held New York in almost the same low esteem as she held this den of inequity. "How nice."

Walter thrust out his hand for Dana to shake, but she held up her bandaged fingers. "Ouch! Guess we'll just say howdy. My name is Walter Schatze, and this here is Mary Lou, my wife. We're from Davenport, Iowa. Glad to meet you."

"Dana Fox," she replied, studying Walter's acne-scarred, flat face. Despite the brim of his unfashionable headwear, he was sporting a sunburn. Or perhaps it was merely a case of mild apoplexy resulting from nearness to so many targets of his contempt. She led them away from the bar entrance.

One guy yelled, "Thanks, Dana," which was greeted with whistles and applause.

Mary Lou looked nervously behind her and tightened her grip on her husband's folded arm. Dana imagined that they slept in that fashion, entwined, lying on their backs. The night-time version of "American Gothic" without broom and pitchfork.

"I don't mean to be inquisitive, but you're a long way from home," Dana began.

"Yep," replied Walter with a quick dip of his head. "We are. It seems like we been here a long while. I miss Iowa. Miss all sorts of things. Why, I sure would like to get my teeth around a thick steak!" This was said with enthusiasm. His set of teeth appeared to be the original model.

"I wouldn't mind that myself," Dana agreed, although the thought made her a trifle queasy. "I guess what I meant is…why did you chose to come to Mykonos?"

Mary Lou was checking out Dana's bruises and tilted her head like a bird to read the Dompke label on Dana's vest. At the question, she produced her happy smile and held up a bible. "The minister of our church told us this place was a regular Sodom and Gomorrah. You know, where sin is acceptable. How everyone parades around…boys doing things to boys, that sort of abomination. Walter and I got to talking, and we decided that as good Christians we needed to do the Lord's work…so here we are."

"I see. Has anyone seen the light?" Dana asked, facetiously lapsing into their style of conversation.

"Three boys," Walter said, sunlight glinting off his silver-framed glasses. "They were by themselves, and I guess they were lonely and in need. We talked to them real good, and they saw the wonder of God's love. We pray for them every day and every night."

"Every day and night," intoned Mary Lou.

"Who were they?" Although she asked the question calmly, Dana felt revulsion wash over her. She reminded herself that she had often encountered distasteful people in her workshops and had developed diplomatic skills to deal with them.

"They were lost souls. Yes, indeed. And they are found, praise the good Lord," replied Walter, two deep lines creasing his liver-spotted forehead.

Were the three murders linked to the three saved men? Dana could tell she wasn't going to elicit more information, such as the names of the "lost souls" or where they were from.

"Well, I don't think you're very welcome here." Dana waved a hand toward the Pink Sphinx. "And I don't think the police are going to sit by and let you picket these clubs much longer. If I were you, I'd consider going home. I appreciate that you feel you're doing good, but that sentiment isn't shared locally."

Walter Schatze leaned back a few inches as if Dana had said something offensive, which, perhaps, she had, and then studied her swollen chin and bruises. "Say, I hear there's an American who got beat up in town. You her? I bet you are!" he said, quickly answering his own question. "Who done this to you, Dana? Was it one of these?" He pointed to some of the lads sitting at outside tables, holding hands and laughing.

"I heard he was Italian," Mary Lou reminded him. "Maybe he's a Catholic."

"I don't know if he's Catholic…" Dana began inanely, since Luca's religion had no relevance.

Mary Lou and Walter looked at each other and shook their heads in unison. "Well, gosh," said Mary Lou, "some of them Catholics don't behave so good, you know. I'm sorry for your trouble."

"Me too," Dana agreed. "But back to the subject, why don't you go home before things get worse."

Walter compressed his lips and gave her a gritty look. "We ain't afraid of nobody. We have our Savior, Jesus Christ, to guide us. While he's by our side, we'll come to no harm." He nodded in agreement with himself and waited for his wife to do the same.

She obliged with perfect timing. "My husband and I will stay here long as we can. This is our mission." Her face was netted with finely etched wrinkles, which deepened when her mouth tucked into a well-practiced smile. A second later, a swarthy bodybuilder in a sleeveless white tank shirt cruised by, blowing the lady from Iowa a derisive kiss. Her smile instantly soured into a crimped line.

Dana sighed. "I wish you would reconsider. These men and women came here to be themselves. They aren't hurting anyone."

"Oh, yes, they are!" Walter tapped his bible with thick, strong fingers. "They're transmitting diseases with their sin. And they got this here plague because of it. God, in his wisdom, invented it so they would be punished for their unnatural ways. We want to save them from dying."

"And they're giving AIDS to our children. You know, our innocent boys and girls that they lure to back alleys and do unspeakable things to! It is an outrage! An abomination!" Mary Lou said with surprising vehemence.

Dana was startled by the power of their convictions. It was clear that the template argument was well ensconced in the Schatzes' hardwiring. Nothing Dana said would shake one wood shaving from their overstuffed heads. Better to leave than lose her temper.

"Well, I have some work to do—"

"Now, don't you mind my wife. She gets riled up real easy. But that's no reason for you to hurry off so fast!" Walter said.

"No reason at all!" Mary Lou insisted, grabbing Dana's arm with a talon-like grip. Her eyes were glittering with intensity.

"I really must—"

"You didn't tell us where you're staying. Maybe we could get together later this evening? You know, visit a while," Walter added, stepping closer.

Feeling cornered, Dana disengaged Mary Lou's hand and took a step away. "I'm sorry. Some other time perhaps. I hope you'll think about what I said…about leaving."

"We have a solemn and worthy mission, my dear. When that's done, we'll head on home. May the good Lord go with you," said Mr. Schatze.

"God bless!" Mary Lou chipped in with her fabricated smile.

Dana turned and decided that if God was speaking through them, God was nuts.

—

A few minutes later, as she was rounding Mitropoleos, Dana ran into Myron, or rather, she ran into his unmistakable fragrance first. He was sweating profusely, his oily skin slick and shimmering in the hot sun. He greeted her politely and asked how she was feeling.

"*Kalá, efharisto,*" she replied.

"Mr. Alessi is in jail, Miss Fox."

"Yes, I know. I'm pleased to hear it. He's not someone I'd like to see again."

"No, he's a bad man," Myron agreed, with sincerity. "We may send him to the mainland. That is what your friend, Officer Karabélias, asked Captain Yalouris."

Amused, Dana replied that Luca deserved to inhale the air of Athens.

This delighted Myron, who, as an islander, harbored a low opinion of cities, Athens in particular. After laughing, he regained his formal demeanor. "Perhaps I shouldn't tell you," he said, telling her anyway, "but we went to Mr. Witten's room last night."

"Oh?" Dana was instantly alert.

Myron nodded solemnly. "Yes, Miss Fox, we did."

Trying to speed up his recitation, she asked, "And what did you find?"

"We found clothes with blood. Mr. Witten tried to wash them."

"Whose blood was it?"

"Ah, yes. We heard an hour ago. It is the dead boy's blood. Mr. Kerr's."

Dana was so surprised that she leaned against the wall. "Really?"

"Yes. We are sure."

"Where is Julian?"

"At the station. We found him with Mr. Garfield. When Mr. Witten saw us, he tried to run away. I think he is the killer, Miss Fox."

Dana couldn't believe that her student was responsible for the murders. The blood evidence, however, was damning and hard to explain. "Could I speak with Julian?"

Myron shrugged. "He is with the two detectives from Athens. They may not let you see him, but you can ask."

—

Sitting on a shady wall, Dana closed her eyes in hopes of chasing away the headache which was reemerging. Though she desperately wanted to go home and take some aspirin and rest, she walked to the police station. When she arrived, Cybele was at her desk.

"Hard at work?" Dana whispered.

Startled, the policewoman pivoted in her chair and looked up; a smile formed. "Yes, I am. And you, you're supposed to be at home." Cybele shook her finger at Dana. "What am I going to do with you?"

"Whatever you like. Later."

"Oh, you're impossible! Now, why are you here?"

"To see Julian Witten."

"How did you hear about this so quickly? I tried to call you a while ago, but obviously you were wandering around town and ignoring the doctor's orders."

Dana smiled and shrugged innocently.

Cybele clucked at her. "Well, yes, Julian is here and might be charged with Bryan's murder. I guess you know that too?"

"Yes. I met Myron in the street. Look, I don't think Julian could kill anyone. Maybe I'm wrong, but I'm concerned for him. Has anyone contacted his parents? Or an attorney?"

"I'll check with Captain Yalouris. And sit down. You don't look well." She wheeled over a chair, and Dana gratefully followed her advice.

When the Captain arrived, he examined Dana with concern. "Miss Fox, you should be at home."

"I know, but I heard that Julian Witten was arrested. Has anyone called his family?"

"Yes. His aunt is making arrangements to fly to Mykonos."

"Good." That was a call she hadn't been eager to place. Curious, she asked, "Do you have any evidence that he killed Malcolm Hall or Virgil?"

"No, not yet. If we could find the wire he used, that would help. Or the cassock or the cosmetics."

Dana nodded. "May I speak with him for a few minutes?"

"I just left him with the two detectives." He paused, considering. "He hasn't admitted anything. Perhaps he'll tell you his story."

—

THE DAY seemed interminable. There was not much the man could do except wait, an activity he despised. His parents had always made him wait. They said that their lives were more important, that he should have no expectations. It was good for a boy to learn discipline, to be respectful, dutiful. If he failed in the smallest way, he was left in his room for a day, without food or water, without the use of a bathroom, the windows nailed shut, the door bolted from the outside. It was a beautiful room—spacious, square, high-ceilinged, looking out over the garden, but he had suffered within its confines. As a boy, he had counted how many strips of wainscoting were on each wall, how many tufts of blue cloth dotted his bedspread, how many books, shoes, and toy soldiers were in his room. The numbers had to be correct. They had to be identical each time.

When the dreams started, he had been ashamed, frightened that somehow his father could read his mind or, worse yet, could see through the thick door, see him touching himself. As he grew older, he realized that the images were empowering. Miss Becker understood. He loved to watch her grow excited, to see her cheeks redden as she listened to his fantasies. Sometimes, Miss Becker made up exhilarating stories of her own, while her hands held him. Over and over, she made him promise never to tell anyone what they did together, what they talked about. She said he must always plan meticulously, that he could do special things, and no one would find out. The cat, Cleopatra, for example. He hated her. He hated the scratches and bites she gave him. That was his first execution—at age twelve.

The man smiled, replaying how he had cut off a tiny section of stiff calico fur and put it in a wooden box. Before long, he had other samples. Over the years, there were many boxes, each labelled with a first name. And now he had started a new one: *Dana.*

CHAPTER TWENTY-ONE

WHEN DANA entered the interrogation area, Julian Witten jumped up and was immediately forced into his chair by Detective Pyrgos and his partner, Pantazakis. Julian looked dreadful, with dark circles ringing his eyes. After a quick assessment of his demeanor, she reassured the policemen that she was comfortable with him, asked for his handcuffs to be removed, and requested a few minutes alone. They refused to unlock the handcuffs but moved to the end of the room. A tape recorder was running, although Julian seemed oblivious to it. He also declined to have an attorney present, though Dana urged him to do so.

"What happened?" Dana took a seat on the other side of the table.

"This is all a terrible mistake!" he insisted.

"Julian, if you didn't do anything, why did you run when you saw the police at the restaurant? And how can you explain the blood on your clothes?"

He hung his head and twisted his hands, clanking the metal cuffs. "I don't know."

He did, of course, know. Little by little, his words gathered force as if they had been pent up inside of him for a long time. He was attracted to men. Avoiding Dana's eyes, he admitted this with shame.

"Julian, you don't have to hide your feelings."

"You don't understand. I can't do this…I can't want those things! I can't!" He was close to tears.

Dana wondered if Walter and Mary Lou Schatze had thumped a bible or two on his head. "Look at how many gay men and women are here on Mykonos. Are all of them evil or sinful?"

"Yeah, they are. We've been given brains to think about our behavior. To make moral value judgments. Just because someone has an urge to do something, doesn't mean he should."

"I don't agree with you, Julian. You're intent on making yourself miserable. If you were so repelled by your desires, why come to Mykonos when you knew this was a gay mecca? Why come to a place where you would feel so unhappy?"

"I don't know," he replied stubbornly, staring at the scarred top of the table.

"I think it's because you want to be surrounded by men and women who share your feelings. Because you want to be one of them."

"No! I can't stand all the guys in dresses and all the dancing and—"

"The open expression of sexual behavior?"

"Yes."

"But you can't resist it, either, can you?"

"No," he whispered in a tormented voice.

"So what about Bryan?"

Julian shook his head and was silent.

"If you're innocent, you need to prove it," Dana told him. "You're in a real mess."

"I know. They think I killed him and Virgil too."

"Yes, they do," Dana agreed. "Let's ask for the tape recorder to be switched off."

"I don't care. Leave it on."

She was worried that Julian would say something incriminating, especially in his clearly unstable mental condition, but the opposite could also occur: He might exonerate himself.

"Okay. Why don't you walk me through Thursday night?"

Julian exhaled nervously. "Well, I went to bed early but couldn't sleep. I kept imagining the music, the fun people were having. The more I thought about it, the more restless I got. Around midnight, I dressed and walked into town to have one drink." He shut his eyes but kept talking. "I stopped at the Pink Sphinx. I don't even remember going in. It's like someone else went there. I didn't have a single drink—I had quite a few. Then some guys started hitting on me. I didn't know whether they were making fun of me or what."

Julian wasn't incredibly handsome, but he was nice-looking. With all the perfect bodies roaming around Mykonos, however, Dana could understand his lack of self-confidence.

"What did you do?"

He opened his eyes, staring at her sadly. "I danced with one of them. A fast dance. I felt like a fool. It was so hot, and he kept getting closer and closer. Before I knew it, he pulled off his shirt and threw it in the air. The guy was really well-built." Perspiration broke out on his forehead.

"And?"

"When the song stopped, he tried to buy me a drink, but I felt too disgusted to stay any longer. I went outside. It was late. I should've returned to the hotel. I wish I had. Without thinking, I headed to Paraportiani."

"That's a popular gay cruising zone. Did you know that?"

Julian's nodded, wiping away a bead of sweat and glancing uneasily at the two detectives. "Yeah, I did. I guess I was trying to tell myself that I just needed to walk, to sober up." He lowered his voice. "On the way there, I saw this blond guy. He looked pretty depressed…like I felt. We started talking and finally we sat down. He told me his name was Bryan. He was upset over an argument with his boyfriend. He said he'd had too much to drink. Well, at this point, I had too. Neither one of us was thinking real straight. Oh, Dana, do I have to go on?"

"Yes, Julian."

Raising his gaze to Dana's, his eyes wide, he cried, "Jesus! The next thing I knew, I was making a pass at him. Me!"

Dana looked at him steadily. "How did he react?"

"Oh, he was nice enough. He let me kiss him." Julian pressed his lips tightly together. "But then Bryan admitted he was in love and not interested. I felt like a complete fool! I was disgusted by what I'd done. I felt sick…so sick."

"What happened next?"

His head sank down on his chest. "I'm not sure. It's a blur. All I wanted to do was forget. I think I ran away from him and bought a couple more drinks at a bar before it closed. It was really late." He rubbed his eyes with his balled fist.

"Which bar?"

"Just a bar. Have no idea which one." Julian exhaled uneasily. "After that, I decided to return to the hotel and got lost. All the streets looked the same to me. Like a maze."

"What time was this?"

"It was still dark." He shrugged. "Eventually, I thought I was somewhere near Little Venice, on the inland side. I stopped and then heard someone cry out. More of a loud gasp, really. I didn't know where it came from. I wasn't sure if it was a sound of pain or…well, whether some guy was getting his rocks off. I even thought maybe the noise came from me. The longer I stood there, the more I wasn't sure if I'd heard anything at all. But I remembered about the murders and was afraid, so I hid behind a staircase. When I thought it was safe, I started walking again but I was so drunk. Fell a few times and stumbled around until I came out on the promenade by the sea. That's where I saw Bryan's body lying against a building…or maybe I was with him all along and never left. Or maybe I came back and…oh, I can't remember."

"Was he dead?"

Julian's voice choked. "Yeah, but I didn't know it at first. I put my hands on his chest. I guess that's where I got the blood on my clothes…but I'm not sure of any of this. I mean, it was like a nightmare. I hardly recall leaving him the first time. Did I? I don't know. But, yeah, I finally understood that he wasn't breathing. It was awful!

He was wearing lipstick and had red circles painted on his cheeks. His eyes were just staring into space, surprised. I'll never forget that…"

"Anything else?" Dana asked him gently.

"His clothes were gone. All I remember is that I touched him again… even though he was dead." With this, he began to sob.

She came around the table and placed a hand on his shoulder. "Julian, don't think about it. You had a lot to drink. You were upset."

"If only you'd let me talk to you… about being gay."

Dana groaned inwardly. So that was why he wanted to be with her! Before she could answer, Julian lowered his head and began to bang his forehead on the table, lightly at first, then with more violence. Suddenly, he stared at her with wild eyes, leapt to his feet, and threw himself against the window. Detective Pyrgos jumped from his chair and caught Julian around the shoulders, but Julian was intent on doing himself harm. He whipsawed his two cuffed hands and shoved the policeman aside. Pantazakis grabbed Julian around the waist and shouted for help. A few seconds later, Theo ran in with Cybele, who immediately hurried to get leg restraints. Once she returned, it took four of them to wrestle Julian into submission before escorting him to his cell. A doctor was called in case sedation was necessary.

Stunned, Dana collapsed in a chair. Detective Pyrgos clicked off the recorder. Captain Yalouris entered and spoke in Greek to Cybele and the two detectives before all of them joined Dana at the table and listened to the replay of the tape. At its conclusion, Captain Yalouris asked her opinion about Julian's story.

Dana wasn't sure what to say. The conversation seemed more elusive after hearing it a second time. "It's very confusing," she admitted. "Both Bryan and Julian had been drinking. Julian walked away and had more drinks—or thinks he did. He doesn't remember the bar he was in. He's not even sure he went to a bar."

"If we knew where he was and when, we could check part of his story. That would help," said Detective Pyrgos.

"Yes, it would. Frankly, I think it's a little surprising that Julian wasn't aware of his location. Even if he was extremely drunk, he knows the town fairly well," Dana said.

"If Mr. Witten's telling the truth, he should have been served about two or three at the latest—most of the bars close by then. Ask around," Captain Yalouris instructed the detectives. "Someone should have seen him."

Dana continued. "He was very disoriented, no matter what he did."

"Do you think he could have killed Bryan and the others?" Cybele asked.

Dana stood up and began pacing. "I doubt he did, even if he feels guilty about his homosexual feelings. Even if he projects his self-loathing onto other gay men."

"He had motive and opportunity," replied Pyrgos.

Dana came to a halt. "For what it's worth, I believe he's innocent, but I can't base that on anything. I mean, if he's the killer, where are the priest's robes and hat? The wire? And where would he keep the cosmetics while he was dancing at the bars?"

"We searched his room, but there was nothing," Pantazakis admitted.

Dana's head was now producing a thunderous beat. Cybele seemed to sense her discomfort and whispered something to Captain Yalouris, who turned toward Dana, thanked her, and suggested that she should return to her apartment.

"I really don't think he's the killer," Dana repeated.

The two detectives exchanged glances but made no response.

Cybele followed her out. "Are you okay?" she asked in the dark hallway, placing a hand on Dana's arm.

"Headache. I promise to go home. No more stops."

"I'll bring dinner."

With Julian in his cell, there was nothing more to do, even if she felt uneasy about his confession.

—

CYBELE SAT at her desk. Instinct told her that Julian was not guilty of Bryan's murder, although she was sorry to have missed watching his conversation with Dana. Analyzing his behavior in person would have been useful as would hearing the earlier interrogation conducted by Pyrgos, Pantazakis, and Captain Yalouris. So far, none of them had uttered a word to the staff, and now the three of them were together in the Incidents Room with the door closed.

As for Luca Alessi, Cybele had heard that his room had been searched. No cassock, hat, garrote, or cosmetics were found. However, it was possible he had another place to hide everything, where he changed into the monk's outfit. The same could be true for Julian Witten.

A minute later, Theo, who was manning the switchboard, informed her that Paul Owens Merrill was delivering an inflammatory lecture near Town Hall and that she and Myron should investigate immediately. The last thing she wanted to do was deal with that arrogant minister. Nevertheless, she had several hours left on duty and no excuse. Sighing, she clipped her police radio to her belt and set off with Myron.

—

Paul Owens Merrill was standing on a slight rise, overdressed in a tan suit, black tonsure clerical shirt, and expensive black shoes. As he enjoined the crowd to pray with him, his Adam's apple chafed against the clerical collar. Cybele had no sympathy for the man—no sympathy for his increasingly red face or for his bellicose message. She was pleased to see that most of the people streaming off the boats from Delos were ignoring him, flowing around him like water around a rock.

Myron informed Merrill that he was obstructing the pedestrians. Merrill raised a bible high over his head and called upon Jesus Christ to save Myron. Myron, who kept a string of brown worry beads in his pocket, was clearly not comfortable with his task. It was obvious to Cybele that while he didn't like the minister, Myron had been indoctrinated to respect men of the cloth.

She stepped forward. "If you don't stop, Mr. Merrill, we will arrest you."

This caught the minister's attention. He gave her an unctuous smile and placed a leaden hand on her arm. "My dear, I am only doing the Lord's work. Surely, you agree with that?"

Cybele shrugged off his hand. "My beliefs are unimportant. You're annoying the tourists. If you wish to preach a sermon, find a church." She gave him a hard look.

The minister sighed as he slowly unfolded a white handkerchief and mopped his brow. "Very well," he replied. As he stepped past her, he shook his head condescendingly and gave her a thin-lipped smile that curdled with hostility. "It's a pity that you don't love God, my dear. One day you will have such terrible, terrible regrets."

—

Hours later, Cybele came upstairs and discovered Dana asleep in bed. She sat down in a chair, which woke Dana.

"Sorry, I did not mean to make any noise. Would you like some dinner?"

Dana sat up halfway. "I missed you!"

She laughed lightly. "I think the only thing you missed was this afternoon, no? And evening? Now, do you wish some of my fine cooking or do you want to go to sleep again?"

"I'll come down with you," Dana said, starting to pull back the sheets.

Cybele placed her hands on both sides of Dana's head. "I think you've done enough. I'll bring up a tray."

—

PERHAPS DUE to all the sleep, Dana stirred before Cybele. They lay close together, Cybele's head resting on Dana's shoulder. When Cybele opened her eyes, she whispered, "Good morning."

"And to you."

"Are you feeling better?"

"Yes, thanks to all of your care. In fact, I'm going to make you breakfast."

Cybele glanced at her watch. "I can't be late."

"Take a shower. I'll start the coffee."

Twenty minutes later, they were on the balcony. Cybele ate her scrambled eggs and then announced she needed to go to work. "And, oh, I forgot. You have a letter. Nikos gave it to me yesterday evening."

"Ah, so he knows who you are?"

She grinned at Dana. "Yes, and he told me to tell you that he approves of me very much."

—

After Cybele left, Dana opened the letter, which was from her financial advisor, confirming their November appointment for her semi-annual portfolio review. Nothing required her to make any decisions, which was just as well considering her condition.

She showered and carefully removed the soggy bandages. The wound on her hand still needed protection, but the one on her cheek was healing well, so she decided not to cover it. However, her face was blooming with a harmonious palette of colors sharing the central hue of violet. No amount of makeup would disguise the damage, though she tried her best.

When she came downstairs, the phone rang: Sandros to see how she was feeling. They conversed for a few moments before Mike Garfield came on the line. Dana asked how his photography was progressing.

"I think I have a few decent pictures. I'd like to show them to you if you're up to it. If you're not, I understand."

"Actually, I feel pretty good. Why don't we meet at my gallery at noon? By the way, thanks for the purchase."

"You're welcome. I wanted to have one of your photographs."

Dana had time to visit *The Pelican* before seeing Mike. When she arrived, Anna was on the phone but quickly ended the conversation. She whistled, knitting her thick eyebrows with concern. A torrent of Greek followed, presumably sprinkled with shocked expletives, little of which Dana understood. Realizing this, Anna migrated into English.

"You look terrible!"

"I do," was the only thing Dana could say.

"Does it hurt?"

"And if I said 'no'?"

Anna whacked her with a folded newspaper. "I wouldn't believe you!"

"Any news?"

"No more murders. Perhaps because Julian Witten and Luca Alessi are in jail." She frowned. "The only problem is the religious Americans. They continue to bother the people at the gay clubs."

"I wonder where their money is coming from?" Dana asked.

"I have no idea, but these people are everywhere with their signs. The police should make them leave."

"The organizer is that minister—"

"From Iowa, yes. Although I believe the couple, Mary Lou and Walter Schatze, are involved. Tassos thinks that they are making the schedules for the others. He tried to interview them, but all they talked about was their mission on Mykonos." She showed Dana the article.

Dana scanned the short piece. At the end of the story, the newspaperman asked Walter Schatze the same question she herself wanted to know: Who was paying? In addition to funds collected from ministry donations, the Schatzes said a generous benefactor was assisting their cause. Did Cybele know who this mysterious benefactor was?

She thanked Anna for the paper and walked the short distance to the gallery.

CHAPTER TWENTY-TWO

WHEN DANA STEPPED through the gallery's open doors, Constantine was displaying a set of watercolors to a prospective buyer. After a peek at Dana, he had the same reaction as Anna: a whistle. Embarrassed, she slipped into the side office and waited for Mike. About five minutes after noon, he came in, his face flushed from the heat.

"Boy, look at you!" he said.

At least Mike hadn't whistled. "Thanks. It looks worse than it is." This wasn't true. A headache had become a constant companion.

"Are you sure you're up for seeing my work?"

"Yes. Show me what you've got."

Mike pulled out four pages of slides and handed her a loupe. Dana examined his images once through, studied them again, and offered her opinion about the ones she preferred, discussing technical problems, and praising him for his extra effort.

He gave her a happy grin and smoothed back his brush-cut hair. "I don't know. I like some of them."

"Mike, they really are good. More than a few. I particularly appreciate some of the night shots that you took. They're eerie … those with the colored lights that wash onto the white walls."

"Thanks. I had a little more time than I thought since Julian was acting so weird. What's the deal with him and the police? Do you know?"

"Actually, I spoke with Julian at the station."

"I tried but they wouldn't let me."

"Well, according to him, he was drunk the night Bryan Kerr was killed. And, as Sandros probably told you, Julian had blood on his clothes—Bryan's."

"Yeah, I understand. But what I don't get is why."

She wasn't sure it was appropriate to out Julian, particularly when he was attempting to deny his sexual feelings. "Julian said that he and Bryan Kerr ran into each other. His story is that he left Bryan and went to a bar. When he was heading home, he saw Bryan's body and touched him. When he recounted what happened, Julian was very muddled. I can't swear that he's telling the truth or that he even knows what the truth is."

"So, he's really a suspect?"

"Yes. His aunt is arriving soon. I'm sure she'll hire a lawyer if she doesn't bring one with her. Julian's in serious trouble. He was so intoxicated that he can't remember anything clearly, which means he's unable to prove where he was when Bryan was killed."

Mike shook his head. "I feel sorry for him. He's not a bad guy. Just a little off center."

"I know. I'll call if I hear anything."

"Thanks. And what about Luca? Boy, he sure went off the deep end, didn't he?"

Dana sighed, not really comfortable with the subject. "He'll be charged with assault."

"I heard you broke his nose and wrist." Mike gave her an admiring glance. "He deserved more than that."

"I think he'll get his reward," Dana replied. "So, Mike, how long are you staying on Mykonos?"

"Probably another day or two. I'm going fishing tomorrow. Then I'll fly home."

Dana patted him on the back and wished him good luck fishing.

After Mike left, she waited until Constantine had completed a successful transaction. He came into the side room, sat beside her, and crossed his legs neatly.

"I always love selling something," he announced, looking pleased. "It's a wonderful feeling to help myself and an artist at the same time."

"Kind of like having your cake and eating it too?"

He furrowed his brow. "Can you explain that?"

Dana laughed. "Not really. Sorry, it's one of those annoying things Americans say. So, is business good, Constantine?"

"It could be better." His standard response. "But your work is doing well. We sold another photograph last night to a woman from a cruise ship."

"Thank goodness for cruise ships!"

"We all say that," he agreed. "Unfortunately, with the murders, another ship has canceled, and I heard that the incoming flights from Athens are running half empty."

"That's too bad."

He nodded and then perked up. "So, are we going to have any more work from you?"

Dana remembered the packet of prints that she'd picked up before Luca's attack. They had been in the back pocket of her vest. Had Cybele thrown them away when she cleaned the blood on the vest or put them somewhere?

"Maybe."

"Good." He gave her a gentle kiss on the better side of her face.

—

Though it was ridiculous to crave sea air on an island, Dana sometimes felt a little claustrophobic in the twisting alleys of town. She headed toward the harbor and found an empty table at a taverna. She ordered a tiropita and some dolmades, both in appetizer portions, and a Coke.

Stretching her legs in front of her, Dana sat there, half in and out of the sun, enjoying the calls of the fisherman hawking their wares. Hercules was standing to her right, posing for the point-and-shoot crowd eager to capture the visage of an authentic Greek merchant, though his participation was contingent upon receiving a few drachmas in a tip bucket. He did this wily impersonation in part because it amused him, in part because it paid well. He had mastered the whole shtick—the finger touching the cap in a little salute, the small bow, the look of humble gratitude whenever someone dropped coins. Although Hercules sold vegetables to some local residents, his primary income was from the hordes of passengers spilling from the cruise ships who bought souvenirs and took portraits. His cart disappeared after departures and returned for arrivals, as linked to the transportation schedules as a dockworker.

Dana finished the cheese pie and grape leaves. Tonight, since she was feeling better, perhaps she and Cybele would dine out and discuss the trip to America. If she agreed to come to New York, there were so many places Dana wanted to show her, so many people for her to meet. Dana also decided to improve her fluency in Greek, a language she found difficult—too many vowels and long words. She and Cybele would concentrate on Dana's ability to read the language and her syntax, which was more or less stuck on present tense.

Standing, she felt slightly dizzy. The glare from the bright sun bothered her eyes. Dana glanced at her father's watch, amazed that it had weathered the fight with Luca Alessi. It was 2:25 p.m. She decided to buy a hat to replace the one Luca had destroyed.

—

THE MAN craved privacy. Layers of it, like the thick walls of his childhood room that shielded his secret activities from his parents. Although they had been dead several years, sometimes he forgot, and the familiar hate for his father and mother rose in his throat. To make the hate fade, he pictured their bodies decaying in cold earth, savored the vision of their corpses moldering in the cheap gray caskets he had purchased. He had opted for burial rather than cremation because he preferred this image of slow deterioration rather than a fiery, fast immolation.

Their deaths had been a relief and a bonus. As an only child, he had inherited everything. He could now do as he pleased; he could indulge his cravings and buy protection to keep his secrets safe.

—

DANA FOUND a new hat. The straw had a greenish cast complemented by an olive band and was similar to her old one—a Greek version of a Panama but with a longer brim. Besides providing shade from the sun, it would also partly obscure her swollen face from the curious eyes of passersby. She paid and decided she and Cybele needed cell phones. She walked to a store, where the owner began a convoluted sales pitch about various models and coverage programs, which caused her headache to gather force. Unable to make a decision, Dana promised to buy one soon and set out for El Greco's, where she made dinner reservations.

In her apartment, Dana took some aspirin and then remembered the packet of photographs she had placed in her vest before the fight. She began a search, hoping Cybele had saved them, and finally located the envelope, slightly damaged, on top of the bookcase. She began boiling water for tea, sat on the sofa, and opened the packet. Some of the shots were good, especially a series featuring the blue sky trapped between the sweeping curves of chapel domes and a second group that captured the labyrinthine streets bisected by long shadows. These would be a hit in Mykonos, but a few might intrigue the Calvin Carnahan Gallery in New York.

As she flipped through the prints, Dana inserted them into paged sleeves, four front, four back. When she was about to look at the first photograph of the protesters by the harbor, the kettle began whistling. She remembered that Tassos had other pictures—some already printed in the newspaper, so these were useless. Nevertheless, Dana stuffed the four prints together in one divisional of the page and hurried to steep her tea. When she returned, she placed all of the pages and negatives in a three-ringed binder, laid it on the sofa, and rested.

At six, Cybele came in. Dana felt considerably better and was eager to show Cybele the new photos, yet she was reticent about doing so because most of her lovers hadn't been perceptive about her work. Not that she sought flattery, but a discerning partner, one who was supportive and enthusiastic, was a luxury Dana greatly desired. She steered Cybele to the notebook on the coffee table.

"I need your opinion," Dana told her.

"You do not need my opinion, but you would like it?" Her brown eyes crinkled with amusement.

"Yes," she replied, sitting beside her.

Cybele opened the cover. In silence, she went through the images and then looked at Dana with respect.

"I think you have two ideas in your mind when you take photographs, yes?"

Dana nodded.

"*Endaksi*. One idea is for the tourists, eh? And the other, it's about making real art."

"Which ones do you like best?" Dana asked, feeling hopeful, since she had understood the dual mentality of the work.

Cybele leafed through the prints a second time and tapped several of the most abstract images of the blue-domed church and of angled shadows falling from exterior staircases.

"I like this one very much," she explained, "because the sky is like the dome. It's round and nearly the same color. I think that's why a dome should be painted blue... so that it looks like the sky. A kind of mirror, yes? They've become friends, these two, and relate to one another."

Each one she selected was Dana's New York style: the less realistic photographs.

"What are these?" Cybele asked, pointing to the prints sandwiched at the back.

"Nothing important. Just pictures of the protesters."

Dana stood to open a bottle of wine. As she did so, Cybele pulled out the four photos, looked through them, and reinserted them into the pocket. When Dana joined her, she asked Cybele to pick her favorite.

"That's easy. This one."

It was an image from a previous roll, one taken with the lens angling up at Little Venice. The picture caught white fingers of foam in mid-air with the buildings in the center. From its skewed perspective, it appeared that the photo had been snapped by the sea itself. Adding to the attraction was the late afternoon sun's glow, which cast lollipop orange reflections on the windows and bathed the entire image in warm light.

"Dana, would it be possible to enlarge this one? To make it very big, very grand? So I will feel like I am home in New York?"

Dana handed her a glass of wine. "Does that mean you'll come?"

Cybele grinned at her. "If you promise to enlarge this picture."

Dana sat beside Cybele and kissed her. "I'm so happy!"

"I want to be with you. But let's call it a visit, okay?"

"Yes, you're right," Dana replied. "But what about your family and your job?"

"They will be here when we return. And if we do not get along, then we tried."

Dana nodded and kissed Cybele again. "What an amazing person you are!"

Cybele laughed. "I'm not so amazing, but thank you." Entwining Dana's arm in hers, she studied the pages again. "I love that you make these creations. They come from a part of you that I'm trying to find, a part that sometimes, when we make love, I see. It is a very silent place. A place where you feel beauty and sadness both. I think that beauty makes you this way. Sad."

"Sad? Yes, I suppose you're right. When I see something beautiful, I often think of my mother. For her, the world was magical, exquisitely so, worthy of constant appreciation."

"And you're sad because you miss her?"

"Yes. That we will never share anything again."

"So you take photographs of beautiful things to share with her, wherever she is?"

Dana realized this was true. "I guess that sounds silly. To believe she sees what I create."

"Ah, but she does, my dear friend. I feel her here with us sometimes. I believe she's happy that we found each other, that she celebrates our joy."

Dana stared at Cybele for a long time. "Yes, I think she's around."

"Good. Let's drink to her and to us." They clinked glasses.

"Would you like to go to El Greco for dinner?" Dana asked.

"I would be delighted if you feel well enough? I have a passion for their stuffed whole squid."

"I'm fine. And the squid is one of my favorites."

—

As they strolled to the restaurant, Dana considered the woman who walked beside her. Cybele seemed to achieve effortless clarity in all things, conveying her perceptions with sureness—such as how she understood Dana's artistic transference. For most of her life, Dana had been fiercely devoted to her work, pouring energy and passion into her photography, seeing the world through the lens. Could her feelings for Cybele intensify her creative vision? Would this also be true for Cybele and her poetry? Dana sensed that law enforcement was a false career for her, one she had chosen for practical reasons or due to guilt about her father. In her heart, Cybele was a writer. Dana could see that plainly. A writer who needed time and a place to work. Dana smiled at the thought. That's where she could help.

At El Greco, they were seated along the half-wall enclosing the exterior dining area. The candle flickered on the small table as the waiter handed them menus. To Dana's surprise, Cybele returned them and began to order in Greek.

"What about the wine?" Dana asked her.

She grinned. "I've taken care of it."

"What did you select?"

"You'll find out when it comes. Now, tell me, why are you so quiet?"

Dana didn't know where to begin, so she spoke tentatively. "I've been with many people who have seen my photography, but none of them have understood how I feel about it. They look at the prints and judge them on whether they like them or whether they are commercially appealing. That's fine, but they don't go further than that."

"They don't recognize the self that is in the pictures." Cybele studied her. "But your work isn't separate…your photographs are like words. Words with colors and shapes and lines. I'm not sure what each one means, but somehow, as a whole, they communicate things about you. I sense that you struggle to find balance in the middle of strong and powerful forces of nature. This is true of you and of your work. Did I say this clearly?"

Dana nodded.

"And you're surprised that I feel this struggle? That I see how you find ways to organize yourself, your pictures, into a strong composition, into a strong self?"

"Yes."

Cybele laughed, her eyes twinkling. "Dana, we come together to complete each other. That is what we do, you and I. We're both strong. We're both weak. But where I am weak, you are strong, and where you are weak, I am strong. That sounds simple, but it's true."

"I think you're right. And perhaps because you are a writer, you perceive things differently than other people."

"That may be so," Cybele agreed.

"Do you have any work in English that I could read?"

"No, but I may try to write something in New York."

Dana grinned at her. "Good!"

The waiter brought a bottle of red wine. Semeli, 1992. He smiled and served it to Cybele. She tasted it and gave her approval. He poured a glass for Dana.

"This wine is from the same mountain that produced the marble for the Parthenon. It's the area of its namesake, the goddess Semeli, who was the mother of Dionysus," Cybele explained. "Mostly cabernet sauvignon with a small amount of merlot. A gold medal winner in the States."

It was indeed a finely made creation that was perfect with the cubes of grilled beef that arrived a few minutes later. With the main course, Cybele ordered a rosé from the same vineyard, which proved to be a beautiful marriage with the stuffed squid and the creamy sauce that floated over it. They finished off both bottles, and at Cybele's request, the chef came out from the kitchen to receive compliments.

After walking hand in hand to the apartment, they climbed the stairs. Dana tossed her keys on the coffee table and looked at Cybele. They laughed and immediately rushed to the bedroom, where they lit candles, removed their clothes, and threw themselves on the bed. Cybele took control, soon bringing Dana to the threshold of excitement and beyond. Afterward, Dana luxuriated for a few moments before turning her attention to Cybele, beginning an intense lovemaking that left both women exhausted and enmeshed in a tangle of arms and legs.

Cybele drifted off to sleep, but Dana lay beside her, staring out the window, frightened to feel so happy, to have so much, and yet also painfully aware that her life had always been about losing people who mattered. She knew this fear was senseless—Cybele was a young, healthy woman—even so, she couldn't stop worrying.

Perceiving Dana's wakefulness, Cybele raised her head and slid her arm under Dana's neck. "Is something wrong?"

Dana was silent, unsure whether to reveal her irrational thoughts.

Cybele waited for a response, and when none came, she said, "Are you afraid I'll leave you? Like everyone else?" She sighed. "I know a little about it, about losing people. My father—he always made me laugh, Dana, like no one else until you. You remind me of him—tall and graceful, charming, and, yes, gallant. That is a word for men, yes? But I think it should apply to women also…to you." Cybele stroked Dana's cheek gently. "We can't be all things to each other. That's not possible. You must find meaning by yourself, and I must do the same. Still, we will be together and that is such a gift, such a wonderful thing that you give me and that I give you."

"How do you know me so well, so completely, in such a short time?"

Cybele considered the question. "It's because you pass through me like sunlight. I feel you and know you clearly. I can't explain this. It is so."

"How can I be the same for you?"

She shook her head slightly. "You do know me. The words will come later. For now, let's just listen and share a quiet place."

"You are so extraordinary."

"Ssh. It is time for you to sleep."

Dana switched positions, nestling Cybele's head below hers, tucking an arm around her shoulders. Dana heard her exhale, expressing the contentment she also felt. They slept.

CHAPTER TWENTY-THREE

The next morning, after dressing, Cybele made an omelet for breakfast. They enjoyed a few minutes together before Cybele departed for the station. Dana washed the dishes and lay on the sofa, reflecting on the previous night. A strange serenity flowed over her as if she were wading through a shallow lake that was warm and still. Her limbs felt deeply relaxed, her muscles loose and languid. Although little had been said, much had been revealed between them. With Cybele there seemed to be no bumps or corners; they poured into each other, and, in the confluence, Dana's wariness and distrust had mostly disappeared. Even so, a small, tight, knife-edge of fear pricked her elation—due to her anxiety about losing Cybele, but also because of an overshadowing dread that seemed very real, very present. Although the police had incarcerated Luca and Julian and one of them was possibly the killer, Dana sensed danger around her. And if it was around her, it was around Cybele too.

Roused by a loud knock on the door, Dana went downstairs to find Nikos with several envelopes in his hand.

"*Kalimera.*" He smiled and handed her the letters, one of which was a monthly check from her gallery in New York, payment for the photography workshops.

"*Kalimera*, Nikos. Thanks. I guess I'll need to go to the bank."

"I have to go myself. Would you like company?"

Dana suspected he was angling after an advance on the rent. "Okay. Just a minute." She ran upstairs to get her wallet and passport, and they headed off with Nikos whistling merrily.

"I think," he said, "that you have chosen well." He accompanied this judgment with a decisive nod.

"You've met Cybele, I understand?"

"Indeed I have. Oh, she is a very beautiful woman! And a police-woman too. That is what you need with all the trouble you get into! You are very lucky to find her, my friend!"

"I know, Nikos. I'm grateful to the gods and goddesses."

He grinned. "She is one of them, I think. For sure."

At the bank, Dana cashed part of the check and deposited the rest. It would easily pay her rent and living expenses until she left Mykonos. She handed Nikos a fat wad of bills, which he cheerfully accepted after feigning surprise.

They returned together, laughing, with Nikos telling stories about some of his clients and their humorous foibles. They said goodbye at Dana's apartment.

Upstairs, the telephone was ringing—Émile de Szasi. He asked how she was recuperating and commiserated with her about Bryan's death. At the end of the conversation, he invited Dana and Cybele for an after-dinner drink at Caprice. Dana accepted with pleasure.

She hung up the phone and descended to the darkroom, where she began heating the water in the color processor in order to print Cybele's favorite photograph and some images for the gallery. The paper was developed in a sealed canister, so when the top was uncapped, the effect was much like opening a present. Now and then a perfect beauty unfurled in front of her eyes.

Dana worked for two hours, took a lunch break, and returned to the darkroom, feeling the build-up of humidity from the processing liquids. Of the Greek photographs, those featuring whitewash were some of the most difficult to print since the slightest cast of incorrect color was immediately obvious. The evening shot that Cybele loved was easier, particularly after mastering other negatives on the same roll. Dana printed five: four for the gallery and one for Cybele.

By late afternoon, she was finished. Leaving the prints in the rack, Dana went upstairs to shower. She removed the bandage on her hand and dressed in a seafoam green knit top and white slacks. After adding jewelry, she descended to the kitchen, defrosted some frozen shrimp and calamari, sliced two cloves of garlic and an onion, and set out a pot and pan in preparation for cooking a pasta dinner. She had just finished tossing a salad when Cybele arrived.

Dana greeted her with a glass of wine. "Not up to last night's standards but adequate."

"I'm sure that it's more than adequate."

They sat together on the couch and talked about the events of her day. Cybele had been assigned to arrest a pickpocket at Ornos Beach. Everyone believed the culprit was a Romani, but Cybele thought it was an Algerian who was sleeping on the beach and begging for money near the cruise ship docks. On other matters, Captain Yalouris and her fellow officers were growing perturbed with the Schatzes and Paul Owens Merrill and were hoping they would tire of their activities and go home.

"They're still at the gay bars. We tried to talk to them many times, but they're stubborn." Cybele was irritated. "I don't understand this need to tell other people how to live, who they should love."

"Nor do I. You know, I read an article in the paper about the Schatzes. It mentioned that their group was being sponsored by a patron —someone they didn't name."

"I heard that too." Cybele rested her head on her hand, thinking. "I wonder if this person is here on the island? Or maybe it's someone in America."

Dana shrugged. "I have no idea, but these protests can't last. It must be expensive to pay for hotels and food for everyone. And I'm sure Walter will eventually miss his meat and potatoes, and the Schatzes' will head back to Iowa."

"Tomorrow is not soon enough."

Dana laughed. She then told her about the date with Émile. Cybele stared down at herself and said that she needed to shower. Without hesitation, she flew up the stairs while Dana set the table.

After dinner, Dana showed Cybele the prints. When she saw the evening shot with Little Venice and the sea, Cybele studied it intently and asked how much it could be enlarged.

"I can scan the negative in New York. Because the image is sharp, it can be printed big."

—

They walked the short distance along the sea wall to Caprice—Dana's favorite place. Its interior was whitewashed with niches cut out of the walls for flowers and candles. The long bar was dimly lit by triangular glass lamps above and by candles spaced along its length. In various alcoves, in various rooms, tables for two or four were placed; the white wooden chairs sported turquoise blue cushions on wicker seats. Dana's preferred spot was at the end of the bar where a couch backed up against a large, semi-circular window that opened to a majestic view of the Aegean. Spotlights outside were angled to reflect on the sea as it sprayed in the air as well as to light the promenade. The view was very similar to her apartment's, but with all the fresh bouquets of flowers, the music, and the friendly staff, it was an enchanting place to have a drink, to dance, to talk with someone special.

"Hello, stranger," said Irini, a barmaid with whom Dana had exchanged subtle flirtations on several occasions.

Cybele and Dana sat on the sofa. In front of them, placed on a low table, was a riotous spray of tall wildflowers, whose stems were held upright in holders set in a wide, flat bowl and submerged in water. Irini lit six tea candles that floated in the arrangement.

"There," she announced, snuffing the match. "Now, who is your attractive friend, Dana?" There was a certain degree of coyness in her question, as Irini frankly admired Cybele. Dana introduced them, and Cybele shook the barmaid's hand. Amused, Dana began to give Irini a drink order, but the waitress waved airily and walked away, returning with three glasses of wine. "To happiness," she said, smiling. Dana and Cybele thanked her and drank to her toast.

Émile arrived, his silver hair perfectly coiffed, his white shirt bright against a double-breasted black blazer. Dana stood and kissed him on both cheeks as did Cybele. He took Cybele's hands in his, tossing Dana a conspiratorial glance. "You look simply ravishing, Cybele! Doesn't she, Dana?" He stepped closer and examined Dana's face. "And you, you look pretty colorful, I must say. What do you think, Cybele? Is she any better?"

Cybele gave him a beautiful smile. "Yes, she is."

He winked at her. "I know you have nursed her with exquisite kindness."

Cybele nodded. "But of course!"

Émile walked to the bar, ordered a bottle of Perrier-Jouët, and returned to sit beside Cybele on the couch, inserting himself between her and a Frenchman, but not without casting an appreciative eye at him.

Out at sea, a ship's horn blew as they toasted each other. They chatted for a while, and then Dana asked how he was managing without Virgil. He grew quiet, his shoulders sagging despite the fine cut of his jacket.

"I really miss him. I'm sad, the house is sad, and I don't even turn my head when a gorgeous young thing passes by…well, maybe I do take a peek. Years of habit, you understand. I'm even thinking of going home early this year. You know I don't usually leave until the end of October."

"Yes, I know," Dana replied.

"Perhaps I'm feeling my age, but I can't imagine finding someone else after my dear, sweet Virgil."

This was a trifle disingenuous since Émile, despite his sixty years, never seemed to suffer the pangs of loneliness for long. However, losing Virgil was a significant loss.

"We'll miss you." Cybele placed a hand on his arm.

"Yes, we will," Dana agreed.

"Thank you," he said. "Oh, well. Maybe during the winter I'll meet someone skiing—some cute instructor who will have his way with me *après le leçon*. You know, in front of a big fire and all."

"Émile has a house in Gstaad," Dana explained.

"Oh, it's just a modest little chalet. But I would love to have you two come visit for a week or two."

"I don't know how to ski, Émile," Cybele told him.

Émile chuckled. "And she thinks all we do is ski! No, the indoor games are far more captivating, *cherie*. Although Dana does look splendid on the slopes. She cuts quite a line coming down the hill. She even has an outfit in this color." He pointed to Dana's aqua knit blouse. "Very stunning against the snow."

Cybele smiled. "I can imagine. And you, how do you keep busy?"

"I'm very creative about that. Lots of parties, lots of planning for parties, lots of recovering from parties. Oh, and there is the occasional guest who can't seem to tear himself away. Yes, I think it is time to head north." He poured another round of Champagne. "This is so cozy, isn't it? Dana and I love this place. We've talked about purchasing it, Dana and I, but the owner loves it as much as we do. It's one of my favorite bars in the world."

They ordered another bottle, brought by Irini with a smile that lingered on Dana. Soon their spirits lifted higher, and the conversation grew more animated. The music became louder, and the crowd thickened, spilling into other rooms and out onto the street and promenade. Cybele invited Dana to dance. Though there was no designated space, everyone understood that the area by the bar was for that purpose. Cybele asked the DJ to play a slow song by a Greek female vocalist with whom Dana was unfamiliar. Leaving Émile to hold their places on the sofa, the two women joined the group of dancers. Cybele placed her arms around Dana's waist, and Dana completed the enclosure, fusing them into one body, locked together. When the song ended, they continued their embrace, moving to the echoes of the music.

Then, distracted, they returned to Émile, who had been watching with amused approval. "*Bravi!*" he cried, clapping soundlessly with his hands. To Dana, he whispered, "I think much more of that and every man and woman here would have been on top of you two."

Dana blushed. "I'm sorry."

"There's nothing to apologize for! This is Mykonos, after all!" Émile replied.

"Even so—" As she began to speak, drops of seawater sprayed through the open window and onto their heads.

"That will cool you off!" Cybele exclaimed, laughing.

Émile clinked glasses with Cybele. Folding one leg over the other, he nestled against his seating partner to the side. When the handsome man turned in his direction, Émile apologized.

The man had large blue eyes, perhaps amplified in their liquidity by contact lenses. He laid a light hand on Émile's shoulder. "You have not disturbed me," he said in slow, accented English. "Perhaps you would like to dance?"

"*Avec plaisir, monsieur,*" Émile replied, taking the man's offered hand.

Cybele and Dana watched the couple. Émile, the older by decades, attempted to lead in a demure fashion. The Frenchmen sized up the situation and moved in under Émile's arms, grasping him tightly to bear pressure in the right location.

A moment later, Émile smiled at his partner, stepped away, and tapped his chest. "*Je suis désolé.*" Sighing, he returned to the sofa. "Too soon. I believe home is where I should be."

Cybele and Dana rose, and Dana tucked some money in Émile's pocket. They kissed him good night and watched him pay the bar bill and walk slowly toward the door.

"Maybe it's time for us to leave too," Cybele suggested.

"Yes. Unless you want to dance with me again?"

"I would love to, my dear, but I think it would be better if we did it at home." She threw Dana a meaningful look and swallowed the last of her drink, as did Dana.

Irini appeared and received a substantial tip. Dana told her, "*Kalini-hta*," but to her surprise, Irini moved in close and kissed her on the lips. The barmaid's intention was unclear, but before Dana knew what was happening, Cybele grabbed Dana's hand and yanked her away. Outside the bar, the next few steps with her were icy. Two chinks in Cybele's armor: she slammed doors and was jealous. At home, fueled by alcohol and a touch of green-eyed emotion, Cybele proceeded to make love with fierce possessiveness. After a kiss, she fell asleep.

Dana stayed awake, weighing her lover's response. In the end, Dana determined that she hadn't provoked Irini's sudden kiss, which she decided had been prompted by youthful spontaneity. Finally, feeling more settled, Dana drifted off.

—

THE MAN VOMITED and cursed himself for veering from eating fish and lighter foods and opting for a heavy, oily Greek stew. Did he have a fever? It felt like it. He rinsed his mouth with water and spat in the sink, wishing he was home in his large, comfortable bed. He thought about late afternoons there with Miss Becker, the sun streaming in through the windows onto his naked back. She liked to invent little punishments after he made up one of his stories. Her punishments were different than his father's. His father used the ruler, the same one the man used now, in the same brutal way.

CHAPTER TWENTY-FOUR

PERHAPS a bit ashamed due to her impassioned performance the night before, in the morning Cybele slipped out without disturbing Dana. When
the phone rang, Dana woke. It was Sandros, who asked how she was feeling and then explained that he had a nice bream courtesy of Mike
Garfield's successful fishing trip. He said the hotel chef had already
cleaned it and asked if he could bring the fish by since he had an errand to
do. She told him that would be fine.

When Sandros knocked on the door, Dana escorted him upstairs, put
the bream in the refrigerator, and offered coffee.

"Has Mike left?" she asked, placing a mug before him on the table.

"Not yet. Mr. Garfield went to pick up his film. After that, he goes to
the airport."

"I'm sorry I missed him. Will you tell him goodbye?"

He nodded and began to discuss an off-season construction project he
was planning, embellishing on his cleverness at negotiating prices. Once
Sandros exhausted that topic, he finished his coffee and left for his hotel.
Dana decided to go to the market with the intention of making repara-
tions for the previous evening, hoping that the way to her woman's heart
would be won by food. A half-block from her building, she ran into Theo,
who explained that Julian's aunt, armed with both an American and a

local attorney, had persuaded the authorities to release Julian into her custody because no additional incriminating evidence had been found. However, Julian wasn't permitted to leave Mykonos until the investigation was concluded. The aunt and nephew were staying at a beach hotel, where they were swimming, dining, and suffering their enforced visit in style.

"It's busy at the station," Theo said. "Our jails are full. We arrested that American protester, Walter Schatze, for blocking the door to a gay club with a wooden cross."

"What about his wife?" Dana asked. "Wasn't she there too?"

"Yes, she was, but it was Mr. Schatze who caused the problem."

Dana shook her head. "Those two are crazy."

Theo agreed. "Captain Yalouris may ask them to leave Mykonos."

"I hope he will. By the way, how is Luca Alessi?"

"Oh, not so good. He has an infection and must go to the hospital. Officers Tsoublekas and Karabélias will be driving him there."

Dana didn't like the sound of that, though she tried to reassure herself that two of them could handle Luca. Theo had errands to do, so she went on to the market, where she purchased eggs, milk, and cake mix. She had tackled dessert-making only once before, with her mother. Even if it was a complete disaster, Dana hoped to win some points for trying. This must be true love: her baking a cake.

By ten, she had combined the batter ingredients and was rooting in the storage cabinet for pans, dismayed to only find ones that had seen better days, probably before her birth. Determined, she forged on, ultimately producing a chocolate cake that would have caused Betty Crocker cardiac arrest. The neat little waves of icing illustrated on the box were a far cry from hers, which resembled a brown tempest. It was probably edible, she decided, laughing at herself.

Realizing she'd forgotten to buy ice cream to accompany the cake, which she feared might be dry, Dana left her creation on the kitchen counter. In front of Nikos' store, she bumped into Steve from the photo shop, who launched into an explanation of the Fuji printer's complex ailments and then asked Dana's advice about a lens he wanted to buy. She offered to show him hers, so he walked with her to the market, talked all the way, and returned to the apartment, where Dana demonstrated the lens on her camera.

—

THE DOOR to the Incidents Room was open, so Cybele walked in. A large black-and-white scanned print of Dana's photograph was pinned on the wall, the one taken on the morning of Malcolm Hall's murder. It was very coarse, with the monk's face—especially the shape of the nose—more obvious but not sufficiently recognizable unless the person were being observed at the identical angle. The hat and its scarf covered the sides and back of his head so that the style and length of his hair were unknown. Of interest, however, was what the killer carried: a shopping bag with Greek letters and a logo. She couldn't make out the type, but the line drawing below the letters was slightly visible. Where had she seen that design before? In Athens? She sat at the table and thought, trying to empty her mind so the connection would be made.

At that moment, one of the other senior members of the department entered.

"We need you and Myron to transport Luca Alessi to the hospital," he said.

"Myron isn't here." Cybele didn't want to drive Luca anywhere and said so. She thought she was on to something of significance with the enlargement.

He stiffened his tone and ordered her to go immediately, without a second officer. Cybele realized she would be in trouble if she refused. With a last glance at the shopping bag, she walked to Luca Alessi's cell.

Luca was no more pleased to see Cybele than she was to see him. Although he began a litany of insults as soon as she appeared, Cybele could see he was sick. A fine sheen of perspiration covered his forehead, and his gait was unsteady. His nose was discolored by bruises, and his left lower arm was in a cast. From what she could see of Luca's protruding fingers, they were swollen tight within their partial confinement and colored a furious purplish-red. Cybele helped him into the back seat of the police car and handcuffed his right hand to the door handle. Luca sat quietly for the ride except for an occasional moan when the car hit a rough patch of road.

Shortly after 10:30, they arrived at the hospital. Cybele uncuffed Luca and escorted him to the casting room, where he lay down on a gurney and closed his eyes. Cybele studied her charge, assessing his physical strength, and decided she could manage him in his weakened condition. A nurse in a lab coat entered the room. She sawed off the white cast and examined Luca's hand. The skin looked infected. In Greek, Cybele asked the nurse what she thought and wasn't surprised to learn that Luca would require intravenous antibiotics immediately. The woman told Cybele to find a male orderly to transport Luca to a room.

Cybele glanced at Luca. His good arm lay over his eyes while the nurse disinfected the other. Since he didn't speak Greek, Cybele knew he hadn't understood the nurse's plan. She should handcuff him to something immovable, but there was nothing suitable, nor could she cuff his hands together because of his broken wrist. Quietly, she opened the door and slipped into the hall, where she saw an aide in the far corridor, rolling a cart. Cybele dashed after him, but he answered a cell phone before she reached his side. She waited and finally interrupted, explaining the situation. He said he would come to the casting room in a minute.

Cybele rushed back. The door was closed, although she thought it had been ajar. Nudging it part way open with her foot, she saw that Luca was no longer on the gurney, and the nurse was nowhere to be seen in the section of the room that was visible. As Cybele took a step inside, the door slammed against her shoulder. She staggered and fell against the nearby wall, landing sprawled across a chair. Looking around, she saw the nurse's body on the floor. To the right was Luca, dressed in the woman's lab coat, a wild expression on his face. As she rose to grab him, he shoved a metal IV pole at Cybele. She protected her face but became tangled in the plastic tubing and bags of saline solution. When she struggled free, Luca was gone. Assuming he ran toward the lobby, she sprinted in that direction. The receptionist at the desk said that Luca hadn't come past. The woman placed a warning on the hospital's intercom, called security, and asked for a doctor to tend to the nurse. Cybele left and sped down the hall, almost flattening a guard turning the corner. They spoke briefly and separated, heading in different directions.

Fifteen minutes later, two hospital guards, three male orderlies, and Cybele convened in the lobby and agreed Luca had escaped. Ashamed and sore, Cybele called in a report and was ordered to return to the station and file paperwork. There, she was informed that she wouldn't be part of the search. Disgusted with herself, she was too annoyed to write up what happened. She tossed her pen and notebook on the desk, placed her belt and equipment in her locker, and signed out. Just before leaving, she walked into the Incidents Room to look at the scan again. Where had she seen that bag before? Suddenly, Cybele knew. Dana's photographs of the protesters! She took off for the apartment at a dead run.

When Cybele reached Dana's, she was out of breath. Inside, she yelled for Dana, but no one answered. As she was about to hurry upstairs, she saw the photo book by the enlarger. Hurriedly, she flipped to the prints of the protest, pulled them out, and stared at the last photo, the one taken at the taverna of a brown-haired man with a dark red shopping bag at his feet. The logo was the same as on the scan. Cybele examined a second photo, but in both cases, the man's head was blurred as if he had quickly turned his head away from the camera. However, the minister, Paul Owens Merrill, was staring at the man with the shopping bag and had raised his hand in greeting.

Cybele checked her watch: 12:35 p.m. What should she do? Police procedure was clear. Call Captain Yalouris and relate her findings. But her judgment had been disastrously wrong once already that morning. If she could learn the identity of the man with the bag, she might resurrect her reputation. Taking the two photos, Cybele raced out the door to Merrill's hotel, which she remembered from her police report.

As she waited for Merrill in the lobby, she wondered if he and the man with the bag were working together. If so, she was taking a chance interviewing Merrill alone, without a partner and without a weapon.

When the minister appeared, he strolled toward her, an expression of distaste engraved on his face. "What can I do for you, Officer?" he asked. "Have you come to find Jesus or have you come to ask me more foolish questions?"

Cybele ignored him. She held up the photographs and tapped the picture of the man sitting outside the taverna. "Do you know who this is?"

Merrill slowly pulled out a pair of eyeglasses and accepted the prints. His face hardened as he seemed to consider his answer. Sighing, he said, "Yes, I know him. Why are you interested?"

"What's his name?" Cybele asked.

"That is Mr. Sirman."

"How do you know him?"

"He's involved in the clinic that I run in Iowa."

Cybele considered her next move. She couldn't hold Merrill without handcuffs, which she didn't have, or without assistance, though she doubted Merrill was the killer, as much as she disliked the man. She hoped her instincts were accurate.

"Is Mr. Sirman still here on Mykonos?"

"He doesn't like to be disturbed. He's on retreat."

"You will either tell me where he is, or I will arrest you immediately!"

The minister studied her, weighing private thoughts. Finally, he told her the address. "I assume you're interested because of the murders."

"Yes," she replied, surprised.

He exhaled a long breath. "Well, go find him."

—

It was a long trek by foot, past the windmills and up the steep hill. The sun was hot and fiercely yellow against the blue sky. As the town disappeared below her, Cybele rounded a curve, walked another mile or more, and arrived at the address Merrill had given her. She stopped and wiped the perspiration from her face, feeling oddly unnerved by the house's scarlet door and the forbidding façade. Only two small, deeply inset windows faced the street; their trim was also painted red. The glass on the one to the left of the door had been blackened, which struck her as peculiar; the other was covered by a heavy dark drape.

Cybele hesitated. Should she be prudent or should she follow her overpowering impulse to take independent action? Deciding that further investigation was a rational move, she skirted the house, maintaining a cautious distance. The building's sides were longer than the front, and the walls were solid and thick, unbroken except for two windows whose glass had also been blackened. The house seemed more like a chapel than someone's home, which wasn't unusual because Mykonos was dotted with hundreds of such places, though the roof wasn't decorated with a cross. The large yard was untidy, full of debris, including a broken truck and a wooden handcart. The nearest neighbors were hundreds of feet away, if anyone lived in those houses. Around the back, Cybele noticed a partially opened door. She paused, knowing it was unwise to proceed, but finding the killer would repair her damaged reputation. And, besides, she was really curious. She stepped inside.

—

THE MAN was relieved that Miss Becker was so prescient. They had been talking about his pleasures, the pleasures that excited her as much as they excited him. Suddenly, she rose to her feet and crept to the front window, fingering the black drape an inch away from the frame. When he joined her, the man was astonished to see a policewoman on the street. Miss Becker let the curtain fall and then told him what to do. He hurried down the dark hall and unlocked the rear door, leaving it ajar.

Miss Becker pulled him into the kitchen and handed him an iron frying pan.

"Don't kill her. Just knock her out," she whispered.

He obeyed, as he always had.

Afterward, he smiled, imaging all the delightful activities he and Miss Becker would devise for the woman.

—

Several hours later, the man stood watch on Solomou and Katsoni Streets, alternating his location to avoid appearing suspicious. He had taken the apartment key and the two color photographs from the police-woman, but he didn't possess the negatives, nor did he have Dana Fox. She had seen the pictures and could recognize him. She had invaded his privacy, threatened his secrets. His secrets and Miss Becker's. She couldn't be left alive.

He moved closer to "Bryan's corner," as he thought of it. There were quite a number of tourists and locals milling about and a couple sitting next to the aqua door. First, they had been talking; now they were kissing—a display that was disgusting. Their proximity prevented the man from entering the apartment because they might remember him. A few minutes after five, a shopkeeper asked what he was doing. The man spun a story about waiting for a woman. Even though the fool accepted it, it wasn't safe to stay. He would return after dark.

—

DANA HAD TAKEN a nap. Feeling renewed, she set the table, prepared dinner, and began playing a CD, a Grieg "Humoresque," to pass the time until Cybele arrived. Twenty minutes later, the phone rang. Damn! Was she going to be late?

"Hello, Miss Fox? This is Captain Yalouris."

"Good evening, how are you?"

"I am well. But we have some bad news."

Cybele? She was instantly in a panic. "Yes?"

"It's about Mr. Alessi." He paused, then said, "I was unable to call you earlier, but I'm sorry to say he escaped from the hospital."

"Oh, no!" Horrified, she swallowed hard. Luca was free?

Before she could ask for details, Captain Yalouris continued. "In the room where they remove the casts, Mr. Alessi attacked the nurse as well as Officer Karabélias and vanished."

What? Was Cybele hurt? In a panic, Dana tried to question him, but several loud voices could be heard from his end. "Excuse me, Miss Fox, I must attend to an emergency. Be careful and keep your door locked. I'll call when I have news." He hung up.

Tight with anxiety, Dana stared at the sea and quickly telephoned the police station. She was told that Officer Karabélias was off duty. With reluctance, the woman accepted a message, though she explained it was unlikely Cybele would receive it until the following day. Dana called Cybele's apartment. No answer. She slammed her fist on the arm of the sofa. What should she do? Was Cybele tracking Luca? Dana tried the hospital, but the receptionist would only say that Officer Karabélias did not require medical attention and had left about eleven that morning.

Despite Luca's infection, Dana respected his capacity for vengefulness. Although the hospital was about five miles inland, he could easily hitchhike into town, where Cybele probably was looking for him now. Dana forced herself to wait for another half hour, expending her nervousness by pacing the length of the living room.

While wearing out the floorboards, it occurred to her that perhaps Cybele hadn't returned because she was still annoyed by Irini's flirtatious kiss. Even taking into account Cybele's jealous nature, Dana had trouble justifying this as a possibility. Nevertheless, the thought kept dripping into her head like acid. She recalled Cybele's over-reaction at Orpheus' Lyre when that jerk had been flirting with her. Could this be the same kind of thing? She couldn't imagine it was. Still, where was she?

Dana phoned Cybele's apartment again, left a message on the machine, and resumed pacing. At 6:30, she was making herself crazy. She jotted a note for Cybele and started for the police station, first at a walk and then at a run. Before going in, she stopped to catch her breath, praying that a miracle would prevail, and Cybele would be sitting calmly at her desk. However, the station was empty except for the receptionist, a secretary, and Theo. When he saw Dana, he smiled and greeted her.

"Do you know where Cybele Karabélias is?" she asked him without preamble.

He shook his head. "I can check to see if she is still on duty, if you like?"

"No, she's not. I called earlier and also heard from Captain Yalouris about Luca Alessi's escape."

"Maybe she's involved with the search for him," he offered.

"I doubt it."

"All I know is that when Officer Karabélias left to find a hospital aide, Mr. Alessi attacked the nurse, and when Karabélias returned, he hit her and ran."

"Is Cybele okay?"

"Yes, I saw her earlier. Perhaps she's at her apartment?"

Dana was greatly relieved to have a second verification that Cybele was unhurt, but her disappearance was ominous. "No, she isn't. I think something is wrong. Will you please contact Captain Yalouris and tell him that Cybele is missing? I'm very worried."

Theo put through the message and confirmed that Cybele wasn't part of the search. Captain Yalouris agreed to alert his staff to look for her and told Theo to give Cybele's home address to Dana. Unsure what to do next, Dana hesitated and then rushed outside. Ten minutes later, she knocked loudly on Cybele's door. No one was there. Where was she?

Her anxiety doubled. And where was Luca? The flights and boats were undoubtedly being screened by the police, so that unless he bribed a fisherman, it would be difficult for him to leave Mykonos without being caught. And Luca couldn't bribe anyone without money—his wallet was probably locked in the station. However, there were numerous places for him to hide. Even on foot, Luca could find a quiet lair without too much trouble.

Dana sat on a wall to consider the situation. Cybele might be at Dana's place, laughing at the chocolate cake. Dana didn't think so. She closed her eyes, trying to empty her mind of all thoughts in order to imagine where Cybele was, but nothing came. Deeply frustrated and growing increasingly more fearful, Dana walked aimlessly, hoping her mind would use her legs like a Ouija board planchette, sending them in the right direction.

After almost an hour of meandering, Dana noticed that the sun was setting, and shadows shrouded the streets. She decided to return to her apartment. It was a long walk back, but when Dana opened the door, she knew the house was empty.

It was just before nine. There were no phone messages. Upset, she sat on the sofa, head in hand. Dana was positive that Cybele would have called, even if she were nettled about last night. She began to imagine all sorts of scenes with Luca that became more macabre as the minutes ticked by. She kept reminding herself that Cybele was trained in martial arts and that with Luca's infected arm, he wouldn't be much competition. On the other hand, he had bested Cybele earlier. Dana wanted to remain in case Cybele telephoned or arrived, yet she was in a fever to move. When the urgent restlessness became impossible to ignore, Dana decided to burn off some adrenaline by searching one last time before contacting the police again.

The town was jumping, with waiting lines at all the restaurants. Dana walked through the dense crowd toward the gay clubs, wondering about Mary Lou Schatze and whether she would find another protester to join her. Cybele had said the Schatzes ate dinner promptly at seven before beginning their nightly harassment, but there was no sign of Mary Lou or any of the other troublemakers. The bars were fairly empty, which was usually the case until later.

A few streets from the harbor, her thoughts turned to the killer. Was it conceivable that he had attacked Cybele? It didn't fit his pattern, but he had murdered Devin Scott for practical reasons. Perhaps he had seen her and Cybele together and realized they were connected. Dana tried to visualize the person in the photograph. Could it have been Walter Schatze? But he was in jail—or had they let him go? And what about that minister? Cybele didn't like him. She hadn't said as much, but it was clear that she was suspicious about his activities. Had Merrill waited near the station for Cybele to leave, then followed her? And though she didn't believe Julian Witten was the killer, he was free again. As much as she tried, Dana couldn't fit the pieces together, which led her to consider whether her photography assignments might benefit her analysis. Everyone had been scouring the island for a subject, a person who would be recognizably evil. In fact, perhaps the killer was striving to be less obvious, more "ground" than "figure." Was he present in a crowd, blending in? Was he a "yin," a dark shadow, invisible in the "yang" of the bright sun? Her mind kept circling back to the angry protesters, the Schatzes, and Merrill, all of whom stood out and were noticed. Were they diversions? The more she weighed the situation, the more she felt that a subtle clue as to the murderer's identity was hidden in the recesses of her mind.

Dana continued to a small square, a favorite haunt of Petros the Pelican. A taverna owner fed him scraps of leftover fish after lunch and again after dinner, hoping to keep the tourist attraction near his restaurant. Petros, however, was elsewhere. Instead, a pack of mangy street cats were scrounging around the door. At the top of Kastro Hill, the whitewashed buildings glowed bluish-white in the moonlight. The thudding beat from a disco reverberated through the ground, sounding—to her ears—less cheerful and more threatening, as if the drums were warning of peril. From a club nearby, bouzouki music, clapping, and shouts of laughter emanated. The typical island exuberance, which usually delighted Dana, now struck her as violently discordant, a painful contrast to her misery.

Exhausted, she leaned against a wall and surveyed the port. The boats were pitching at their anchors; metal stays and rigging whined in a breeze that was beginning to freshen. Dana shivered. Somewhere on this barren rock of granite was Cybele. Was she hurt or lying dead on a street or deserted beach? Had Luca or the killer abducted her? "Oh, where are you?" she cried.

Dana started walking. The wind blew over her shoulder, following her up from the harbor, whistling in the tunnel of the alleyway and flapping a rainbow flag hanging outside a jewelry store. Tears came to her eyes and slipped down her cheeks. She felt lost, too tired to stitch together any course of action. Helpless, like on a dark Nantucket night long ago. Covering her face in her hands, Dana stopped as anguish overtook her. Sobbing, she wanted to sink to her knees, to collapse onto the pavement. However, the chance she might find Cybele kept her upright. After taking a large breath, Dana wiped her tears and continued to Little Venice. The waves were crashing onto the narrow beach below, but she scarcely heard them, nor did she notice the crowd of people sitting outside Caprice, although they were laughing and talking loudly. Facing the sea, Dana let the wind evaporate the moisture on her face while she fished in her pocket for the house key.

As she made her way down the promenade, Dana looked up. Someone was leaving her apartment! Someone who wasn't Cybele. The man's back was to her. He was dressed in black, wore a baseball cap, and carried a bag. She should call the police, but there wasn't time. The man would disappear.

Dana dashed after him, checking as she went past her door that the lock was intact. How had he opened it? With Cybele's key? Her heart pounded. She increased her pace, matching his, and observed how deftly he followed the shadows along the street, drifting left and right, so that he was sometimes invisible before breaking again into a small section of light. The man was a phantom exploiting the darkness.

Who was he? Why had he been in her apartment? And where was Cybele?

CHAPTER TWENTY-FIVE

THE MAN KNEW he was being tracked. From a shadowed area, he peeked over his shoulder and noticed the woman's blond hair. It was Dana Fox! Laughter burst out of him. He had been waiting in her apartment, hoping she would return so that he could kill her there and finish this business with the photographs; he had the prints and had just removed the matching negatives. A pity that he had departed too soon, but leaving Miss Becker alone with the prisoner had concerned him. But now what should he do? Hide and attack Dana Fox here above the town? Or was it safer to lure her into the house, as he had done earlier with her dark-haired partner? If she were successfully captured, he and Miss Becker would have leisure time for their special, private experiments. The man smiled at this agreeable prospect. Dana Fox was chasing him, but the hunter would become his prey.

—

DID HE REALIZE Dana was following him? The man walked briskly past the windmills, the community parking area, up the hill above the town, and entered a neighborhood of modest houses, most owned by local residents. Fewer people were on the street, and as she rounded a curve and the houses thinned, she saw no one except the man ahead of her. The area was darker, with only occasional lights emanating from homes, and the moon was now choked by clouds. Dana navigated a rough section of road, and, when she looked up, the man had disappeared. Where was he?

Had he entered the house on the left? It was thick-walled, with a curtained window and one window whose glass had been painted opaque black. Nothing was visible inside—not even a glimmer of light. Was the place deserted? Dana approached the door and turned the knob. Locked. Placing her ear against the wood, she listened and heard no sounds. Maybe the man had entered from the back? As she crept through the tall grass and mounds of junk littering the grounds, she sensed Cybele's presence. Her pulse quickened with anticipation and fear.

At the rear of the building was a second, smaller door. This one was partially open. Should she enter? Not without a weapon. Dana scoured the backyard and found a two-foot metal post lying on a pile of wood. Grasping it tightly, she walked through the weeds, edged near the door, and peered inside. An empty, dark hall led into blackness, though she could faintly see closed interior doors. All was silent until Dana heard a voice. A woman's voice? It was muffled, yet it sounded like Cybele! Dana rushed forward, shouting her name. Then, just behind her shoulder, she saw an object flying toward her head. Instinctively, she threw up her arm, but it was too late.

—

When Dana regained consciousness, her hands were tied together in front. Her fingers tingled from lack of circulation. She had no idea as to the hour, though she vaguely recalled someone sticking a needle in her arm. She was lying on a narrow pallet. The room was dark and smelled of the sea, damp and cool, but there were other scents too: candlewax and lavender incense and cigarette smoke. Dana looked for a window, saw none, and assumed she was being held in an interior area. Remembering the curtains and blackened glass, she thought the house's owner was pathologically secretive. Of course, a killer would be.

Dana knew she had to escape, but when she tried to sit up, her body felt extremely heavy. Any movement produced dizziness. Flopping over on her side was the best she could do. Dana slept.

She was awakened by hands clamping her arms and legs and another sharp needle jab. Though her eyes wouldn't focus well, Dana perceived a black figure standing in front of a niche lit by two tall, white candles in gleaming brass holders. Between the candles was a large Byzantine icon, a painted Jesus on a cross with his head wreathed in a gold-leaf halo that pulsed with light as the candles guttered. She closed her eyes to dispel the gauziness, but the drug slammed into her brain, powering swiftly through her nervous system.

At some time later, Dana floated out of oblivion. She heard rhythmic chanting, low and deep; the words were undecipherable. When the voices stopped, someone cried out her name. Cybele? Or was that a hallucination? Silence. And then more sounds nearby. Dana fell asleep. When she opened her eyes again, she gasped. A person in a black head-scarf and robe stood beside the bed. A man or a woman? The Monk? The dark form was silhouetted against the glow of the candles. Although she was terrified, Dana was having difficulty staying awake. Her consciousness felt slippery, as if her mind couldn't gain purchase.

"Where is Cybele?" she whispered.

"Is she a friend?" A stern, male voice asked. "Or is she your lover?"

Dana didn't answer.

"Ah, it's as I suspected. You have sex together." The figure stepped closer. "Do you repent?"

She shook herself, trying to stay focused.

"You must repent if you are to live purely…and you must be pure. You have done sinful things, but now you must see the light of God."

"What are you talking about?" Her speech was slurred.

"What abominations you and that woman have practiced! That is what I'm talking about! Boys lying with boys, girls lying with girls.

Abominations! Unnatural practices!" The voice was practiced, preachy. A minister?

"Who are you?"

"I am your savior, your light, your guiding angel!" The man's laughter was chilling. "I will save you from the degradations of your misguided choice."

An American. Where had she heard the voice before? Walter Schatze? Luca? The faint rasp was distantly familiar. Surely not Mike. Julian? Julian's voice was too high. Then she wondered about David. She hadn't actually seen him leave the island, but, no, it couldn't be David. David's tone was creamy, like a bass opera singer, and David was taller. Looking through the narrow slit in the man's scarf, Dana noted that the skin around the man's eyes was white.

"What's your name?" she asked.

A low chuckle rose from his throat. "My name is appropriate for my calling."

Suddenly, Dana became aware that her breathing was labored, that it took more effort to draw air into her lungs. Not serious, but not normal.

"Where is Cybele?" she demanded again.

"We will bring her to you in time. After you have totally acquiesced. When you no longer want her, you may see her."

"How are you going to do that?"

"There are ways. Most women are weak. God made them pliant so man would have control. You have rebuffed the ways of God, declaring that you are like a man yourself, that you may lie with a woman as the man should. This is depraved and wicked. In your heart and soul, you want to return to your natural state. We will help you."

Dana didn't like the sound of that. She tried another angle. "Where am I?"

"You are in my sanctum, on a bed that is beholden by the eye of God. He is considering your story, observing you. Soon, he will touch your mind and your body when he deems that you are ready. He will do this through me. I am the instrument of his divine forgiveness or his divine retribution. You will do whatever I wish." The figure turned and walked toward the shrine, where another person in black faced the gold icon, head bowed in prayer.

A touch of rebellion oozed through her lethargy. "Why will I?"

"Women must bend to the wishes of men. Men dominate women," he said over his shoulder.

"Why did you kill Malcolm, Virgil, and Bryan? And Devin?"

"Devin was a nuisance," he scoffed. "The others were weak, addicted to receiving each other's sacred fluids. Their souls couldn't be rescued. When a man corrupts his body, he has defiled himself forever. It was a mercy to end their lives. And necessary so that they could not spill their seed and taint the bodies of other young men." His voice sounded distracted as if he were aroused by the imagery he described. "Every night, I watch them, coupling in alleyways, their pants down around their ankles, thinking they are alone, unseen by God and his servant. But I know where they walk, where they seek each other out. I go there and find them. Wait until they fornicate, and then I follow in the darkness, and when God instructs, I fall upon them. They are blessed with a quick death." From within a pocket of his robe, he removed a wire that was formed at the ends into loops wrapped with tape.

The garrote.

He hid the wire again and continued in a sing-song voice reminiscent of an incantation: "And the Lord told me that the boy should be judged in the naked flesh just as he was issued naked through the womb of his mother." The man paused, breathing through his mouth as if to control himself. "So I removed their clothes. In two of the boys, their members were upright, pointing to God. Because these two would go to heaven, I blessed their members, as the Lord blesses mine. I was also told to paint their bodies like women, to sully their flesh, to mark their shame." His voice constricted slightly, and suddenly he walked from the room followed by the second person. Dana could dimly see a connecting passage to the left of the shrine.

She tried to work her hands loose, but the ropes were tight. Then she remembered hearing Cybele. Had it really been her?

"Cybele!" Dana intended to shout, but the drug ravaged the volume. Even marshalling her thoughts seemed to take gargantuan effort. Had she been injected with an opiate? Morphine? Her body seemed curiously free of pain, which might support this theory. Dana shook her head, trying to remain conscious, yet she felt so drowsy.

—

The candles, disturbed by a faint draft from the adjoining hall, were pooling wax on the floor. Dana heard a door open. A woman in black entered the room—or at least it appeared to be a woman. The robed figure stood in front of the crucifixion. Kneeling, she began to pray. "God bless us this day for we do your work. Bless us with your pure love. Shine down upon us and these misguided souls. Let your wisdom prevail." She mumbled other words before turning and walking toward Dana. Her face was partly obscured by a large black scarf, and her figure was backlit by the candlelight. Even so, Dana sensed the woman was smiling.

"We hope that you'll chose to be saved, Dana, my dear. I have prayed for you and your friend. Your fate is in the hands of the Lord and with yourself. He has directed us to provide a sacred liquid for when you are ready to receive it, when you shall be blessed."

"Where is Cybele?" Dana whispered urgently. "Please, tell me! What have you done to her? Is she all right?"

"She is near. But you must no longer think of her with lust in your heart. You may love her only like a friend."

When the woman's scarf dropped a few inches, Dana saw a glint of bright white teeth. And the voice? Dana recognized it. "Mary Lou! It's you! Untie me! Help me get loose!"

"I can't do that."

"Then free Cybele. Let her go."

"It isn't within my power. She has sinned."

"Please! If you release her, I'll renounce anything you wish. I'll do whatever you want. Anything."

Mary Lou was silent for a long time.

Dana couldn't stay awake, as frightened as she was. When she opened her eyes after a brief sleep, the woman was still present. "What time is it?"

"It doesn't matter to you," Mary Lou replied with frightening serenity. "Let yourself go; forget where you are. Let the Lord take you into his embrace."

All this heavenly palaver was not helping Dana's disorientation, which was, of course, the intention. "Can I have some water? And may I use a bathroom?"

"He does not like any attention to the body," Mary Lou replied ambiguously, "but I will ask."

Mary Lou blew out the candles and disappeared into the blackness. Once Dana's eyes adjusted, she saw a dim light from the hall that adjoined the room. A few minutes later, Mary Lou returned with the man, whose face was almost covered by a piece of black material. Both passed in front of the light, hands were placed on Dana's arms, and she was raised to her feet. Her legs wobbled as they half-carried her across the room. In the hall, a glow emanated from under a door.

"Cybele!" Dana cried out.

There was no response. Though she tried to resist, she was too weak and was dragged forward into a bathroom lit only by a faint light that pierced through a tiny section of the window where the black paint had been chipped. Whether it was night or day she couldn't tell. While the man stepped into the hall, Mary Lou remained. She unzipped Dana's pants, handed her some toilet paper, and then left. While relieving herself, Dana worked frantically to reach the knots but had no success before the door opened again. Mary Lou gave her some water.

"Nothing to eat?" Dana asked.

"No. You must fast before your purification."

Purification didn't sound entrancing. She was pulled to her feet and immediately staggered against the wall. The man, smelling of cigarette smoke, joined Mary Lou in the near darkness, and together they guided her into the room with the candles and icon and eased Dana onto the mattress. Mary Lou lit one candle, and the black-robed figure—was it The Monk or was it Walter Schatze?—held her down while Mary Lou tricked out another syringe, filled it, and jabbed it home. He grunted his satisfaction and exited the room.

"What are you, a nurse?" Dana whispered, trying to fight the potent effect of the drug.

Miss Sweetness was unperturbed by the sarcasm. "No, but I assist my husband. He's a vet. Large animal practice."

This was getting better and better. The injections were being monitored by an amateur who was used to cows and horses. Dana realized that too high a dose or injections too close together could be fatal. Respiratory failure, coma, death—all possible. And was Walter the man in black or were there two of them? If it was Walter, why hadn't he administered the shot? And why hadn't the man's voice sounded like Walter's?

"Say your prayers. We really do want you to be saved," Mary Lou said. "Put all lustful thoughts out of your mind and think only of God."

Whether it was the opiate making her feel ill or Mary Lou's speech, Dana didn't know. "What are the steps to salvation?" she mumbled.

"Oh, honey, there are many, many steps. You must give yourself over so that you may receive God and his righteous sword."

The morphine hit like a brain-numbing warm wave. If this was supposed to be pleasurable, you couldn't prove it by her. Dana tried to concentrate on what Mary Lou was saying. Something about receiving God's sword? That conjured up some frightening images. She wasn't well-versed in the Bible, but this wasn't any text she knew. As Mary Lou blew out the candles and left, Dana shuddered into sleep.

—

THE MAN WALKED down the dark hall, opened the door into the kitchen, and switched on a lamp. Although he was pleased to gratify his teacher's desires, the presence of Dana and Cybele would distract him from his mission. When he was conceiving his visit to Mykonos, the plan had been to kidnap gay men and bring their drugged bodies to the rented house, using the morphine to subdue them while he and Miss Becker conducted their physical investigations. But, regrettably, the rental agent had misled him about the distance from the house to the gay bars, and he had been forced to satisfy himself with a more expedient pleasure—using the garrote.

Pulling out a stool, the man sat down. He possessed the negatives, the photos, the photographer, and her lesbian consort. Because no one else had approached the house, he was probably safe. But how had the policewoman found him? She refused to say. For now.

He reached into a cabinet and poured two tots of vodka. Miss Becker joined him, and they discussed what little dramas might be planned for the two captives. She was fond of his tale about the woman he'd picked up in the MG long ago, but the man desired more spectacular, protracted activities for the two women. With all the wondrous possibilities, they were unable to select their favorites. Miss Becker reminded him that the schedule of injections needed considering. At first, she had been timing them so they had an opportunity to sleep while the women were unconscious, but, during the day, she had been testing dosages to ascertain what would be enough to control the women but not enough to knock them out. After all, it was important that they participate in the experiments. The man agreed, imagining Dana Fox's eyes wide with fear as she begged him to stop, begged for his benevolence, a scene that was delightful to contemplate. Although the photographer wasn't his usual fare, he harbored special hatred for her because she had made his visit to this island so complicated.

—

IT WAS ASTONISHING how bewildered she felt. Her head was clearer, so Dana presumed it was four to six hours later, if the injected drug was similar to morphine, which she had received in a hospital after the car accident. But four to six hours later than what? The space was so black that she began to hallucinate: First the room appeared enormous, then it suddenly collapsed into a coffin-sized space, airless and suffocating. Her labored breathing didn't help dispel this last delusion. Terrified, Dana tried to convince herself that the place was large, but the crazy claustrophobia consumed her reason. Her skin prickled and she felt sick. Tears stung her eyes and etched hot trails down her face. Slowly, the room changed again, tilting sideways and producing vertigo and disintegrating her spatial orientation. She envisioned herself stuck between two glass planes, which threatened to compress like giant microscope slides. Dana wanted to close her eyes and make it all go away, but, when she did, the sensation was inside her, zooming around crazily. She opened her eyes again and saw the black Mercedes coming straight at her, faster and faster, engulfing the narrow road as it accelerated. Instinctively, she sat bolt upright. As she did, Dana realized the car didn't exist and there was nothing immediately above her head. The mental imagery of being trapped disappeared. Scared and shaken, she forced herself to swing her legs over the edge of the bed, to recall the actual construction of the room—where things were and how far away. As best as she could remember, the area was bare except for the two candleholders in front of the shrine. Dana gritted her teeth and made herself step into the blackness. Trying to use sensory radar, she inched forward, hoping her shaky legs wouldn't collapse. After several steps, she encountered the wall that backed up on what she supposed was Cybele's room. Trailing her hands along it, Dana reached ahead for the door. When she found the knob, it was locked. Silently, Dana cursed.

Another blitz of dizziness struck. Leaning against the wall, she tried to steady herself, to chase away the panic and devise a plan. She recalled the look of the candlesticks: heavy, brass, about three feet high. One would be a formidable weapon. The trick would be to grab one in the dark without knocking either candlestick over and making noise. After what seemed like twenty yards, her outstretched hands touched cold, carved metal. She curled her fingers around it, appreciating its weight, and retreated to a corner that wouldn't be immediately visible if the door opened. Dana sat cross-legged on the floor and gripped the candlestick between her knees. She removed the thick candle from the holder's sharp point, placed the candle behind her, and began rubbing the two-inch point against the rope bound around her wrists. It took an eternity before she felt the binding fray and finally release. Her heart pounding, she listened for any sounds of movement in the house. All was still. Mary Lou had probably overslept or forgotten the next injection. Dana was willing to praise the good Lord for that. A fickle atheist, indeed.

She then contemplated her method of attack. The metal point would cause a vicious wound if thrust dead on, but this wasn't possible because she would need to stand to the side of the door, so that when it was opened and light shone in, she couldn't be seen. Dana hid the rope in the corner and crawled into position. Who would be first? If it was Mary Lou and not the man, knocking her out wouldn't help much because it would warn him. Even so, the candlestick would provide some defense.

She grasped the candlestick, though it was so heavy that she rested its tip on the floor. Another bout of sleepiness hit her. Shaking her head to make herself more alert, Dana waited.

—

CYBELE HAD HEARD the noise in the hall when Dana arrived, although at the time she hadn't been sure it was her and not another victim. When Dana had cried out a little while ago, however, Cybele recognized her voice. She would have responded except for the duct tape across her mouth.

Her hands tied, Cybele lay on the bed, agonized with worry, yet hopeful that the next injection might be delayed. Already, the side effects of the opiate were receding.

CHAPTER TWENTY-SIX

PEOPLE WERE speaking in a quiet murmur. Dana rose unsteadily, her muscles aching, and lifted the heavy candlestick to a batting position. Down the hall, a door opened. To Cybele's room? A second afterward, the door closed, and footsteps approached. A key was inserted in the door's lock. They wouldn't send Cybele in first, would they? No time to hesitate. A figure walked inside; Dana swung hard. Solid contact, the crunch of bone. Mary Lou cried out as she slumped heavily to the floor. Dana drew back for another blow, but Mary Lou was doubled over, whimpering with pain. Stepping over the woman's body, Dana crept to the next door on the left, the one she thought led to Cybele. She turned the handle and gave a tiny shove. A sharp angle of light crossed the threshold. With a pounding heart, Dana raised the candlestick and pushed the door open. Lying on a mattress, her mouth taped, her hands bound, was Cybele. She was shaking her head, her eyes wild with fear. Dana entered and there was a sudden movement as a silver wire sliced through the air. Instinctively, Dana jerked the brass candlestick upward and managed to get it within the wire as it tightened around her throat. She turned and saw the man in the black cassock. The cold green eyes staring at her were those of Ray Johnson, the man who had bought her a drink at Orpheus' Lyre.

They exchanged looks of profound hatred. Then he began to twist the garrote. As the wire bit into the sides of her neck, Dana surprised him by jolting backward. They crashed to the floor, and he released the garrote. Dana rolled onto her knees, shook the wire off, and thrust the point of the candlestick into his cheek, drawing blood. Ray grasped the candlestick with his left hand and tugged it away, ripping a deeper wound and unbalancing Dana. He raised his body against the wall, swung his right fist, and delivered a blow above her ear. Stunned, she tilted away, but when Ray was about to throw another punch, Dana jerked upright and swiftly whipped the candlestick to the left, lodging it against his throat. His hands flew up to grab it and his knee raised, bumping Dana forward and pushing the point into his windpipe. Ray's eyes popped open in shock. Like a fish sucking for air, his mouth gaped wide. She pulled the candlestick out, and his fingers rushed to cover the hole in his trachea. Blood instantly clogged the passage, gurgling and spilling over his fingers until the last whistle of air hissed through his windpipe, and his arms slithered lifelessly to the floor.

Leaning on her hand so she wouldn't topple over, Dana inhaled and exhaled, frantic to breathe. She felt lightheaded and sick, wired from adrenaline and dulled by morphine. As she slowly stood and turned toward Cybele, who was trying to shout despite the tape, Dana glimpsed movement by the door. Mary Lou stepped into the room. Her posture was hunched from the earlier blow; her mouth formed a taut line. A carving knife was in her hand.

Dana swung the candlestick around. "Mary Lou, put down the knife."

Mary Lou glared at Dana, and then she saw Ray. Her expression turned from alarm, to horror, to fury. She lunged at Dana and sliced her left forearm with the knife. Blood poured out, and Dana dropped the candlestick to clutch the wound. As Mary Lou was about to strike again, Cybele rushed from the bed and slammed into her. The blade caught in the epaulette of Cybele's uniform and grazed her shoulder. Although Cybele twisted free, Mary Lou had a good grip on the knife and drew it back for a second attack. Quickly, Dana picked up the candlestick, balanced, and swung hard, smashing Mary Lou's hand. The knife skittered onto the marble floor, and Mary Lou seized her crushed fingers. Uttering a piercing scream, she crumpled on top of Ray.

Dana faced Cybele. The candlestick slid from her hand and landed with a thud. In a daze, she removed the gray tape covering Cybele's mouth.

"Dana! Look at your arm! Stop the bleeding!"

She didn't answer because she couldn't feel anything. Without speaking, Dana grasped the knife and cut the rope binding Cybele's hands. As the room began to spin, she gazed at the blood on her white shirt and trousers and coating her hands, astonished that most of it was hers. The red seemed to pulsate and spread, threatening to blot out her vision.

Just as Cybele was about to help her, Mary Lou staggered to her feet.

"You killed Ray!" She raised her fist, but Cybele blocked the punch and kicked Mary Lou's leg from under her. As Mary Lou tried to stand, Cybele delivered a chop to the top of her head. The woman pitched forward, unconscious.

Dana began swaying as if the floor was undulating beneath her. Her legs buckled and she tumbled against the bed, painting the sheets with blood, and then fell onto the floor. A moment later, she was turned over. With half-closed eyes, Dana watched Cybele shred a cotton sheet with the knife, bind her arm, and secure the cloth by splitting one strip in two.

Elevating Dana's arm, Cybele pressed hard on the wound to stop the bleeding. "Dana! Stay awake!"

Dana was feeling a curious spinning sensation as she stared at the ceiling. "Everything feels so heavy. "I—"

"Here, squeeze tightly." Cybele replaced her fingers with Dana's and hurried to Mary Lou, who was moaning. Grabbing a roll of duct tape that had been used on her, Cybele trussed the woman's hands and dashed out of the room.

Dana heard Cybele speaking to someone on the telephone. Unable to stay awake, Dana passed out. When she awoke, her head was resting on a pillow, and Cybele was sitting on the floor beside her, applying pressure to her arm. Dana attempted to sit up, but Cybele held her down.

"You are not moving, my friend. Captain Yalouris and an ambulance will be here soon."

Dana drifted again until she heard loud footfalls. Opening her eyes, she saw Cybele with Captain Yalouris and two men lowering a stretcher.

Cybele took Dana's hand. "I'll be with you in a little while, okay?"

"No, I'm not leaving without you. You're too hard to find."

"Miss Fox is right," Captain Yalouris said. "Go with her. I'll come to the hospital later." He turned to look at Cybele closely. "And have yourself checked by a doctor."

—

On arrival, Dana was injected with a painkiller. The doctor removed the saturated cotton strips, and the bleeding started again. Dana was sent to the operating room. She dreamed that her mother was hovering above her, watching with a tender expression that made Dana's heart ache with longing. She yearned to reach out and embrace her, but Dana's arms were immovable. She called her mother's name. No one answered.

Slowly, Dana broke through into the busy reality of the recovery area. When she moved her head, she was overjoyed to see Cybele seated beside her. Although Cybele looked exhausted, her stained uniform was covered with a hospital gown, and her hair was uncombed, she was the most welcome sight Dana could imagine.

"Are you all right?" Dana whispered.

Cybele stood and squeezed Dana's hand. "I'm fine. Just a scratch on my shoulder. How are you?"

"Okay, I think."

Cybele stroked her cheek. "You better be. I have a date with you later."

"A date?"

"Yes, we're sharing a hospital room for the night."

"How did you arrange that?"

"I have a small concussion from being whacked with a frying pan. It's just a precaution."

Dana had many questions but was too unfocused to ask them. Instead, she gazed at Cybele and smiled.

"I love you," she whispered.

Cybele looked surprised, then her face transformed into happiness. "I was wondering when you would tell me." She gave Dana a long kiss. "I love you too."

As much as Dana wanted to treasure the moment, she closed her eyes and slept until a nurse and an orderly arrived with a gurney. Once the nurse was satisfied with her condition, Dana was brought to a room. With Cybele lying on the adjacent bed, Dana succumbed to exhaustion.

—

The next morning, Dana was more alert; she was off the IV painkillers by afternoon and onto pills. Dr. Michaelidis, the same physician who had tended her after Luca's attack, explained that besides a mild concussion, the loss of blood, and the deep wound on her forearm, no serious damage had been sustained.

"You have very bad luck, Miss Fox," he told her.

"I'm always in the wrong place at the wrong time," Dana agreed.

"I think you both can go home tomorrow morning."

"That would be the right place at the right time."

Cybele smiled and shook her head.

—

They were ready to leave by mid-morning. Dana was instructed to watch for fever, vomiting, temperature, infection, or a sudden increase in pain, and Cybele, who was almost recovered except for a headache, was warned to call Dr. Michaelidis if either of them felt worse.

"Do you think you can climb your stairs at home?" the doctor asked Dana.

"Yes. My legs have had a nice rest," she replied with more bravado than she felt.

"Very well. Your companion has been given several days off to care for you. Mind her well. I'll see you tomorrow."

—

The trip home was a tortuous trial because no roads ran near the apartment. They traveled the first part by taxi, whose bumpiness was painful, and then by foot. Cybele supported Dana as they walked and helped her up the two sets of stairs inside the apartment. Once Dana was lying on the bed with Cybele beside her, she could stay awake no longer.

Several hours later, they opened their eyes. Both were hungry, so Cybele heated some leftovers. After they had eaten, she brought the tray downstairs, made a phone call, and then rejoined Dana, who began to barrage her with questions.

"Who was Ray?"

"His last name was Sirman…"

"Not Johnson? Hmm. He said his name was appropriate for his calling."

Cybele gave her a quizzical look but continued. "You can explain that later. I just spoke with Captain Yalouris. When he made inquiries in Iowa, the authorities said Sirman was wanted for questioning about the murders of four gay men—all done with a wire. One guy, who fought him off and escaped, provided a partial description. They also have a hair sample from the killer, so we're sending one of Sirman's to see if they match."

"Did you learn anything else?"

"He comes from a very wealthy family and inherited a fortune from his parents. No brothers or sisters, no wife or lover that anyone knows about. The police say he has a record of juvenile offences and is suspected in the arson of a neighbor's barn. He attended college but was asked to leave school. And, though he didn't go to seminary, he was a minister."

"It's easy to get a piece of paper saying you're a priest. You can get one over the Internet. A real racket."

"That's probably what he did," Cybele replied. "He met Paul Owens Merrill about two years ago. Merrill had a small church and was preaching against homosexuality. Sirman offered to fund a clinic to convert gay people. The two traveled to several states, but Merrill denies that Sirman was using him to access gay men, yet deaths occurred in towns where the two had been staying. Merrill admits he heard complaints, but no charges were ever brought. Merrill claims he never had suspicions about Sirman until they arrived here."

"Hard to imagine. And how did Mary Lou and Walter get hooked up with all of this?"

"Ah, that's an interesting story. The Schatzes were introduced to Merrill by Sirman. They became members of Merrill's church and were active in the clinic. What is most fascinating is the strange relationship between Sirman and Mary Lou Schatze. She taught him at home until Sirman was fourteen years old. Something sexual happened then and his parents found out. When Mary Lou and I were at the house while Sirman was searching for you in town, Mary Lou talked about him like he was a god, like she worshipped him. She said they shared many secrets but didn't tell me what they were."

Dana shivered. "That sounds like a really sick relationship." She took Cybele's hand. "So, how did she meet Walter?"

"Walter took care of the horses on the Sirman farm. When Mary Lou was dismissed from service, Walter quit his job, they married, and he enrolled in veterinary school. The police think the murders started later, though no one knows exactly when. Last month, he was questioned about one death, but his attorney helped to delay charges. We believe Sirman left the United States to continue his killing, using Merrill and the protesters as cover and the Schatzes as coordinators—especially Mary Lou. All of their activities drew attention away from him. He told everyone he was on a retreat and wasn't to be disturbed, except for Mary Lou, who was often at the house."

"Which allowed Ray to come and go as he pleased…particularly late at night."

"Yes," Cybele said.

"And none of the men and women made the connection with the deaths in Iowa? When the same thing began occurring here?" Dana asked incredulously.

Cybele shrugged. "We're interviewing Merrill's followers, including Mary Lou and Walter Schatze. Walter might have guessed at his wife's disturbed relationship with Sirman, but he admired the man, saying Sirman praised Mary Lou and himself for being perfect examples of Christian living."

Dana snorted. "Such a nice, sweet, little couple."

"For sure," Cybele said. "Walter mentioned that they met you one afternoon near a gay bar. And when they told Sirman, he instructed them to find you."

"Yes, we did meet," she replied, "but I don't understand why Ray was still looking for me. He had Devin's photos and the negatives by then."

"Ah, well, this is the part I figured out. The first photograph you took of Ray Sirman was after the Malcolm Hall killing—when he was dressed as a monk. Later that morning, you took a second set of photographs at the harbor."

"I did, but—"

"Sirman was sitting at a taverna…in street clothes, without his beard and priest's cassock. At his feet was the same shopping bag he had carried with him earlier. The bag in the 'priest' photo, taken in black-and-white, didn't show the store's logo well, but the later color photo by the harbor did. The bag's background was in dark red and the lettering was dark pink—"

"So the value similarity in the black-and-white image made the design difficult to see."

Cybele smiled. "Exactly. When I saw the enlarged scan of your black-and-white photo at the police station, I knew I'd seen the logo on the bag before—from a costume shop in Athens where my mother often purchased theatrical items, where he bought his disguise. The identical bag at both scenes linked the man to Hall's murder. I ran back here to check your color pictures and found two prints showing Merrill waving to the guy with the bag. Since I knew where Merrill was staying, I brought the photos to him. He identified Ray Sirman and gave me Sirman's house address."

Dana squeezed Cybele's hand. "Pretty fine detective work."

"Thank you. Now, rest. More later."

CHAPTER TWENTY-SEVEN

DANA OPENED her eyes as the rays of sunset flushed the room with orange light. Cybele was sitting in the chair by the window, gazing at the sea. Hearing Dana stir, she turned. "Ah, you're ready for cocktail hour?"

"I think I'll skip it tonight, if it's all right with you."

Cybele rose and kissed Dana on the forehead. "I'll make some tea instead." She went downstairs and returned with two mugs and two slices of cake. "Your cake is very beautiful," she said with undisguised irony.

"It's a very special cake!"

"Oh?"

"Yes. It's the first cake I've baked since I was a child. I made it for you."

Cybele laughed gaily. "It was a little crooked, you know."

"I planned it that way."

"Well, my friend, your cake is a success in that case. But perhaps I'll be the baker in the family, yes?"

"I relinquish my title to you with pleasure." Dana ate a bite. "At least it doesn't taste too awful."

"No, it doesn't," Cybele agreed. "However, I'm sorry to say that I had to throw away that big fish. He wasn't so fresh."

"Too bad."

They were silent for a few minutes, eating, and then Dana asked her about Mary Lou Schatze's involvement in the murders.

"I spoke with Detective Pyrgos while you were asleep. He spent several hours at the hospital with Mary Lou, who has a few broken ribs and fingers thanks to you and your candlestick."

"I'll pray for the darling woman."

Cybele laughed. "Well, my friend, religion aside—"

"The best place to put it."

"Yes, I agree. Now, here is what happened. Mary Lou admitted that she and Walter followed us home on the night we dined at El Greco. Later the next day, Mary Lou gave Sirman the address. However, her story is very confused. Sometimes, she says she is innocent and knows nothing about the murders; at other times she takes credit for Sirman's behavior. Whichever is the truth, Sirman's death was too much for her. She isn't always in her right mind." Cybele drank some tea. "Mary Lou's maiden name was Becker, which Captain Yalouris learned from the police chief in Davenport. When Sirman was a teenager, his mother walked into her son's room and found him burning hot candlewax on Mary Lou's breasts while she was sexually manipulating him. Mary Lou was arrested but then released when Mr. Sirman asked the police to free Mary Lou because he didn't want the family's name in the newspapers. The chief did so but he made notes in a file."

Dana exhaled a long breath. "If only someone had stopped the two of them then, all of the deaths might have been prevented."

"Probably Sirman's pathology was already fixed by that point," Cybele said. "In an interview, Walter told Detective Pyrgos that Sirman had described a vision. A flash of green light in which God ordered him to change homosexuals into heterosexuals, and, if this wasn't possible, to kill them quickly and without pain so that they could do no harm to innocent children."

Dana rubbed the side of her neck where the wire had cut the skin. "I don't think it was very painless."

"According to Walter, he and Mary Lou were upset by the conversation."

"Ha! I doubt it. He must share some of their sickness to be involved with her." Dana remembered her application of the figure/ground photographic assignment to the situation. "You know, Ray was clever to front his activities with all these people. He knew the police would suspect the protesters, Merrill, and the Schatzes because they were so visible about their anti-gay beliefs. I wonder if he planned to incriminate them more directly."

"You're very perceptive, my friend. When Merrill's hotel room was searched, we found a wooden cross on a priest's prayer rope—a match for the one in your photo. Merrill said it wasn't his but reported that Sirman had used his room one afternoon to change so that he could swim in the hotel pool."

Dana finished her tea and set the mug on the table beside the bed. "I wonder why Ray was so obsessed with killing gay men? Was he gay himself?"

"I suppose so. I didn't tell you before, but after the men were dead, he raped them—not Devin Scott—that was not the same kind of killing. He also sodomized them using an old wooden ruler, which was found in the house along with the cosmetics. Mary Lou Schatze hinted that the ruler had a connection to abuse that Sirman received when he was young."

—

Cybele went downstairs to make dinner, which she brought up on a tray. Although Dana was hungry at first, her appetite soon deserted her. She thanked Cybele and accepted a dose of pain medication.

"Let me clean the dishes and I'll be back," Cybele said, lifting the tray.

Dana nodded and settled against the pillows. A short while later, Cybele returned, changed into a nightgown, and eased into bed. "How are you feeling?"

"Slightly better. And you?"

"I'm fine. Just a headache and tired." Cybele propped herself on an elbow.

Dana stroked Cybele's arm and considered some of her other questions. At last, she asked, "Okay, so exactly when did Mary Lou tell Ray where my apartment was?"

"Mary Lou wasn't able to speak with him until the evening after our El Greco dinner."

"Why didn't Ray do anything then? He wanted to get the color photographs and the negatives, didn't he?"

"Yes," Cybele replied.

"So, I guess when he was standing near the spot where Bryan was killed…he didn't know where I lived yet…"

"What do you mean?"

Dana shook her head, feeling the initial effects of the drug.

Cybele's eyebrows arched. "There are things you haven't told me…"

"I'll explain in a minute. As to why Ray didn't come after me sooner —he might not have had a good opportunity because on Thursday I was either home or with someone." She listed all of the various meetings and activities. "But you never told me what happened at the hospital with Luca?"

Cybele shook her head. "Ah. Him. What a fool I was! I let him escape. I was very upset with myself. But when I returned from the hospital to the station, I realized where I'd seen the shopping bag the murderer was carrying. Because of my error with Luca, I wanted to make things right, so I didn't follow procedure. After getting the address from Merrill, I went to Sirman's house alone. The back door was open, and I stupidly walked in and was hit over the head."

"That's what happened to me. I saw Ray leaving my house—"

"He took my key…"

"Yes, I figured that. Anyhow, there wasn't time to call the police, so I did exactly what you did."

"We're quite a pair! Really smart." Cybele chuckled. "Now, you didn't answer me…you said something about seeing Sirman where Bryan was killed?"

"I didn't know who he was then." Dana sighed. "You remember the night at Orpheus?"

"How could I forget!"

"The man that was standing with his hand on my neck?"

"Yes."

"That was Ray Sirman."

"No!" she replied, aghast. "He could have killed you!"

"Yes, he could. I thought he was just flirting with me. He was very smooth. Now I know that he was trying to get me drunk in order to make his job easier. I told him my name was Marilyn—"

Cybele giggled. "Marilyn? Oh, come on!"

"He must have learned my real name from the bartender. Then he went to my gallery hoping I would have work there, and they would know where I lived—he asked Maria for my address, but she refused to give it to him. And last Monday I was sitting on the balcony and saw a man standing on the corner. It was Ray."

"You didn't tell me!" Cybele cried.

"Well, all I knew was that he seemed familiar. Besides, after your reaction, I didn't want to ever mention the guy again."

She gave Dana a weak smile. "No, I was very jealous. That's true."

"So, he was probably even angrier at me because I'd walked out on him."

"Good work! You insulted the worst murderer Mykonos has ever known, at least since the Ottomans invaded."

"I suppose I have good instincts even in an inebriated condition." Dana was quiet, realizing how lucky she'd been. "What else did Ray tell you at the house?"

"Not much. He talked on and on about how it felt to use the garrote. For you, however, he had decided on a special plan."

"Tell me. It's better to get this all in the open so we can forget about it."

"He said something about 'God's sword' and how you would enjoy it."

"He was planning to rape me?"

She nodded and swallowed hard. "Perhaps, but I believe he meant his threat literally."

A chill ran down Dana's back. She looked at Cybele in alarm. "Did he try anything with you?

Cybele put her arms around Dana. "No, he didn't, except for hitting me on the head and drugging me, but, after he was finished with you, he would have killed me. And how he would have done it, well, I'd rather not imagine."

—

Émile came to say goodbye—he was leaving for the season—and, an hour after he left, Dr. Michaelidis arrived. He replaced the bandages, checked Dana's eyes, and told her to stay on the antibiotics and to use the pain medication as needed. Satisfied that there was no infection, he instructed her to call if anything changed.

Since the Mykonian crime rate had been greatly decreased by the death of Ray Sirman, the imprisonment of his partners, and the departure of the religious protesters, Captain Yalouris insisted that Cybele stay home for several days. He then came for a visit.

Dana was sitting on the balcony wearing drawstring cotton pants and a loose-fitting blouse. He sat down, accepted a coffee from Cybele, and explained that a fisherman had discovered Luca Alessi lying unconscious in the cockpit of his boat.

"He was trying to steal the boat but apparently fainted because of the infection, which turned poisonous. In the hospital, the doctor scraped the diseased bone, and IV antibiotics were administered. Even so, it's possible that Alessi will lose his hand. The assaults will mean time in jail."

"He deserves it!" Cybele said with vehemence.

"And then we have Mary Lou and Walter Schatze," Captain Yalouris continued. "Walter Schatze probably didn't participate in the murders, but we're not sure if he knew Sirman was killing gay men in Iowa and here. Mary Lou Schatze was definitely involved and will be charged for abduction, administering illegal drugs, and attempts to kill both of you with a knife. She encouraged Sirman, but he appears to be responsible for the four deaths. As for Paul Owens Merrill, we've learned that Sirman paid for Merrill's hotel and other expenses for the protesters. We believe the minister had suspicions about Sirman and ignored them. Mr. Merrill will remain on Mykonos until we're sure that he's innocent, as will Mr. Schatze."

"It sounds like Ray planned what he was going to do before he left Iowa," Dana remarked, setting down her coffee mug on the table. "I mean, why else did Mary Lou bring morphine here?"

"Yes, it does," he agreed. "We're coordinating our investigation with the American authorities." Yalouris swallowed some coffee. "And, by the way, when we searched Sirman's property, we found an oil drum in the yard containing burned clothes—probably those of the three men—and remains of the negatives, the prints, and the shopping bag. In the house was a cassock and hat and a suitcase full of boxes labeled with names, each holding hair samples—all excellent evidence."

The policeman came to his feet and carried his cup into the kitchen. As Cybele and Dana followed him to the stairs, he turned. "I'm sorry all this happened but thank you both for what you did."

—

Dana held two consecutive workshops. Nine days after the second one, Cybele and Dana dined at Edem Restaurant and then walked to Caprice where Dana, unbeknownst to Cybele, had reserved the couch —a request that had amused its owner, who left a folded white card perched on the blue cushion. When Cybele saw the card, she laughed and sat with a grand flourish. A circle of patrons applauded the comedy and began to buy drinks for them: two rounds from friends of Malcolm Hall's and another from a man who knew Virgil. Irini, not to be outdone, proffered two flutes of sparkling wine.

Despite the convivial atmosphere, Dana sensed the nostalgia spreading throughout the room as many people were preparing to return to their winter residences.

Cybele read her thoughts. "It's sad to go. And yet I'm eager to see all those tall buildings in New York." She sipped her drink. "And that large bed of yours."

Dana chuckled and hugged Cybele. "I think you'll like it."

"Shall we go home and finish packing?"

They set down their glasses and stood to leave, a little unsteadily. To Dana's surprise, Cybele walked over to Irini and placed both hands firmly on her shoulders. After a mischievous glance at Dana, she gave Irini a steamy kiss. The barmaid staggered a step, half-confused and half-pleased. All three women erupted in laughter.

"I am very, very, very jealous!" Dana said to both of them.

"Trust me!" was Cybele's naughty response.

Irini shook her head and clapped Dana on the back. "She is all yours!"

"She certainly is!" Dana gathered her wayward lover around the waist and escorted her onto the promenade. Hand in hand, they strolled along the sea-slicked stones, speaking of love, speaking of their future. At the aqua door, they paused. Cybele rested her head on Dana's shoulder, and together they watched a white ship leave the brightly lit port and steam into the darkness.

ACKNOWLEDGMENTS

I am grateful to Interlude Press for honoring the novel with publication and also wish to thank Annie Harper, Executive Editor; Candysse Miller, Director of Marketing and Communications; and C.B. Messer, Art Director, who did a lovely job on the cover design—thank you for selecting my photograph, "Mykonos Steps," for the illustration. Special thanks to Kristin Pape, an insightful developmental editor; the excellent copy editor, Nicki Harper; and the sharp-eyed proofreader, Linda Morris. It has been a pleasure to work with all of you.

Many dear friends have supported me during the writing of this book and others, especially Beverly Harris, Carol Oberle, Karla Linn Merrifield, Dr. Dwight Wilson, Julie and Tom Stewart, and Vicki DeVico, who also provided my author's portrait.

Photo by Vicki DeVico

ABOUT THE AUTHOR

Laury A. Egan is the author of *The Outcast Oracle, Fog and Other Stories, Jenny Kidd, Fabulous! An Opera Buffa,* and *A Bittersweet Tale.* Four poetry volumes were published in limited edition: *Snow, Shadows, a Stranger; Beneath the Lion's Paw; The Sea & Beyond;* and *Presence & Absence.* She has spent several months in Greece, with three visits to Mykonos, where she photographed the island and found inspiration to write *The Ungodly Hour.* Her website: www.lauryaegan.com